# LAST STAND

## A TOM ROLLINS THRILLER

## PAUL HEATLEY

INKUBATOR
BOOKS

Published by Inkubator Books
www.inkubatorbooks.com

Copyright © 2023 by Paul Heatley

Paul Heatley has asserted his right to be identified as the author of this work.

ISBN (eBook): 978-1-83756-132-2
ISBN (Paperback): 978-1-83756-133-9

*For Aidan*

# PROLOGUE

It's dangerous alone on the streets.

As a woman, a black woman, alone and homeless, the streets of Santa Fe feel extra dangerous, especially at night.

Day time is bad enough, but the day at least provides some semblance of security. The light keeps the worst of the threats at bay. In the day, so long as she stays close enough to others, to civilisation, it keeps the savages away. Those who would beat her, kill her, rape her. Come the night, that's when the danger increases. Civilisation recedes. It sleeps. The savages are free to play.

For Rhonda, that's why she got with Jim. At first, it was convenience. He could keep her safe. Then it grew into something more. Grew so that she actually cared for him. It became a relationship, and not just of convenience. He cares for her, too. Tonight, though, they're not together. They haven't seen each other in a couple of days. This isn't uncommon. Right now, Rhonda wishes she had a way to get in touch with him.

She's being followed. She's sure of it. The feeling began

earlier today. On the street, she's become attuned to her paranoia. If she feels like she's being watched, it's usually for a reason. If she feels like she's being followed, likewise. She's felt both today. And, more than that, she's caught glimpses. The same two faces, over and over, at a distance, but there too often for her to be comfortable with, until she became certain it wasn't just coincidence. Everywhere she went, there they were. Every time she thought she'd managed to slip them, they'd turn back up.

There's nothing distinct about them. They just look like regular guys. Both of them white, one of them with a shaved head and the other with dark hair looking in need of a cut. The bald one has a beard and the other is clean shaven. They wear jeans and shirts. The bald guy wears a denim jacket and the other wears a bomber. They don't look like cops. Which means they could be any number of other things.

It's late, now. It's dark. Rhonda is tired. She hasn't stopped moving all day. She's hungry, too. She hasn't had a chance to get anything to eat, to stop and search for something, or hold out her hand on a street corner. Now she just wants to rest. She tries to find somewhere she can hunker down for the night, hide out from her two pursuers. She wishes Jim were here. Tomorrow, she'll have to find him. Even if the two men are still following her – *especially* if the two men are still following her – she'll have to somehow find Jim.

She stays where it's built up, moving between the Pueblo buildings. She hasn't seen either of the men in an hour now. She remains vigilant. Peers around every corner before she steps out. As a rule, she tries to stay away from crowded areas when it's dark, even though they tend to be better lit. Tries to give the nightclubs and restaurants a wide berth, as she knows from experience the wrong kind of crowd leaving those kinds of establishments can be dangerous to her. A group of horny frat boys looking for trouble could emerge, or some drunken businessmen who aren't ready to end the night just yet. Tonight, though, she's thinking about making an exception. Taking a chance on either of those groups doesn't feel as risky as the two men who have been following her all day. No one follows for so long without having bad intentions.

She heads for Grant Avenue, and she'll make her way from there. Keeps her head on a swivel as she goes, looking around, checking her back. She thinks about how Jim would say she was 'watching her six'. She needs him to watch her six right now. To watch her whole damn clock.

It's quiet. She feels all alone in the city. It wouldn't have to be Jim – she'd settle for any familiar face, or any homeless stranger who would understand the position she's in and offer her shelter. She can't see anyone. No one at all.

Until she turns, and she *does* see a familiar face, but it's not one she wants.

It's the bald guy. He spots her, and this time he doesn't keep his distance. He's not following. He's *chasing*.

Rhonda doesn't hesitate. She turns and she starts running. Behind her, she can hear his heavy footsteps drawing closer. Rhonda screams, but she knows as the sound leaves her throat that it's useless. No one will come. If anyone hears, they'll pretend they don't. This is how it is on the street. This is how it always is.

She's aware she hasn't seen the other man. The one with hair. He could be anywhere. She wants to turn her head while she runs down the middle of the road, to check the alleys and corners, but she can't, knowing she can't risk a stumble, a fall.

Ahead, she can hear the roar of an engine. A black van comes into view, cutting across the road, blocking her way. She can't see the driver, but it doesn't matter. The intention is clear. Rhonda veers, turns to the left, aiming to cut down another street, to get away from the man behind her and the van blocking the road.

She doesn't get far enough. From the shadows, the man with hair emerges, wrapping his arms around her and lifting her from the ground. She's running so fast he almost loses balance, but he spins with her, keeping upright. Rhonda's legs kick out into the air. She finds herself wondering, briefly, who was driving the van. If all day there's been a third man she hasn't seen.

This thought doesn't hang around long. Instead, she's soon struggling, trying to break free, but the man's grip is strong. Out the corner of her eye she sees the bald man catching up to them. The one holding her calls to him. "Hurry up!" he says. "She's getting loose!"

These words motivate Rhonda to struggle harder, to twist harder than she was before. Her arms are pinned at her sides by his own, which are bigger and more muscular than hers, but she stamps at his feet and kicks at his shins. The bald guy is getting closer. He's reaching into his pocket. Rhonda ignores him, and instead deals with the task in hand, fighting for her life.

She does it – she breaks free, escaping the binds of the man's arms. Her feet hit the ground and she braces, about to start running, but the bald guy is already here, and he's clamping a hand over her mouth. He's holding a rag, and it's damp, covering her mouth and her nostrils, and Rhonda involuntarily breathes in the chemical tang that has soaked it. Almost instantly, her head begins to swim. Her legs buckle. The bald man is still holding her up. If he wasn't, she'd have fallen. Her brain fogs, her thoughts are slow and clouding, but she thinks the rag has been soaked in chloroform.

She hears the van pull up beside them, and the side door is slid open. The last thing Rhonda is aware of is being bundled into the back of it, and then everything goes dark.

# 1

---

"**Y**ou seeing Hayley tonight?"

Tom was pulling on his jacket at the time. Del had a gleam in his eye as he asked. Sixty-three years old, and it made him look like a schoolboy.

It was the end of the work day. The store was closed, the door locked, only one light left on while they prepared themselves to leave. Tom could see out across the town square. A literal square, with breaks at each corner for the roads. Del's store was in the row at the top, with a large supermarket directly opposite at the bottom, taking up the whole row. In the middle of the square was a large grassy area, with some unkept flowerbeds in the centre, and a few benches arranged around the outside. There was a bus stop near to Del's. A couple of the units neighbouring Del's store in the row were empty, out of business. In the other rows there were a couple of cafés, a craft store, a gun store, and a couple of bars. He turned back to Del. He nodded. "I am."

Del smiled. "Been on a few dates now, haven't you?"

Tom nodded again. "A few."

Del beamed like a proud father. "Sounds serious. Two of you knew each other a long time ago, isn't that right?"

"High school, yeah," Tom said, already halfway out the door.

"And now all these years later, you're getting reacquainted," Del said. "That's real sweet. Like something out of a movie. Where you taking her? Somewhere nice?"

"To the diner," Tom said. "We thought the options around here were limited when we were young, but it turns out they're still limited now."

"Well, I tell you what," Del said, stepping closer and reaching into his pocket. "Get yourselves a couple of drinks on me." He pulled out a twenty and forced it into Tom's hand.

"You don't have to do that," Tom said.

"I know I don't," Del said, patting him on the arm. "Yet here I am, doing it anyway."

Tom remembers this as he pays the bill, putting down Del's twenty to round out the tip. "By the way," Tom says, "Del said to tell you hello."

The diner isn't busy. It's about half full, and people talk at a low, comforting murmur. There's a pleasant atmosphere. It's relaxed. The food came quick, and it was good.

Hayley grins. "Tell him I said it right back," she says. "It's been a while since I last needed to go into his store. DIY isn't one of my main hobbies."

"I'm sure he would appreciate the visit," Tom says. "Most people we get in a day are just coming by to say hello and talk with him."

"Well, Del's an institution, isn't he? He's been around long enough."

Hayley uses both hands to brush locks of brunette hair behind her ears. The action takes Tom back almost fifteen years. He remembers her making the same gesture back when they were sixteen, seventeen, eighteen. She sees him watching, and she smiles. It's a beautiful smile. She's an attractive woman, even more so than he remembers her being when they were younger. She's aged better than he has. She doesn't have anywhere near as many scars.

They bumped into each other a few weeks after Tom returned to town. Tom was in the supermarket, buying his weekly groceries. He was comparing pastas when her voice broke through. "Is that Tom Rollins, or am I just being wishful?" It sounded like she knew it was him for sure.

Tom turned toward her, and he felt his face breaking into a beaming smile that matched her own. "Hayley Teller," he said, pasta forgotten. Next thing either of them knew, they were in each other's arms. They promptly arranged to meet up soon for coffee and a catch-up.

Tom left Hopper Creek when he was eighteen, to join the Army. It turned out Hayley left not long after, to attend college. She's a nurse now. She returned to Hopper Creek to work at the hospital – Hopper Creek Medical Centre. "I suppose I could've gone and worked anywhere," she told him. "But sometimes it feels like you've just got to come back home. Like that's where you want to be, more than anywhere else, even if you've never realised that before."

Tom is smiling at her. Hayley reaches across the table for his hand. "You keep looking at me like that," she says. "I don't hate it."

Tom squeezes her fingers. "I'm glad to hear that."

She takes a sip of her drink, a coke, and strokes the back of his hand. "You know," she says, "you still haven't told me what you're doing back here in Hopper Creek."

"I was passing by," Tom says. He shrugs. "I hadn't been here in a long time. I thought I'd call through, see how it was holding up."

"And why'd you hang around? Find you miss it? Or

maybe you were hoping we'd bump into each other like we did that day in the store?" She winks at him.

"That's the one," Tom says, nodding. "You caught me. That's what I was holding out for."

"You charmer," she says. "I know that wasn't the real reason."

Tom shrugs. He doesn't want to tell her the real reason. "I didn't have anywhere else to be," he says. "So I thought I might hang around. See how things are before I move on."

"And how are things?"

"They're coping."

"I think we both know that's not true." The town looks like it has problems. It's run down. There's more graffiti than there used to be. Weeds are sprouting untended through the cracks in the pavement. Tom has spotted a couple of dogs running free, collarless and homeless.

"Well, I found a better reason to hang around longer," he says.

"There's that charm again. You've never really changed, have you? Even in high school – I remember, everyone was scared of you. You, and your brother, and your dad. And you were intense, there's no getting around that. I swear, sometimes it was like you never blinked. Y'know, for a little while, I used to do prison visits. The guys in there, how they moved, they would remind me of you. They could never relax. Always watching their backs. Their shoulders were so tense, all the time, raised up almost to their ears. They were like coils, like snakes, ready to spring into action, always ready for a fight. You're a little more relaxed now, but I can still see some of it. Anyway, my point is that, no matter how intense and scary you always seemed, whenever people actually spoke to you they always came away shocked, because you weren't what they expected. You were polite. You were *charming*. I remember that's what I always thought. I mean, you certainly charmed me. We were together for two years. That didn't just happen."

"Everyone was scared of me?" Tom says.

Hayley laughs. "As if you didn't know."

He grins. Hayley smiles back at him, but then she looks behind him, over his shoulder, toward the diner's door. Her face drops a little. She looks dismayed. She runs her tongue around her mouth, over her teeth, and then takes another drink of coke, like she's suddenly tasted something bad.

Tom looks back over his shoulder. He recognises the man who has entered the diner and is at the counter, paying out dirty, crumpled bills as he picks up a bagged collection. It's Kyle Hobbs. Tom and Hayley went to high school with Kyle. Recently, Tom has come to know of him better through his activities in the town. He doesn't let Hayley know this, as he turns back to her. "Kyle Hobbs?" he says, keeping his voice low. "What's the problem?"

Hayley raises her eyes to his. She lowers her head, likely so Kyle won't notice her. Tom wonders if something has happened between them, or if it's just that she's aware of what Kyle is up to, too. "Have you seen much of Kyle Hobbs lately?" she says. "Around town?"

Tom shakes his head. It's a lie.

"He's a drug dealer," Hayley says. "There's a whole gang of them. You remember Donny Bradshaw? He's their ringleader. The reason Hopper Creek looks the way it does now is because of them."

"How do you mean?"

"Don't pretend you haven't noticed. The place is a dump. All the graffiti, all the litter, all the junkies stumbling through this town like zombies. You've seen that, right?"

"I suppose I have."

"It's because of *them*, and what they're selling, and what they're doing to people." She shakes her head in disgust.

"They're scum," she says. "They're killing people. They're literally killing them, and the ones who aren't dead yet are rotting alive. And it's not just here. It's bad over in Bittersweet, too. All around us, the whole county nearly. I see them, the users, the victims, day in and day out, and we just don't have the capacity or the funding to help them all properly. To help them the way they need."

Tom doesn't say anything. He's seen this all for himself. He feigns ignorance, however. He has plans, and she's not going to be a part of them. Keeping her in the dark about what he's going to do will keep her safe.

"I'm sorry," she says, running a hand down her face. "There was... We had an overdose at the hospital. Just yesterday. I guess it's still...it's still fresh in my mind. You should have seen her, Tom. She was younger than us – she was only twenty-four, but she looked about thirty years older. And now she's dead." She shakes her head again.

"Well, well, well. Hayley Teller. Imagine bumping into you here."

Hayley looks up. From the expression on her face, Tom doesn't need to turn to see that it's Kyle who approached them. Hayley battles to maintain her composure. "Kyle," she says, practically spitting the man's name.

"And this isn't Rollins, is it?" Kyle says, turning toward Tom with surprise.

Tom nods at him. He sees that Kyle is holding onto his bag of take-out. He can smell the greasy fries and burgers within.

"Shit, man, I'd heard you were back," Kyle says. "What a trip, right, bumping into you both here? Oh man, this is crazy – it's like being back in high school. So, what's happening here? The two of you looking to rekindle that odd-couple thing you had going on way back then?"

"We're having dinner," Hayley says, and it's clear she's

battling not to erupt on Kyle, to spew out the venom she feels for him and his friends. Tom needs her to keep it together. He needs her not to draw attention to herself, or him, from any member of the gang, even a clearly low-level member like Kyle.

Tom clears his throat, draws Kyle's attention away from Hayley's sneer and toward himself. "It's been a long time since we last saw each other," Tom says. "And I was passing through, so we thought we'd catch up, for old time's sake. Been almost as long since I last saw you, Kyle. How are you doing?"

"I'm good, man, I'm good," Kyle says, seemingly oblivious to Hayley's stare. "Hey, I just remembered – I saw you on the news, man. Few years ago, now."

"That so?"

"Yeah, man. Like, you stopped that bomb from going off, right? I was trying to tell my girl at the time, *Hey, I know that guy!*" Kyle laughs. "She didn't believe me. She didn't believe much I said. Was always rolling her eyes. Guess that's why we're not together anymore." He laughs again.

"That'll do it," Tom says. "It's been good to see you, Kyle. We're just finishing up here. Maybe I'll bump into you again some other time."

"Sure, man. Maybe. It's a small town." Kyle turns back to Hayley. "Catch you later, Dr Teller."

"I'm a nurse."

"Uh, Nurse Teller." He makes gun fingers at them both, then leaves.

Hayley watches him go. "I need some air," she says.

## 2

"Look, I'm really sorry about back there," Hayley says.

They walk through the town, Tom escorting her home. It's a pleasant evening. Warm. It's still light, the sky orange in the distance as the sun moves closer to the horizon.

"Don't worry about it," Tom says. "You explained yourself. You weren't even that bad. It didn't look like Kyle could tell you were pissed at him."

"I get the impression Kyle doesn't often know what's going on around him," Hayley says. Tom is walking with his hands in his pockets. She hooks one of her arms through his and rests her head on his shoulder. Tom catches the scent of her shampoo. She smells like vanilla. "He's high on pot most of the time. I'm surprised he didn't stink out the diner."

Tom nods. "He was high. I could see it in his pupils. The smell was there, but it was faint. It had sunk into his clothes. Is that what he and the others are selling? Weed?"

"I wish," Hayley says. "What they're selling is a lot worse than that."

She doesn't continue, and Tom doesn't prompt her. "That's unfortunate," he says. "How you feeling now? Better?"

"Yes," she says, squeezing his arm. "I was ready for some fresh air."

"There's one thing Kyle said that I keep thinking about," Tom says.

"What's that?"

"He referred to us as an *odd couple*. Was that how people saw us?"

Hayley laughs. "I mean, maybe? I don't know. If they did, no one ever said anything like that to me."

"I was probably the odd one."

"Well, everyone knew about your dad. They all knew he was a doomsday prepper. Someone like that, they're gonna become a character, and I guess that's gonna reflect on their kids, whether that's fair or not. How *is* your dad, by the way?"

"He's still a doomsday prepper," Tom says. "He lives on a commune."

"Oh, really? Are you serious?"

Tom nods.

"I suppose I shouldn't be surprised. What about your brother?"

Tom hesitates. He clears his throat. "I haven't seen Anthony in a while. A few years now. We weren't getting along too well the last time we saw each other."

"That's a shame."

"It is what it is."

They walk in silence for a few paces. Hayley speaks first. "Y'know, people might've thought we were odd together, but I never thought we were. I thought we fit right, you know? And it's not like... I mean, I wasn't the most popular girl there or anything. I wasn't a cheerleader, or on any sports team. I was just some nerd who was good at biology."

"You were the prettiest girl there."

She nudges him. "There's that charm again."

"I mean it."

She shakes her head, smiling to herself, and then turns back to him like she's just remembered something. "It surprised me when Kyle said he remembered seeing you on the news. It must have left a real impression on him."

"I never saw the report myself," Tom says.

"I remember where I was when it came on," Hayley says. "I was at work, on break. The TV was on but I wasn't watching it. I just kind of saw it out the corner of my eye. And then the next thing I know, they're flashing up a picture of you in your Army uniform, and saying that you stopped a group of terrorists from setting off a bomb. As soon as they flashed your picture, I don't know what happened, it was like I just teleported to that television so I could hear what it was saying." She laughs. "Where was that again?"

"Dallas."

"I'd like to hear the full story of that sometime," Hayley says. "The reports weren't exactly clear."

"And I'll maybe tell you sometime," Tom says. "But I'm not sure how much of it you're going to believe."

They reach her street. They're not far from her house. They stop when they reach the foot of her porch steps. Hayley turns to him. "Would you," she says, then shrugs like it's no big deal, "would you like to come inside?"

Tom would. He would like that very much. He would like nothing more. But he has something he needs to do. "I can't, tonight," he says. "I need to get back to my place. I'm expecting a call from my dad." This isn't true. He doesn't like lying to her, but it's necessary.

"Oh, of course, sure," Hayley says. "No problem."

"Next time," Tom says.

"You're hanging around long enough for a next time, huh?"

"Seems like it."

Hayley smiles at him. She leans in close, a hand upon his chest, and kisses him on the corner of his mouth. "Until next time, then." She turns and heads up the porch steps, and Tom watches her go, his mouth tingling where her lips brushed his. She unlocks the door and turns back before she goes inside. She waves. Tom smiles and waves back, and then she closes the door. He hears her lock it.

Tom turns. His smile fades. It's time to focus. He parked his car, an older Chevy Impala that he bought cheap from one of Del's customers looking to sell, at the end of the street when he first arrived to pick Hayley up for their date. He walks toward it now. He needs to head back into town. He needs to get into position before darkness falls.

He's not through with this night. Not yet.

# 3

Tom Rollins has been back in Hopper Creek, his hometown, for three months. He's renting a small place on the outskirts of town, only a few miles away from where he grew up. He has a job. He works in a hardware store in the town square for a man named Del Nowak. The store is called, imaginatively, 'Del's Supplies'. Around town, he sometimes sees people he knew back in high school. Some of them recognise him and some of them don't. The ones who do always stop to say hello, and ask how he's been and what he's been up to. Some of them have seen him appear on the news over the last few years. They mention this, and he sees that they're desperate to ask more, to find out all the details the news reports didn't reveal, but they never do ask and Tom never offers to tell.

Tonight, though, after dropping Hayley at her home, Tom isn't at the hardware store. He isn't at home. He isn't waiting for a call from his father like he told Hayley. He isn't bumping into people around town whom he used to vaguely know a long time ago. Instead, tonight, he's crouched low, lying in wait, wearing a long-sleeved shirt and leather gloves, and a balaclava that feels hot against his face. He's been here for hours. Since before it got fully dark. He hasn't moved. Lying in wait, a predator awaiting its prey. He knows they'll be here soon enough. For weeks now, he's been watching their movements. He knows how they operate. He knows *where* they operate. He knows where every single one of them lives, all seven of them. He's been watching, and now he's ready to start making his move.

The two that work this corner are brothers. Max and Micky Simmons. Tom didn't know them when he lived in town. He doesn't know them from high school. Max is older than him, and Micky is younger. They should get here soon.

Tom stays low behind a dumpster, peering down the back of it and the side of the building, toward the entrance of the alley. He can hear voices. He stays very still, and watches. They're outside the alley, to the left, obscured by the building. A group of voices, talking. He knows what's happening. Max and Micky have arrived, and they're seeing to a deal. The buyers are trying to haggle. The brothers aren't interested in hearing it. They have all the leverage. Eventually, the sale goes through. Tom sees the two buyers pass by the alley's opening. They wear T-shirts, despite the night growing colder. They're both thin and pale. Look like they haven't tasted food or felt sunlight in weeks.

Tom has seen many others like them around Hopper Creek. In the few brief months he's been here he's seen their number grow. He's not comfortable with this. He's seen what can happen to a small town when the drug dealers are left to run free.

The younger brother, Micky, enters the alley, talking over his shoulder and unbuttoning his jeans. He laughs about something. Tom can't hear what they're saying. The older brother remains out of view. Micky takes up a position by a wall on the other side of the alley, in the shadows, and starts to piss. Tom stands.

He moves quick and silent, and Micky doesn't sense his approach. He's almost done pissing when Tom slams his head into the wall, grazing his forehead against the brickwork, and then clamps an arm across his throat, blocking his carotid, cutting off the blood flow to his brain. Micky doesn't put up much of a struggle. Before long, he's unconscious. Tom leaves him lying in his own piss. He pats Micky down, but he's not carrying the stash. He's not armed, either. Tom isn't armed. He's carrying his KA-BAR, but he doesn't expect to need it. He's noticed that the dealers never carry anything heavier than a bar or a bat. They don't wield guns. Hopper Creek is too small and too quiet for that. The dealers have gotten comfortable. They're too confident. It's made them soft. Tom is counting on it.

He disappears back behind the dumpster, and waits for Max to come looking for his younger brother. It doesn't take long.

"Yo, what're you doing down there?" Max says, poking his head into the alley. "You taking a shit or something?" He can't see his brother in the shadows, not straight away. He steps closer, closer, until he's almost tripping over Micky's prostrate form. Micky groans, stirs a little, but doesn't wake.

Max leaps back. "Jesus Christ!" Then he realises who he's almost tripped over and drops to his knees by his brother. He sniffs, and his face twists. "Shit, Micky, have you pissed yourself? What've you done – passed out or something?"

Tom makes his move. He locks the same chokehold on Max, cutting off his blood and his oxygen, and then drops him over his brother. He pats him down. Max is carrying a switchblade. Tom drops it in the dumpster. More importantly, he's also carrying their supply. It's wrapped in a plastic bag and stuffed into his jacket. Tom pockets it, and then leaves the alley, slipping off his balaclava once he's far enough away.

He returns to his car and opens up the bag. It's filled with smaller baggies. The baggies contain white and pink crystals. Flakka. Also known as gravel. Also known as zombie. A designer drug. Its effects are similar to bath salts. It can be smoked, snorted, ingested, and swallowed. It makes its users feel euphoric. It makes them feel focussed. It increases their sex drive. It can also make them paranoid, give them panic attacks, and make them see hallucinations. It's easy to overdose on. It's easy to kill yourself with it. Tom has seen around the town what it can do. He's seen the condition of the men and women who use it. Sees the way their clothes hang from their skinny frames. Sees how their eyes have sunken into their skulls, and their cheeks have become emaciated. Sees their knotted, dirty hair. Their pallid skin tones. Tom didn't know much about flakka before he came back to Hopper Creek. He's had to look into it. It's as potent as meth, and more addictive.

Tom gets rid of the flakka. He crushes the crystals under his boot, then finds a dumpster to dispose of it, stuffing it into another trash bag. He moves on. He's not done yet.

He drives across town. The Simmons brothers might be awake, but if they are they'll still be dazed. Confused. Trying to work out what's just happened to them. They won't yet have spread the word of what happened to them. They'll both stink of piss. They could be too embarrassed to talk about it. The rest of the crew are still living in ignorance.

Seven of them all told, including Donny Bradshaw, the head of the operation. Tom remembers Donny. They didn't have anything to do with each other in school. Tom kept mostly to himself. Even if he'd been up for socialising, Donny's circle was one he would have stayed far away from. Donny was loud, obnoxious. A jock and a bully. Tom never had any trouble with him. Tom didn't have any trouble with anyone. Well, that's not entirely true. Early on, people tried to run their mouths, and push him around. They did the same to his brother. Tom and Anthony didn't allow themselves to be pushed around. They dealt with any trouble that came their way, and after that the trouble dried up.

A couple of the others ran in Donny's crew even then. Willie Shaw and Shawn Stark. Willie was born big. He's always been a hulk. He's always been Donny's muscle. Shawn was, and probably still is, a sycophant. He snivelled at Donny's power, and leached off it, and did everything that was demanded of him to stay in Donny's good graces. Kyle Hobbs wasn't in their circle, not back then, and Tom finds it curious that he should be among them now. He wonders how it came about. Even in high school, Kyle had been a stoner. Perhaps over time he found himself drawn to other varieties of drugs. Perhaps coming to sell them was a natural progression.

The others Tom does not know from school. Max and Micky Simmons, and Hal Redford. He doesn't think Hal Redford is from Hopper Creek. From what Tom has gleaned, it seems Hal was a later addition to the crew.

For now, Tom goes to the home of Willie Shaw. Tom has been watching them all closely. Willie is still Donny's right-hand man. Even after more than a decade, Willie has never grown up, never grown apart, never tried to become his own man.

Willie is home. Tom can see his lights on inside as he drives by, shining out from around the sides of his blinds. Willie lives alone. Tom parks a couple of blocks away, and around a corner, keeping the Chevy out of view. He continues on foot, through the back yards of Willie's neighbours. He stays in the dark, in the shadows, out of view of security lights. He pulls the balaclava back over his head on the way.

Willie's home has a security light, too. Tom sticks close to the fence, edges around the circumference of its sensor. Gets closer to the building. The lights are off at the back of Willie's home. The blinds here are open. Tom peers inside. It's a bedroom. The bed is unmade. There are dirty clothes in piles on the floor. There's a weight bench in the corner. The closet door is open. Tom eyes it, and wonders if there is a stash in there.

Ducking under the light sensor, Tom goes to the back door. It leads into the kitchen. He tries the handle but it's locked. He picks it and slips inside, as quietly as he can. From the front of the house, he can hear Willie watching the television and laughing. It's clear he hasn't heard about the Simmons brothers.

Tom moves silently through the house. He reaches the living room door. It's open a crack. He peers inside. Willie is lounging on the sofa, a beer in hand. He takes a drink and some liquid sprays from his lips as he laughs again. Tom doesn't know what he's watching. A sitcom. Tom doesn't watch much television.

He pushes open the door and moves fast. Willie is raising the bottle to his lips again and he turns at the sound. Tom moves fast. Willie is bigger than he is. Tom slaps his hand upward against the bottom of the bottle, slamming the top of it into Willie's teeth and lips, cracking and bloodying them. Willie cries out. His eyes close with the pain. The bottle flies across the room, spraying foamy beer. Tom grabs his flailing left arm by the wrist, takes control of it. He pulls him forward, raising his weight from the sofa, and puts his other hand on the back of his neck. He drives him down into the ground, slamming his face into the carpet. A blow to the back of Willie's head renders him limp.

Tom makes sure he's still, not faking, and then heads through to the bedroom. He checks the closet first, and finds the stash. It's packaged the same as what he took from the Simmons brothers. Smaller baggies inside a plastic carrier. He stuffs it into his pocket, and then tosses the rest of the room to make it look like he had trouble finding it. Going through the house, he messes the rest of it up, too. Makes it look like he's had a thorough search. Then he leaves, and when he reaches his car he disposes of the bag of flakka the same way he did the last one.

He heads home.

Three dealers down. Two stashes disposed of. The drugs are not manufactured in town. He's been having trouble finding where they come from. Tonight, he's generated some chaos. Made it clear that someone is targeting the dealers – perhaps, so far as they're aware, multiple people. A rival gang, maybe. He wants to panic them. He wants them to slip up.

Next, he finds out where their drugs are coming from, and he destroys the source.

# 4

J im Belafonte has spent the morning with his hand out. He hates doing it, but a man has to eat. The little cardboard sign he carries under his arm reads 'Hungry and Homeless, Ex-Army veteran, Anything helps, Thank you'. He knows some people lie about having been in the military in the belief it'll earn them some extra sympathy, but in Jim's case it's true. If quizzed, he can name his rank, regiment, and commanding officer. He can list off all the places he's served. He hasn't been quizzed for a long time. About a year. Not since a white cop tried to push him around, questioning the veracity of the claim on his cardboard sign. The cop's partner, also white, got him to back off, then he sent Jim on his way.

He's managed to earn himself enough for a sandwich and a coffee, and he calls into a café he knows won't hassle him to purchase them. He heads to the park to eat, taking a seat on the grass under a cedar tree. He scans the area while he does, looking out for familiar faces. It's not until he's finished eating and he's nearing the end of the coffee that he finally spots someone he knows. Edgar is across the way, trying to be subtle while he sits on the edge of a bench and rummages through the trash can next to it. Jim goes to him.

"If you'd got here a little earlier I could've split a sandwich with you," Jim says.

"Kind was it?" Edgar says without looking up.

"Ham and cheese."

"Mayo?"

"Yeah."

"Seeded bread?" Edgar sits up now, finally looks at Jim.

"Yeah."

"I don't like mayo," Edgar says. "Or seeded bread."

Jim sits down next to him. "You're awful choosy for a man picking through a trash can."

"I still would've taken half," Edgar says. "I just don't like them, is all."

"Can't be choosers," Jim says. "Y'know, when I first got put out on the streets, I used to be a vegetarian. Didn't last too long. Being choosy was another way of saying you were gonna go hungry."

Edgar grunts in agreement.

"You seen Rhonda around?"

Edgar shakes his head. "Not for a while. You looking for her?"

"Been looking for a while now."

"Thought the two of you were going together?"

"We are. Doesn't mean we're joined at the hip."

"Well, I ain't seen her. How long's it been?"

"Just over two weeks."

Edgar whistles low.

Jim knows what the whistle means. Two weeks is too long. It's not a good sign. "I know how it sounds," he says. "But I ain't heard anything. I've been keeping an eye and an ear out. Listening for descriptions. I've even been checking newspapers. Nothing's turned up yet."

"Hope you find her."

"Me too."

"You usually spend this much time apart?"

"Few days, max."

Edgar whistles again.

"I *know*," Jim says.

"Been some others go missing," Edgar says. "A lot of faces I used to see a lot, I don't see them anymore. Elias. Mark. Sally. Rizzo. Lamb–"

"You don't have to name everyone," Jim says. "I've noticed it too."

"People always disappear, but this feels different. Too many people, too fast. You understand?"

"Yeah," Jim says. "I understand."

"Been about six months. People started disappearing about six months ago, and I don't see them anymore. They don't come back. Don't hear about them. Don't know where they go."

"It doesn't have to mean anything negative's happened."

Edgar shoots him a look. "Rarely anything positive on the street. Where else they go? Everyone get clean at once? Everyone's lottery numbers come up? Everyone's family finally come to get them? All too much. Too many people, too fast. Like I said."

Jim stares into Santa Fe, through the gaps in the buildings that surround the park. He thinks about Rhonda. He worries about her. Worries something bad might have happened to her and he wasn't there to keep her safe. He grinds his jaw and feels muscles twitch in his cheek.

"I hope Rhonda's okay, though," Edgar says. "Maybe *she* got lucky. Somebody had to."

"I hope so, too," Jim says, but he doesn't say what he's thinking. That if Rhonda *had* got lucky, if she'd found a way out, she would have told him. She wouldn't have left him worrying like this.

Jim stands. "If you see her, let her know I'm looking."

"Will do," Edgar says.

Jim hesitates. "And if you hear anything, let me know that, too."

"Okay." Edgar nods. "Okay. What you gonna do now?"

Jim shrugs. "Try and get some money. Get another sandwich. Find somewhere to spend the night. Ask around and see if anyone else has seen or heard from Rhonda."

"You gonna try and find her?"

"I'm already trying to find her."

"I mean, you gonna go knock on doors? Look in windows, turn over every rock?"

"I wouldn't know where to start. I'm just gonna do what I've already been doing – ask around and hope for the best."

"I'll keep my fingers crossed that works out for you," Edgar says. He turns and peers back into the trash can, and resumes his earlier foraging.

Jim leaves him to it and heads back into the city. On his way, his thoughts race, thinking of Rhonda. It happens every time he asks about her and comes up with an unsuccessful response. Edgar is another in a long line of people who haven't seen or heard from her. With every step, he feels his concern growing. Feels himself becoming weighed down. He tries to shake these feelings loose. He needs to stay sharp on the streets. Rhonda is always in his thoughts, but he can't allow her to dull his edges.

He finds a corner and takes a seat, positioning his cardboard sign in his lap where people can read it best. He puts out his hand, and looks up at every passing black woman's face, hoping that one of them will eventually be Rhonda, walking toward him with a big smile, a big smile just for him.

None of them are.

# 5

Tom keeps an eye on the town square from the store window. He can see the dealers at their usual spot, close to the supermarket, but there's more of them than usual. They normally either travel alone, or in pairs. This time, there's four of them. Kyle Hobbs, Shawn Stark, Hal Redford, and Willie Shaw. Willie has a plaster across the bridge of his nose, and he's regularly rubbing at the back of his neck and head, twisting side to side like he's trying to work out a deep kink. He pops pills, most likely painkillers, and gingerly probes at his lips and teeth. There's no sign of the Simmons brothers. No Donny, either.

The four stick close together, and they look solemn. Usually, the dealers he can see will be laughing, joking around, shoving each other, acting like they're still in high school. They're not so playful today. They look over their shoulders. Their mood is sombre. Someone is striking at them, and they're worried about it.

"What you looking at, Tom?" Del says, coming through from the back, carrying a box of hacksaw blades in plastic packaging. The storeroom is only a little smaller than the store itself. It has a couple of rows of shelving where items are kept neatly ordered, and the rest of the space is mostly filled with boxes – boxes of packaging, and of nuts and bolts, of screws and nails.

"Just thinking what a beautiful day it is," Tom says. A bus pulls to a stop on the opposite side of the road and obscures his view of the dealers, so he turns around.

Del grins. "I assume the date went well?"

"It did. Thanks for the drinks, by the way. Hayley said to make sure I sent you her regards. She said she'll try and call in sometime, but she's usually busy at the hospital."

"I'm sure she is," Del says. "Especially with everything going on around town. I assume those boys are over there again?"

Tom nods.

Del shakes his head, looking more disappointed than anything else. He starts hanging up the packaged blades. "I've lived in this town my whole life. I'm not gonna pretend I know everyone who lives here, or what they're like, but I at least recognise most of the faces I see. These days, there's some folk that are so ravaged by whatever it is they're taking, I can't tell if I've ever seen them before or not. And those boys that are selling it to them..." He sighs. "Y'know, Shawn Stark used to work here when he was in high school. He worked here every Saturday, never missed a shift. He was a good kid. I don't know what went wrong. Fell in with the wrong crowd, I guess. Donny Bradshaw, more than likely. I never knew him, but I heard plenty about him. And he's the ringleader, from what I hear. You went to school with him, didn't you?"

"Yeah."

"What was he like?"

"He was an asshole. It sounds like he still is."

Del grunts. "Guess some people never change."

"Something I've been wondering," Tom says. "How come

the cops aren't doing anything about it?" Tom knows exactly why, judging from what he's seen. He's curious to hear what Del has to say on the matter, and if he's seen anything.

"I've wondered that myself," Del says. "At least, I used to. But I've seen cops roll up on them before, from the same vantage point you're enjoying there, and they're all nicey-nicey. Hopper Creek is a small place, and I get the impression the dealers and the cops know each other. Know each other too well. They're friendly. Friends of friends. Enough that the law is turning a blind eye to what's happening in this town. They're gonna turn their blind eye until it's too late and this place is a ghost town. It's happened other places, it could happen here."

This is what Tom has seen, and theorised, too. Much like Del, he's seen it from the same window. Has seen the dealers lean into the open windows of the cop cars, on the rare occasions they come by, and they're all laughing and joking, real friendly.

Behind him, he hears the bus pull away. Tom turns back around, looks toward the dealers. He realises two of them are missing. Shawn and Hal. Tom can't see any sign of them. He watches, waiting. He doesn't think they could have gone far. He scratches at the side of his chin. Del finishes putting out the hacksaw blades.

"How long you gonna watch them for?" he says.

"I'm not sure yet," Tom says. He sees Kyle deal with a customer. The exchange is brazen. They make no secret of what they're doing. No attempt at subtlety. The junkie takes his baggie and hurries away.

Shawn and Hal come back into view. They leave the supermarket. They're not carrying anything. They haven't picked up any groceries. There's nothing in their pockets. They return to Kyle and Willie, converse briefly. Tom wishes he could hear. He's too far to read their lips.

A car speeds by the store, a metallic blue Subaru, going too fast – far faster than it needs to. It tears up the roads around the town square, pulling to a screeching stop where the dealers are. They all stand up at the Subaru's approach. The driver's door swings open. Donny Bradshaw gets out.

Tom is intrigued. Donny doesn't come out into the streets. He doesn't get his hands dirty. He holds back, lets the others do the work for him. He stays at home. Tom has only seen him from afar. It took him a while to realise he was the one behind the operation in town. The others go to his home, meet up with him there.

Except for today. Tom wonders if his assault last night has spooked them so much it's brought Donny out in public. Tom straightens, intrigued. He doubts Donny would come out just to visit his boys on their spot. He never has before. He figures it would have to be something important to bring him here today.

"Del, I'm gonna take my lunch now," Tom says, heading for the door.

Del is behind the counter, standing by the till. "Sure thing," he says without looking up. Del is laid back. He's easy going. He's not going to protest, or ask too many questions. The shop isn't exactly overly busy. Tom often thinks Del gave him the job more for the company than the actual assistance.

Tom strides calmly and casually around the outskirts of the town square, keeping his distance from the dealers. He walks on the shadowy side of the street, keeping close to the store fronts. He watches the crew out the corner of his eye. They don't look his way. Don't even notice him. Tom gets past them on the opposite side of the square, then slips down an alley. He watches them from deeper in the shadows. Donny is talking to his boys. He keeps glancing at his watch, checking the time. Like he could be expecting someone.

Or maybe he's expecting something.

Tom waits. The minutes pass. Donny looks back down the road, over and over. Tom is sure – something is coming. Something important enough that it's brought Donny out here the day after his crew has been attacked. Soon enough, Donny perks up. He slaps Willie on the arm with the back of his hand, draws his attention to it, too. Whatever it is, it isn't close enough yet for Tom to see. He doesn't move from where he is. Doesn't attempt to get into a better vantage spot. He's patient. He's always patient.

He hears the rumble of an approaching truck. It drives straight past the dealers, but they all turn with it, watch it go. Tom watches it go, too. It travels around the back of the supermarket, out of view. It's a supply truck for the store. Tom is intrigued.

The dealers start moving. Donny motions for them to follow him. They get into his Subaru. He drives, but slower this time. He follows the truck around to the back of the supermarket.

Tom leaves the alley. He crosses the town square, and enters the supermarket. He walks straight through it and heads toward the back. He doesn't look side to side, or behind him. He strides with purpose. He steps straight through into the storage room and slips to the side, hiding himself behind boxes of tins. He can see the loading bay, and people in the store's uniform unloading the truck. There's a man in trousers and a white shirt with a charcoal grey tie who must be the manager. He doesn't help to unload. Instead, he heads outside, where Donny and his boys are standing, waiting, by Donny's car. He talks with them. It all seems very friendly to Tom. The manager glances back inside, toward the truck, to see how his workers are getting on. It looks like they're almost done.

Tom can see inside the truck. There's a lot more produce

still on board. It looks like the driver has more than a few stops left to make.

The manager goes inside the back of the truck now. Donny motions for Kyle and Shawn to go with him. The manager talks with the driver, and then he steps in a little deeper, and when he emerges he's carrying a box. It looks like he's struggling with the weight. A moment later, Kyle and Shawn follow him with boxes of their own. They head back outside. Donny opens the trunk of his car and they put the three boxes inside.

Tom looks toward the other workers nearby. They're busying themselves with putting away the newly arrived stock. They're all ignoring what's happening outside. None of them looks that way.

As the manager and Donny exchange parting words, Tom slips out from his hiding spot and heads back through the store. He pulls out his phone as he goes and calls Del. "I'm sorry, Del," he says, "but something's come up. I'm not going to make it back in today."

"Hope it's nothing serious," Del says.

"Could be." Tom hangs up. He heads to his car. Off to his left, he sees the delivery truck driving away from the store. Soon after, he hears the roar of Donny's Subaru. He reaches his car and waits a moment. Gives Donny and the others a chance to get away. Leaves a little space between himself and the delivery truck.

He starts the engine, and he follows.

# 6

Tom has been following the truck for a couple of hours. It's hit two other towns so far. They're in the third town, now. He sits in the Chevy down the block, with a view of the back of the store. It unloads. For the third time it unloads and there aren't any dealers in sight. The truck is unloaded by the staff. The manager doesn't come to supervise. The truck gets emptied of this store's order, and it moves on.

Tom considers this. The influx of flakka hasn't spread this far – not yet, anyway. He's asked around, subtly. He's read newspaper reports. And now, here, he can see it for himself. The lack of graffiti. The better care taken of the plant life, as opposed to it being abandoned, signifying the dying of the town. The lack of zombies, shuffling along on the sidewalks, desperate for their next hit. He drives on, following, wondering if this will change at the next town, or the one after. He wonders how long he'll be following. He wonders how much stock can be left on the truck.

The day is warm. Tom drives with the window down. He listens to Springsteen. *Darkness On The Edge Of Town*. His favourite album by the Boss. Always has been. Now, when he listens to it, it reminds him of Taylor. He thinks about her, in Portland with her brother and his wife. They still keep in touch. He still writes her letters, and she still writes him back, but they're not as frequent as they used to be. It's been almost two years now since he helped her out with her stepfather, and the church/cult he was involved in. Taylor is getting older. He reminds himself that kids grow fast at that age. The things that matter to them so much one month don't matter so much the next. He doesn't take it personally when she takes her time responding to his letters, or when she bemoans the fact that he won't just email her, or the instances when she doesn't respond at all.

He smiles to himself, remembering her. Wherever she is, whatever she's doing, he hopes she's well. He hopes she's happy.

He focuses back on the task in hand. The truck up ahead. They're on the highway. Tom has left space enough for three cars to slip between them. The truck is big. He's not going to lose it.

They drive another fifteen minutes before they turn off for the next town. It's far from the highway. They drive for another half-hour. It's a small town. Tom doesn't think the truck will be here as long as at the others.

While he waits, and watches, his phone rings. It's Hayley. "Hey," she says. "I actually stopped into the store today, and you weren't there. Del said you had to rush off?"

"Yeah, something came up," Tom says. "It's nothing serious."

"Del said it sounded like it might be."

"I just had to look in on a friend."

"Oh really? Anyone I know?"

"I don't think so." Tom changes the subject. "How long ago did you swing by? Have you just got away?"

She chuckles. "No, no, Del didn't keep me talking this long – though he tried. It was very sweet, in fact. He seemed very pleased to see me. My dad used to shop there all the time, and Del used to always give me a lollipop. I'd always get real excited when my dad said he needed to go, and I'd tag along with him."

"They must've been great lollipops."

"He always had red, which was my favourite."

"We've still got red. Did he give you one today?"

"No, but I was tempted to ask." She laughs.

Tom watches the truck get unloaded once again. It looks like they're already nearly done. A quick visit, as he'd expected. "I didn't have candy much as a kid," he says. "Maybe that's why my dad didn't take me along whenever he went to Del's."

"He didn't let you have candy?"

"Not often. Anyway, we're getting off topic."

"Yes, we are, but trust me, they were great lollipops. So no, Del didn't keep me there talking about old times, though he did try. I've just finished lunch and I'm about to head back to the hospital, but I wanted to check how you were doing first."

Tom checks the time. It's nearly three. "That's a late lunch."

"I'm on a late shift. We've got the blood drive later, too, so I'm making sure I eat enough. I don't want to pass out when I donate. If you're back in time you should call by, give some blood. We usually get a good turnout but we can always do with more."

"I'm not sure I'll be back in time."

"Ah, okay. Have *you* eaten, by the way?"

Tom realises he hasn't. "Yeah," he says, not wanting to concern her.

"Okay, well, I just wanted to check in. So long as you're okay."

The truck is leaving the store. It's getting back on its way. Tom wonders how long they're going to be on the road. How far it's going. "I'm good," Tom says. "I appreciate you calling. I'll talk to you later." He follows the truck. He'll follow it as long as he needs to. He has a feeling the driver won't be heading home tonight, not when he's already come so far. And if this is the case, later, when it's dark, when it's quiet, Tom will make his move. He'll find out where the flakka is coming from, and he'll find out who's supplying it.

# 7

---

J im still hasn't heard from, or about, Rhonda. No one
has. His concern rises with every passing moment. At
this point, he knows realistically that the next time he
hears anything about her, it's likely to be bad.

Jim walks through the dark city streets. He heads back to
the park to spend the night. It's late and he's tired. He runs his
hand down his face, thinking of Rhonda still and wishing his
thoughts didn't skew so negative. Well, not necessarily negative – he's a realist. That's probably worse.

He knows where in the park is safe, and where to avoid.
The safe spots are quiet. He takes a seat on a bench, not far
from where he sat with Edgar earlier today. The spots around
him are empty. He's glad. He wants to be alone tonight. Needs
to try and clear his head, before his thoughts can drive him
crazy.

The sky is clear. The stars are bright. Jim turns his face
toward them, counts the biggest of them until his eyes begin
to close. He takes deep breaths, and feels most of the tension
go out of his shoulders – most, but not all. He can't relax
completely. Never. He needs to keep his sharp edges. He

needs to keep some tension at all times, even when he's preparing to sleep. *Especially* when he's about to sleep. He rests light. It carries over from when he was in the Army. The slightest noise, and he's awake.

He balls up his jacket and lies down on his side on the bench, using the jacket as a pillow. It doesn't take long for him to fall asleep.

It feels like, just as quick, he's awakened.

The sound that wakes him isn't close, but it's enough to sit him bolt upright. He scans the area, makes sure he isn't in any immediate danger. There's no one near. He hears the sound again, and his head snaps in its direction. Opposite, but over a hill. He can't see what's happening.

The sound isn't a mystery. It's familiar. Someone is being attacked. Someone – male, young – is crying out, screeching for help like their life depends on it. Someone else is trying to silence them. The cries are repeatedly muffled, but the screamer must be struggling hard. He keeps breaking loose enough to cry out.

There's a struggle. Jim can hear it. He can hear the screamer being beaten, the hard thud of flesh on flesh. The screamer is finally silenced.

Jim knows he shouldn't get involved. He should mind his business. Stay exactly where he is. Chances are, though, the person being beaten is just like him – homeless. It could even be someone he knows.

He thinks back to the Army. You help your brother. You rely on your brother. You don't leave your brother behind.

He grits his teeth and gets to his feet, looking around as he goes to the hill, peering over it toward the struggle. He sees three dark shapes, out of reach of all nearby light, but it's still a clear night. Two big guys, beating on someone smaller. It's too far and too dark for Jim to be sure whether he knows the person being assaulted. That doesn't matter, though.

Whoever the men are – a couple of drunken assholes, or perhaps just general assholes – they're taking advantage of someone less fortunate. He can't stand for that.

Jim looks around. The area is clear. There's no one else approaching. No one else is going to help. The two men are distracted. Jim runs at them. He shoves aside the first one he reaches, then jabs at the face of the other. The attackers are caught off guard by his attack. In the distraction, the man they were beating on scrambles away.

Jim turns, ready to make his own escape, but the man he shoved aside is on him, wrapping his arms around him. Jim attempts to headbutt him, to break his nose and his grip, but the second man has recovered from his jab and is landing shots of his own into the back of Jim's head, dazing him. The man holding him is squeezing the breath out of him. Jim feels his vision is fading.

An engine idles nearby. Jim is no longer upright. No longer being crushed. He's on his back. He thinks he must have blacked out. He turns his dazed head, sees a van has appeared.

"He's coming around," someone says.

Jim tries to look, to see who has spoken. All he sees is a boot, coming right for his face.

## 8

E arly evening, the truck driver checks into a motel.
Tom lets him get comfortable, lets it get a little
darker, and then he makes his move.

He goes to the truck first. He picks the lock on the back
and slides the door up enough for him to roll inside. Using
the torch on his phone, he looks around. The truck is empty.
Tom checks it thoroughly for any hiding spaces, anywhere
the flakka could be secretly transported. He doesn't find
anything. He leaves the back of the truck and closes it up,
then moves onto the motel.

Peering into the driver's room, he can see him lying half-
asleep on the bed, the television blaring on the stand beyond
his feet. The driver is middle-aged, thin, and tired. Struggling
to keep his eyes open. He chuckles sleepily at something. He
doesn't look like a fighter to Tom. He's not going to be much
trouble. Tom scans the rest of the room, too. No sign of any
weapons. No handgun on the bedside table, or a holster
hanging over the back of a chair.

Tom doesn't bother with anything fancy. He goes to the
room's door and knocks, hard and loud enough to stir the

driver from his daze. Tom has to knock again before he receives a response.

The driver calls something, most likely asking who's knocking, then clears his throat. "Pizza delivery," Tom says, putting his mouth close to the door as he calls through.

This time, he makes out what the driver says. "I didn't order any pizza."

"Man, I've got a pizza here and it's getting cold, and I was told to come *here*."

"I told you I didn't order any pizza." The driver is protesting, but Tom can hear him coming closer to the door.

"Man, I'm not in any mood for games – just come get your pizza so I can get back to work, huh?"

The driver unlocks the door. Tom doesn't wait for him to open it. As he twists the handle, Tom pushes the door open and forces his way in. He pins the driver against the wall. "Don't make a sound," Tom says, but his forearm is across the driver's windpipe, and any noise beyond the choked gasps he's managing would be impossible.

With his spare hand, Tom throws the door shut behind him. The driver is staring at him, wide-eyed. He's afraid. As Tom suspected, he's not a fighter. There's no struggle in him. He doesn't attempt to break Tom's grip, or to push himself off the wall. His hands rest on Tom's forearm instinctively, hoping to loosen it for a little more breath.

"I'm gonna ease up," Tom says, "and you're gonna take a seat over there on the chair by the window. You make noise, try to call for help, and I'm gonna have to hurt you. That clear?"

The driver nods as much as he's able. Tom slowly removes his forearm. The driver takes a deep breath, but he doesn't attempt anything. He goes to the chair by the window and Tom follows. The driver sits, but Tom remains standing.

"What's your name?" Tom says.

"Smitts."

Tom assumes this to be his last name. "Full name," Tom says.

"W-why?"

"In case I need to know it later." Tom holds his eye.

Smitts shrivels under it. "Leland Smitts," he says.

"I'm gonna be checking your ID, Leland Smitts, so that better be the truth."

"It's my name, I swear. Look, I don't know what you think you're gonna get from me – my truck's empty. I've done my route. I'm going home tomorrow–"

"Stop talking," Tom says.

Smitts promptly shuts up.

"There's only one thing you transport that I'm interested in," Tom says. "The flakka. Who's making it, and where are they?"

Smitts's jaw works. He's not able to say anything straight away. Throat dry, he asks, "You a cop?"

Tom stares at him.

"I dunno – what is this, man? You another dealer or something? I – I don't wanna get involved in anything more than I already am."

"But you *are* involved, Smitts. You're in deep. Deep enough to have answers to my questions."

Smitts squirms in the chair. "Why – why do you wanna know?"

"That's my business."

"Man, I can't tell you – they'll *kill* me."

"What do you think *I'll* do to you?" Tom has no intention of killing this man, but Smitts doesn't know that. However, the look he gives Smitts lets him know that he's more than capable of following through.

Smitts swallows. There's a dry click in his throat. "They're...they're in Bittersweet."

Only a couple of towns over from Hopper Creek. "How many towns do you supply, Smitts?"

"I don't – I don't *supply* anyone. I just drop it off, that's all. I'm paid to pick it up, drop it off, and turn a blind eye. That's all I do. I don't make the shit, I don't use it, and I don't sell it."

"And yet you're just as complicit," Tom says. "How many towns?"

Smitts sighs. "Basically, from Bittersweet to Hopper Creek."

"You drop it off in supermarkets all the way?"

He nods. "That's why they roped me in."

"How'd you get into this?"

"I didn't. I've only been driving this route six months. It was the guy I took over from. He's retired now, but he took the deal originally. To top up his retirement plan. So it just kinda fell into my lap. Not that I had much choice..."

"You were forced into it?"

"Basically."

"I'm sure the money doesn't hurt."

Smitts doesn't say anything to this. He looks away.

"Who makes the flakka?" Tom says.

"I don't know their names. The guy before me, like I said, he set it all up. I think they were buddies of his, but I didn't wanna know. Figured less I knew, the better."

"In this instance, it sounds like you know just as much as I need. Whereabouts do you make the collection in Bittersweet?"

"It's like, it's this compound just outside the town. I think it used to be part of a mine or something years ago, before it shut down. It's been abandoned for decades."

"And is that where they make the flakka?"

"I think so. I mean, it's gotta be – it's so remote. Do you want me to – to give you the address or something?"

"No need," Tom says, turning. He goes to where the landline is on the bedside table, and tears the cable out of the wall.

"What're you – what're you doing?" Smitts says, though he's staring at the cable and it's clear he knows he's about to be tied up.

"You're coming with me," Tom says. "You can give me directions on the road."

"But – but–"

"You know my face, Smitts," Tom says. "I'm hardly gonna leave you all alone while I go off to check out this compound, am I?"

Smitts opens his mouth to protest, but he promptly decides against it. His mouth clamps shut. His shoulders slump. He sighs and holds out his wrists, waiting for them to be tied.

# 9

Kendis Dukes shivers as he gets out of the
passenger side of the Lexus and looks up at the
old hospital. It's not a cold night, but the sight,
and the knowledge of who is inside, still gives him the chills.

"Jesus Christ, you see that?" he says, turning to Big Ron as
he gets out of the driver's door. The car is Kendis's, bought
brand new, but he's never driven a mile in it. That's what he
has Big Ron for, among other things. "This creepy motherfucker is giving me the shivers, now."

Big Ron grunts. "He's a fucking ghoul, all right." Big Ron
more than lives up to his nickname. His real name is Ronald
Savage. He used to play football, but a knee injury stopped
him from turning pro. He's six-foot four, and two hundred
fifty pounds of solid muscle. He may not have been able to
pursue his footballing ambitions, but he's maintained the
physique – if anything, he's gotten bigger since those days.
Kendis found him working as a doorman for a nightclub. Saw
him bust three skulls, some assholes who had been getting
obnoxious with one of the female bartenders, and Kendis –

who had been waiting for his old driver to pull around – hired him on the spot. So now Big Ron is his bodyguard, and has been for the last five years. Officially, for tax purposes, he's listed as Kendis's driver.

"That's what I get for hiring a white boy," Kendis says, heading inside. "They're all fucking ghouls."

Big Ron chuckles at this. A lot of the men on Kendis's payroll are white.

Referring to Alec as a boy isn't entirely accurate, though handling him sometimes feels like dealing with a child. He's fifty-four, fifteen years older than Kendis himself. He's ageing well, even after his stint in prison. His hair, despite being mostly white, is full, and he's in good shape. Lean, like an athlete.

Kendis and Big Ron head through the abandoned, but not empty, hospital, heading up to the top floor where Alec makes his office. On the way, they pass a few of Kendis's men. They stand to attention as he approaches, like they're in the Army and he's their commanding officer. It's not true, and Kendis knows it probably looks a little silly, but it still brings a smile to his face. He nods at them, says hello, and fights the urge to tell them, *At ease.*

"Quiet tonight," Big Ron says, as they ascend the stairs.

"The patients must all be tucked in and out for the night," Kendis says. They reach the room Alec uses as his office. There's loud music coming from inside. Classical. Kendis doesn't know anything about classical music. He steps inside without bothering to knock.

Alec Hill leans back in his chair with his feet upon his desk. His eyes are closed, listening to the music. He turns a little, looking to see who has intruded upon him, though he probably already knows – no one else would barge in like this.

Alec does not stand to attention. He doesn't lower the

music, or even take his feet off the desk. "Kendis," he says, with a slight nod. He doesn't attempt to raise his voice to be heard over the music, and Kendis has to strain to make him out. "I thought you'd probably drop by. Your visits are becoming more and more regular."

Kendis motions to Big Ron. "Turn that shit off," he says.

Big Ron goes to the stereo in the corner, hits the power.

Alec cocks an eyebrow. "Brahms is not *shit*," he says.

"I could give a fuck," Kendis says. "You know why I'm here."

"Indeed." Alec finally takes his feet from the desk. He doesn't stand. He leans back in his swivel chair, but he at least turns it so it's facing Kendis and Big Ron. He laces his fingers in his lap.

When it becomes clear he's not going to continue without prompting, Kendis says, "*Well*? How many you pick up tonight?"

"Three," Alec says. "Two males, one female."

"Any trouble?"

"Not really. A couple of your men got into it with someone in the park, one of them ended up with a bump on the nose, but nothing serious."

"You had a chance to check their bloods yet?"

"I've checked," Alec says.

"*And*?"

"No luck, I'm afraid. But, Kendis, you know, I've already told you it's a *very* rare blood type. AB-negative is the *most* rare. Our chances of finding someone, especially plucking these people off the street, is very unlikely."

"Unlikely, but not impossible," Kendis says, hiding his disappointment. "And if the chance arises, I want to know about it." If they find someone with AB-negative blood, they can make a *lot* of money off them. Kendis doesn't say this part out loud. Alec doesn't need to know what kind of money they're making.

"That chance has not arisen tonight, I'm afraid."

Kendis folds his arms. "I feel like you don't care, Alec."

"Of course I care, Kenny." Alec rocks side to side in his chair. He smiles. It's a tight-lipped smile, but his always are. He never expresses humour, or much in the way of emotion. Just smug self-satisfaction. An aloofness. Alec spreads his hands. "I do the best with what your men supply me."

"They can't tell blood type by sight, Alec."

"And neither can I, Kenny. And it's *Doctor* Hill."

"Used to be."

"You never lose it."

"The medical register would disagree."

Alec chuckles, but it's without mirth. "Fuck them."

"Uh-huh. And it's *Kendis*. None of that Kenny bullshit." Kendis takes a deep breath. Calms himself. Alec is too valuable to him, and Alec knows it. "What have you been doing tonight?"

"Working."

"I mean specifically."

Alec smiles, and this time there is genuine delight in it. Kendis can even see some of his teeth. It's unnerving. "There's a fresh lung on ice, two beautiful brown corneas, and a kidney."

"You've been busy," Kendis says. "That's a lot. How many did you operate on?"

Alec is still smiling. It deepens. "One." He looks pleased with himself.

"*One?* They all come from the same person?"

Alec's smile shows all of his teeth this time, and that's answer enough.

Kendis's skin crawls at the sight. "How – *how*?"

"Because he's young, and he's healthy. But mainly because I'm damn good at what I do."

"Where's he now – in the basement?"

Alec shakes his head. "There's still some use to be had out of him. He's my pet project."

"How are you keeping him alive?"

"A lot of machinery, and a lot of drugs."

Kendis's eyes narrow. "And how much is this costing me?"

"You can afford it."

"I'm not in the business of losing my money on your experiments."

"I've crunched the numbers," Alec says. "You're not in any danger of running out, no matter how long I keep him alive for."

"And how long do you expect that to be?"

"That's what we're going to find out."

Kendis shoots Big Ron a look. Big Ron looks as uneasy as Kendis feels. Kendis is ready to leave. He feels like he's already been here long enough. This operation is his, this business is his, but he hates it here. Alec has turned this empty building into a butcher shop. It's clean, and everyone here is clean, and it's calm, but whenever he walks through he expects to see blood on the walls, and to hear screaming, like trapped, dying animals crying out.

"From now on, when you get people in," Kendis says, "first thing you do, I want you to check their bloods. You got that? That's your priority. Job number one. And then you contact me – not just for the AB-negative. I wanna know everyone's bloods."

"Why?" Alec says.

"Because I want it to be in your *head* that I want to know the fucking blood types. I want to know when we have an AB-negative. And when you don't get in touch with me, it feels like you don't give a shit, Alec. So get into the habit. That clear?"

Alec shrugs. "Sure. I'll get one of your lackeys to relay that information to you while I work."

"No – *you*. *You* are going to contact me, and *you* are going to tell me the bloods. I want to know that this is getting done."

"If you don't believe I'm checking, ask your men."

"Oh, I *do* ask them," Kendis says. "And yet I still feel the need to have to come down here and check in on you, because you don't keep me up to date. You're gonna keep me up to date, Alec."

Alec smiles, and it's back to being humourless. "Of course," he says. "Anything to make you happy, Kenny. I mean, Kendis. And, if it stops you feeling like you need to come down here, that's all the better."

"What's that supposed to mean?"

"It's so much more peaceful when you just leave me be. I like to work at the fresh meat while it's still fresh, and when you come, it just distracts me from my patients."

"You didn't look particularly busy when we got here. *Brahms*, was it?"

"All part of the process."

Kendis grunts. "Mm." He taps Big Ron on the arm and nods his head toward the door. "Keep me up to date, Alec. I don't like to have to ask."

Kendis and Big Ron leave the building. Once they're outside, Kendis feels better. The air is cleaner. The atmosphere isn't so heavy. He shakes his head at Big Ron before they get into the Lexus. "You were right," he says. "He *is* a fucking ghoul. Dr fucking Frankenstein in there."

"I don't like him," Big Ron says. "And I don't like how he talks to you."

Kendis waves this off. "Don't worry about it. I know how

to handle him. Asshole can be as pompous as he wants, but once we get that AB-negative liver we ain't gonna need him anymore. My buyer's getting desperate, and what he's willing to pay, we'll be retiring to the Bahamas."

Big Ron grins at this. "Sounds good to me."

"Hell yeah, it sounds good," Kendis says, laughing at he gets into the car.

## 10

It's early morning. Tom and Smitts arrived in Bittersweet after midnight. Smitts gave him directions to the lab. It's outside of town, like Smitts said, and the road was quiet. It looked unused. Tom left his car parked at the side of the main road, and he and Smitts continued on foot through the darkness.

"This all looks different on foot," Smitts said. "I'm used to driving down here pretty fast. It's all a blur. In and out."

"Take it all in," Tom said. "This'll be the last time you need to come this way."

It wasn't too far from the main road. Twenty minutes of cautious walking. It would take less if they weren't being so careful.

They found a covered spot in the trees where Tom had a clear view of the lab opposite, and they settled in.

Smitts has been on his best behaviour. He's never attempted anything. Never said anything out of line. He's been placid the whole journey, in the car and on foot. He's doing what he's told, isn't trying to cause any trouble. For the past couple of hours he's been napping off to the side. Tom has kept his wrists bound, though, and wrapped the wire around a nearby tree. Smitts hasn't protested this.

The lab is an old mining building, as Smitts described. It's concealed by overgrown bushes and unkempt trees, and the outside of the building is covered in creeping vines of ivy. Tom has spotted signs of life within, though, and there is a foul smell hanging in the air around the area. It smells a little like burnt plastic, and it's enough to give Tom the edge of a headache.

Tom knows that cutting off the drug supply and destroying the source will not fix all of Hopper Creek's problems. He's not a fool. He knows, too, that drug addiction is often a symptom, not a cause of what drives the user to drugs in the first place. What they really need is treatment, not the likes of him destroying the poison they're putting inside themselves.

But this is something that can be tackled at a later date. Tom isn't going anywhere. For now, though, he deals best in immediacy. And, immediately, he can see that his home town is dying. It has a cancer. He needs to curtail that death. He needs to cut out the cancer. *This* he can do.

From inside the building, he hears the occasional raised voice, or a burst of laughter but it's mostly quiet. What sounds he does hear are more like a social gathering than an operational lab. The windows closest to the road that lead to it have been covered on the inside with black-painted wood. The glass in the windows has all been smashed. The windows closer to the front of the building are still intact, however. The view inside is obscured with old rags, but they don't conceal much. Earlier, when Tom gagged Smitts and got closer, he could see lights on inside. He got close enough to the windows at the front to get a good look at the people within.

There were two of them. One of them was armed – a

Glock tucked carelessly down the back of his ill-fitting jeans. The lab didn't appear to be in operation, and Tom figured the two men present were here to guard it. They aren't doing a very good job. Not once, in all the hours he's been here, has Tom seen either of them perform a perimeter sweep. He hasn't even seen them come to the windows to look out. The closest they've come to stepping outside was leaving the front door to take a piss into the weeds at the side. They leave the front door unlocked – careless of them, but an important detail for Tom. When he was closer, the one without the gun was swinging in a chair and smoking something – potentially flakka, though he looked too calm for it to be that. Whatever it was, he and the armed guard passed it back and forth.

It looks too easy. Tom has waited to be sure. They're as laid back here as Donny and his dealers were in Hopper Creek, before Tom struck at them. He wonders if Donny has spread word of this attack and if perhaps the guard detail inside is the manufacturers' response to a potential threat. He doesn't think so, though. He thinks this is likely how it always is. They're lazy. They're unconcerned. They don't believe anything bad can happen to them. This spreading operation has been so good for them for so long, they've forgotten what it can be like when bad things happen.

Tom is ready. He doesn't think this is going to take long. He nudges Smitts. "I'm gonna have to gag you again," he says. "You've behaved yourself this far, don't go and fuck that all up now by trying something stupid."

Smitts nods. "Nothing stupid," he says.

Tom gags him, then, ducking low, heads back to the lab. He checks through the window on the guards. The armed guy is leaning against the wall, flicking through a nudey magazine. The other is asleep in his chair, his head hanging back at an uncomfortable angle and his mouth wide, a trail of thick drool running from the corner of it. Tom can hear his snores through the glass.

Tom goes to the back of the building, by the road, and he kicks down one of the black-painted boards on the inside. It falls to the floor in an empty room with a loud bang. Tom doesn't hang around. He rushes back down the side of the building, toward the front, pausing as he goes to check in the windows again. Both men are looking back toward where the sound came from. The sleeper has awakened, and is twisted in his chair to look back, wiping at his mouth. Tom watches them, window to window, as he goes.

They debate among themselves. Tom can't hear them through the glass. The armed guard pulls out his Glock. He holds it out in front of him, sideways, like he thinks he's in a movie. The other gets out of his chair and huddles in close behind him. Tom reaches the corner of the building. He watches. The armed guard shrugs the other guy off and motions for him to stay where he is, then he heads toward the room. He opens the door and fumbles for the light switch, then steps inside to investigate.

Tom moves fast. He gets in through the unlocked front door. He's quiet. It's not a big room, and Tom is able to cross the space quickly. He reaches the guard standing in the centre of the room, waiting for his friend, and clamps a chokehold on him from behind. He pulls him to the side, dragging his feet along the ground, and slips through a door into another room, next to the one the armed guard is investigating. When the guard in his arms goes limp, Tom lowers him to the ground.

The other guard steps out into the lab. "The hell?" he says. "Yo, where'd you go?"

Tom stands very still, listening. He's left the door open a little, and he stays close to it.

"Yo, this supposed to be funny? I ain't laughing, man."

Tom pulls on the door, opens it a little wider. It creaks. Enough to get the other guy's attention.

"What're you doing in there?" the guard calls. "You playing hide and seek? You think this is a joke?"

Tom can hear him approach, stomping across the ground.

"Man, I'm gonna whoop your ass – you trynna scare me or something?"

He storms into the room, and Tom is ready for him. He slams his left elbow across the guard's jaw. It's a precise shot, and the armed guard crumples to the ground, out cold. Tom retrieves his Glock, tucks it into his own jeans.

Tom pats both of the men down. The unarmed guard has a lighter. Tom keeps hold of it, then grabs him by the ankles and drags him out of the building, far away from it. He goes back and does the same to the other, lying them side by side. He returns to the lab. He goes to the boxes in the corner, and opens one up. It's filled with the familiar baggies he found in Hopper Creek. The white and pink crystals mixed in together.

There are half a dozen boxes in total. Tom drags them into the centre of the room. He moves around the lab and finds every chemical container that he can. He soaks the bottom box and then piles the rest of the chemicals, still in their containers, at the base. Taking the Glock from his waistband, he ejects the magazine and places the empty weapon on top of the pile. There are six rounds in the magazine. Using his KA-BAR, he separates the bullets from their cartridges, and pours the powder onto the ground at the base of the wet box. He makes a trail leading away. When he's emptied all six cartridges, he presses the lighter to the gunpowder trail, and steps outside.

He watches through the open door as the boxes catch fire. It spreads to the chemical containers, which burst, and the flames begin to spread around the room, carried on the liquids. He looks back. The two guards are beginning to stir, but it's too late for them to do anything. Tom walks away, back toward Smitts.

It's dawn, now. The sky is gradually lightening. Smitts is where he left him, sitting cross-legged and watching as the lab begins to burn. It's clear he hasn't made any attempt to escape. He shakes his head as Tom approaches. Once Tom removes the gag, he says, "You're burning it? I thought you were gonna rip it off. Who the hell are you?"

"You don't need to worry about it. Let's go."

They head back toward the main road, travelling through the field to avoid anyone that might come rushing to the burning lab. Again, Smitts does not grumble. He does not try to escape. Tom wishes all hostages could be like him.

They get back to the car in time to see other vehicles go racing down the old road. Probably the most traffic it's had on it at one time in a long time. None of them are emergency vehicles. Two cars and a pickup, only the pickup carrying an extra passenger. The two cars contain only the drivers.

"You recognise any of them?" Tom says.

"They were going too fast," Smitts says, "but even if they weren't, I doubt it. Like I've told you, I have as little to do with these guys as I can." Smitts looks where they've gone, the road they've disappeared down, and then he looks back to Tom, concerned. "What – what're you gonna do now?"

"I'm gonna take you to a bus stop," Tom says. Smitts looks relieved at this, but he also raises an eyebrow, like this is not the answer he was expecting. Tom isn't concerned about the men racing to the burning lab. The lab is destroyed. That's what he came here to do. It'll take them a long time to get their operation up and running again, and, if they do, Tom will be back to shut it down all over again. By then, he'll have cleaned up Hopper Creek. "I'd take you back to the motel, but I'm in a rush." He starts the engine, gets the car moving, pulls onto the road and heads into Bittersweet. He glances at Smitts while they drive. "I'm going to need your silence, Smitts. It's in your interest to keep quiet. To forget my face. Do you understand me?"

"I don't even know your name, man."

"No, but I know yours, Leland Smitts. I tracked you down once, and if I have to, I can find you again. I don't want to have to do that."

Smitts doesn't respond, but Tom knows he understands.

They reach Bittersweet and Tom pulls to the kerb opposite from the bus stop. He loosens Smitts' binds and dumps the wire in the back of the car. He hands him a twenty for the bus. "Make sure I don't see you again."

Smitts gets out of the car. He leans in before crossing the road to the stop. "I'll do my best," he says. He takes a deep breath before closing the door. "Well, it's really been...*something*. I truly hope I don't see you again, aggressive stranger."

Tom watches him cross the road, then turns his car around and heads back to Hopper Creek. He hopes that Smitts will stay quiet, won't tell anyone what he's done, but he can't rely on this. While he believes him when he says he wanted as little to do with the operation as possible, the fact is he did still partake in it. Tom can't trust him. He needs to move fast from here on out.

But that's fine, because that's exactly what he plans on doing. Everything has gone how he's wanted it to so far. He's on track. Now, he strikes at the heart of Hopper Creek's drug problem.

Now, he goes for Donny.

# 11

J im wakes.

He's dazed. He's confused. He knows all too well the difference between a post-beating state and a post-drugged state. This is the latter.

Except, the last thing he remembers happening, he was taking a beating. He hasn't touched any drugs in a long time, now. Not since Rhonda got him clean.

The best thing he can do right now is close his eyes and clear his head. He does, taking deep breaths, in and out through his nose, while he counts down from one hundred. While he does this, the air around him becomes clearer. His awareness returns, taking in everything he can feel. He's lying on a thin mattress, and something about it reminds him of being on a hospital bed. He can feel the cold metal of a cuff on his left wrist, and if he moves he can hear it jangling. Somewhere nearby, he can hear beeping, and a strange kind of compression, like artificial lungs. It *sounds* like being in a hospital, too. He opens his eyes and the room he's in comes into focus.

As he suspected, it's a hospital, but something about it

feels off. There are no lights overhead. The room is dim. There's a lamp without a shade in the corner. It's on, but it doesn't produce much light. The walls aren't exactly dirty, but something about them doesn't look as clean as he would expect in a hospital. Not as well maintained as they should be. Then, off to his right, there is a window. A blind is pulled down, keeping out the outside world. Jim is about to turn away from it when he realises there is masking tape running down either side of the blind, holding it down and in place, blocking out all outside light. Stopping anyone from looking out.

Or from looking in.

He looks down at himself. It hurts to move. He's in a white gown. He scans the room, and off to his right, in the corner, he can see a small pile of clothes. They must be his.

Jim lets his head fall back into the pillow and tries to pinpoint where he's hurting. It's his back, on the left. Low down. All the pain is emanating from that point.

He turns his head toward the sound of the beeping, and the respirator. It turns out he's not alone in the room. Across from him, there's another bed. The man lying in it is unconscious. He's young, and white, and he's covered in bandages. One covers his eyes. Jim forces himself up on his elbows, trying to get a better look at him through the dim light. He grimaces at the sight.

As well as the bandaging obscuring his eyes, there's a clear tube running into his mouth, held in place with tape on either side. It pumps air into him, and Jim watches as his shallow chest rises and falls, ever so slightly, with its pressure. It looks like there was a blanket on him, but it's down around his feet. He's wearing a gown, too, but his legs are clad in compression socks. There are various IV's running into his arms, and the backs of his hands. The monitor which shows his heartrate does not look as active as Jim would expect it to be. Whatever has happened to him, he looks in a bad way.

Jim isn't sure how he came to be in a hospital. Wonders if perhaps the men that beat him down left him lying somewhere, and then some Good Samaritan dropped him off here. He has no recollection of it. But then he remembers the feel of the cuff on his left wrist, and he looks toward it. He's cuffed to the bed railing that's there to prevent him from falling out. He wonders if the police brought him here. He's not sure what could have happened that would make them think they needed to restrain him.

Then, out the corner of his eye, he spots something on his neighbour's bed. He pushes himself up a little higher, until he's sitting upright, so he can see better. The man in the next bed is cuffed to the railing, too. He doesn't look like he's in any condition to go anywhere anytime soon.

Jim doesn't like this. The whole situation gives him an uncomfortable feeling. This place feels off. He's pretty sure he's visited all the hospitals in Santa Fe at least once, and this one doesn't look familiar to him. Sure, he hasn't necessarily been in an overnight room in all of them, but still. This doesn't feel right.

He deliberates calling out, but then notices there isn't a buzzer at the top of his bed, or at the side. Nothing to get a nurse or a doctor's attention. He realises there's not even a bedside table. There aren't any chairs, either. It's the same around his neighbour's bed. Jim's eyes go back to his clothes in the corner, just dumped there. They haven't even been folded.

He looks toward the room's door, to the small window in it. Beyond, out in the corner, he can see light, but again, it's dim. Like out there is lit by the same kind of lamps as in the room. He watches for a few minutes and doesn't see anyone walk by. He can't hear any kind of activity out there.

Jim decides against calling out. Instead, he thinks back to being attacked in the park. He has no idea what happened next, after the brief skirmish. It could be that those men, whoever they were, brought him *here*. Wherever *here* is. It makes sense. It's about all that makes sense right now.

More than that, when he woke up he felt drugged. It's fading now. Whatever dose they hit him with, it probably wasn't strong enough. Jim has been clean for a while, but when he was using he managed to build up a high tolerance. Whoever drugged him, they probably weren't expecting it to wear off before morning.

Speaking of morning, he's not sure what time it is right now. He thinks it's still night, but it could be close to dawn.

Jim stares at the cuff. He sucks his teeth while he thinks, looking around the rest of the room and plotting his next move. Whatever he decides, he needs to put it into motion fast. Hanging around here doesn't feel like a good idea. No one has looked in on them yet, but that could be just a matter of time.

He gets to his feet and inspects the railing on the side of the bed closer. If he had tools, he'd be able to get it off, but there aren't signs of anything like that in the room. Instead, he's going to have to use brute force.

The bed is on wheels. He knocks off the locks and pulls the bed closer to the wall, so he can brace himself. It's out of sight of the window in the door, too, in case anyone wanders by. Before he starts properly, he gives a practice tug, just to test how firm the railing is. It rattles a little, like its screws and bolts could do with a tightening. It still feels solid enough, though. Enough to cause a challenge.

With his back against the wall, Jim grits his teeth and starts pulling on the link, hoping to twist the railing. He gives it sharp yanks, but this makes more noise that he would like. His eyes dart toward the window. No one comes to investigate. He looks toward his roommate, too, but he doesn't stir. Jim isn't surprised. At least one of those IV's, if not more, are likely pumping him full of drugs. A bomb could go off and he wouldn't wake.

Jim tugs on the cuff as hard as he can, pulling on it with both hands. It cuts into his left wrist. He realises he's bleeding, but he tries to ignore this. He raises a foot to the bed, to brace, and then finds himself standing on the bed and pulling upward. He bites his lip to avoid screaming out in frustration.

Finally, the railing begins to give. This motivates him. He pulls on it, harder and harder, not caring about the noise anymore, driven to break free.

The railing breaks away from the bed and Jim falls back. He hits the wall with a thud, and his momentary elation is halted as a sharp pain runs up and down his spine, and then his whole body. He gasps at the sharp agony on his left side. His ribs ache. It feels like he's been stabbed. There's a burning at the back of his throat and his stomach does a somersault. It feels like he's about to throw up, but he swallows it down. Then, he freezes, looking toward the door, the window, to see if anyone comes running to investigate the noises he's made. He listens at the wall. If he and his roommate are next to another room, if they have neighbours, they don't shout their protest at the sound of his slamming into the wall.

Jim lets out a long breath and gets off the bed. The railing is still attached to the cuff, but now he's off the bed it'll be easier to disengage.

He gets down onto the floor and twists and pulls at the metal of the railing, bending it back and forward out of shape, until finally it begins to tear. He works at this, until he's able to pull the cuff through. There's nothing he can do

about the cuff attached to his wrist right now, but at least he's
not going to be hauling a bed railing around with him.

His body screams for rest, but he ignores it. He can't stay
put. He needs to keep moving. To take advantage of what he's
gained so far. The last thing he needs is for whoever brought
him here to come in and cuff him to the other side of the bed,
and up his dosage of the drugs.

Crawling, glancing back toward the window in the door,
he goes to his pile of clothes. His tattered old boots are
hidden beneath them. He's glad of this. After tearing off the
gown, he pulls on his jeans. Loose change jangles in his pockets. He slips into his boots, and then pulls on his shirt. Whilst
buttoning it, he goes to the door. Peers out the window. He
can't see anyone out there. Carefully, he tries the handle. It's
locked.

"*Shit.*" Jim sucks his teeth while he looks it over. It's a
heavy door, and he's too weak to make any kind of attempt at
busting it open. He checks the lock. Peering through, he can
see it's locked from the outside, and the key is still in the lock.

Leaving the door for now, he crosses to the taped window.
He tears a strip off so he can peer around the side, take a look
at what's outside. If they're not too high, he can potentially
escape out the window.

It's too high.

Looking down, Jim estimates he's about four storeys up.
He's never had much of a head for heights at the best of
times. He looks around. Looks further. Is shocked to find
he's not far from the city. They're on the outskirts, still
within the city limits. He realises he knows where he is. This
*is* a hospital, though it's long been defunct. He can't
remember the name of it but he knows it closed down about
six years ago. Some people he knows used to take shelter
here, but then the building was bought. He doesn't know
who by, or what their plans were. He'd heard they might

convert it into a hotel, but then time passed and nothing changed.

It's clear to him now, being inside, that the hotel story was just a fabrication, most likely to distract the city from what is really going on in here.

Jim isn't entirely sure what it is that's *really* going on in here, but he's quite certain it's nothing good. Whatever those men in the park were attacking the kid for, before they settled on taking Jim with them, he doubts it was to offer him an overnight stay in a homeless hotel. They didn't strike him as the philanthropical types.

Despite the darkness in the building, it's getting light outside. It's after dawn. There are cars on the road, and a scant few people moving on the sidewalks. Jim can see a bus stop nearby. He rummages through the change in his pockets, counts it up. It's not much, but if he's able to get out of here it's enough to get him far enough away from this place to rest and regroup.

The rising light is worrying, though. With the day coming, whoever is outside the door could start doing rounds. Looking in on the unwitting patients. Jim needs to figure a way out of here, and he needs to do it fast.

His eyes settle on the various monitors hooked up to his roommate. The heart monitor. Jim has a plan.

He moves his own bed back into position, away from the wall. If it's where it should be, it's less likely to draw attention. He goes to the door again, looks out the window. There's still no one near. Presumably, though, the heart monitor is rigged up to somewhere outside this room. A makeshift office, perhaps. If it crashes, it should bring them running.

He hopes, at least.

He gets close to the bed. To his roommate. The closest he's been to him so far. Over the top of his gown, Jim can see a deep and fresh scar that looks to run down the centre of his ribcage. He pulls the gown down so he can get at the monitors, and sees that he's right about the scar. Except, a scar implies that it's healed. This wound is still fresh. Puckered and pink. Jim winces. The man looks like he's had his chest cracked open.

Moving fast, he pulls off the monitors and then gets into position behind the door. A moment later, the machine makes a long, steady buzz, as if the patient is flatlining.

It doesn't take long before Jim hears footsteps pounding down the corridor. He can hear raised voices. The clattering of a trolley. Then, the key scrapes in the lock. The door is thrown open. Jim presses himself against the wall. He catches the handle. No one seems to notice the door is held open for them.

Three men race into the room. A fourth follows them. He looks like a doctor. He wears a white coat, which matches the colour of his hair. He beckons to the man who has pushed in the trolley. "Get the paddles ready," he says. "I had high hopes for the longevity of this one. I'm not going to lose him so soon after I've told Kendis about him."

Jim doesn't hang around to watch or listen. He slips out of the room and lets the door close behind him. The key is gone. He can't lock them in there. That doesn't matter. He's out now, and he needs to keep moving.

The corridor is clear. There's an elevator at the end. Jim goes to it, but it doesn't work. Turning, he spots a doorway leading to the fire escape stairwell and hurries toward it. He knows it's only a matter of time before they realise the other bed is empty. He wants to get as far from the room by then as he can.

Four flights down is a long way to go. The pain in his back increases, but Jim does his best to ignore it, gritting his teeth through it all. The stairwell, luckily, is empty. As he goes, he wonders how many of these rooms are occupied. He could exit the stairwell and check a couple of rooms, but it's not worth the time, or the effort. He doesn't dwell on these thoughts. He can't. Soon after, he hears raised voices above. He hears pounding steps on the stairs. Distant for now, but they'll soon gain. They've realised he's gone. They've realised there was nothing wrong with his roommate's heartrate.

Jim reaches the bottom of the stairwell and peers out. It's an empty corridor beyond. He sees the glass door at the end of it. He slips out of the stairwell, the people above still too far away to have noticed him, and races for the exit.

"Hey!"

The call comes from nearby. Someone already on the ground floor. Jim doesn't turn to look. He hears them give chase. He keeps running. Spots that the main door is blocked – when it was a functioning hospital, it looks like it was a rotating door, but now it's been jammed shut to stop anyone from getting in.

Jim doesn't let this slow him. He spots an open door and dives into it, finding himself in an office, most likely an administrative assistant's. He slams the door closed behind him. There's a window at the back of the office, and it's not boarded over, or taped shut. Jim runs for it. The window is high up, but there's a desk nearby. He drags it to the wall and climbs. As he gets the window open, the office door is forced open. He crawls out the window, feeling grasping hands graze his boots as he falls to the ground below.

It's a rough landing, but not as rough as if it had been four storeys. He reminds himself of this as he forces himself up to his feet and runs for the road, forcing his way through the overgrown bushes that obscure the chain-link fence from his view. He scrambles over the top, and has another tough landing on the other side.

Grinding his jaw, Jim pushes on. He sees the bus stop up ahead. Can see a bus pulling up to it. He pushes on. There aren't many people around, but he notices how some of them all look his way. A wild, wide-eyed homeless man, running for a bus. They stay out of his way.

Jim manages to get on before it closes its doors. He keeps the handcuff concealed within his sleeve, and keeps this arm pressed against his body to further conceal it. All the way, he hasn't looked back. He's gone on the assumption that he's being chased, whether he was or not. It kept him moving.

The bus driver looks up at him with a raised eyebrow. "Where you going, buddy?"

Jim is breathing hard. He pulls all the change from his pockets and drops it onto the plate. He swallows and says, "Far as that will get me."

The driver rolls his eyes and sighs at the change. While he counts it up, Jim looks toward the hospital. He can't see anyone following, and he wonders if that means he was able to give them the slip. He hopes so. He ran like devil dogs were behind him.

"All right," the driver says, printing his ticket. "Take your seat." The bus's engine rumbles into life.

Jim stumbles down the centre aisle, relief washing over him. He stuffs the ticket into his pocket. Doesn't bother looking yet to see where he's going. He drops into a seat and, as the bus pulls away, he allows his exhausted eyes to close.

---

## 12

Donny Bradshaw paces his kitchen floor, running his hands back through his dark hair. His men are gathered, sitting and standing at the table, watching him warily. Donny blows air.

It's evening. Eight. Donny didn't receive the news of what happened to the lab in Bittersweet until an hour ago. The cooks said they were trying to salvage what they could, but it was hopeless. The building, their lab, all their work – all the flakka, shy of what had already been shipped out – was gone. They don't know who was responsible. The two men who were guarding the building didn't see who attacked them. He, or they, got them from behind, and they were fast. What they find curious is that he – or they – dragged them outside, and dumped their bodies far out of reach of the fire.

Since finding out, Donny has paced. He called his crew in. Willie arrived first, and Donny's left it to him to inform everyone that's arrived since.

Donny isn't sure how he's going to react. He feels like he might explode. He feels like he wants to hit someone, but he knows no one present is to blame. He bites at his lip. He's been biting at it for the last hour. It tastes of blood.

Finally, he stops pacing and wipes his mouth with the back of his hand. The blood smears darkly. He sighs, then turns to his crew. They're all present. Willie Shaw. Shawn Stark. Hal Redford. Kyle Hobbs. The Simmons brothers, Max and Micky, with their bumped and bruised faces, similar to Willie's. All six faces are turned to him, watching expectantly, bracing themselves.

"Well," he says, looking at them each in turn. "You've had an hour to think. What you got for me?"

They all look to each other in alarm. It's Willie who speaks up first. It's always Willie. That's why Donny likes him best. "Uh, what do you mean?" he says, licking his split lips.

"About who the *fuck* could be behind this?" Donny says. He barks it. They flinch. He doesn't care. "First we get attacked, and then the lab gets burned down? The biggest stash of flakka that we've got left is *right here* – so what are we gonna do? We need to know who's striking at us, and we gotta put them in the fucking ground. So – who've you got for me?"

No one has an answer.

Donny shakes his head to show his disappointment. He goes to the counter and folds his arms, staring at them all, waiting. "I need ideas," he says. "I need suggestions. I wanna know how we're gonna handle this. Give me some fucking thoughts."

Everyone is silent. They can't meet his eyes.

Donny thinks of the stash of flakka down in his basement. He does quick calculations in his head. Math was never his strong suit in school, but ever since he went into business for himself and he's had to work out his potential earnings, he's found himself getting a lot better at it.

After Willie and the Simmons brothers were attacked and their stashes stolen, he ordered more to make up for them.

Now, he's extra glad he did. At the rate they usually sell it, he estimates they roughly have enough to get them through the next couple of months, into the early fall, but that's not enough. Nowhere near. Winter is always busy. Christmas, particularly. The drugs are the only things that keep the junkies warm. It's all that brings them Christmas cheer.

Donny sucks his teeth, now calculating his potential losses. It's depressing. His stomach sinks. He feels sick.

"Couldn't we maybe make our own lab?" Shawn says, first to suggest something even if it is a terrible idea. "Start producing it ourselves?"

Donny looks at him. "Do you know how to make flakka, Shawn? Cos I sure as hell don't, and I don't believe anyone else here does, either. Unless, of course, one or two of you are holding out on me? Or maybe someone has a degree in chemistry they've never felt like telling us about?"

Shawn grunts. "I don't believe those boys over in Bittersweet had any kind of degrees."

"No, they don't, but they've been cooking for fucking years," Donny says. "And years we don't have. Besides, you think they'd be happy if we tried to start a lab of our own? We're already under attack, I ain't interested in going to war with them, too."

It's Kyle who speaks next. He clears his throat, scratching at his cheek and then tugging on his chin like he's thinking. Like he's still trying to decide if he wants to say anything.

Donny stares while Kyle marshals his thoughts. From across the room, Donny can smell the weed smoke clinging to his clothes. He rolls his eyes, and finally Kyle speaks.

"Y'know, I was thinking," he says, but then stops again.

"Just spit it out, Kyle," Donny says.

"The other night, when I went to get some food, I saw Hayley at the diner," Kyle says.

"Hayley who? Hayley Teller?" Donny says, and Kyle nods.

Donny remembers Hayley from high school. He chuckles. "She still a babe? Goddamn, she was a good-looking girl. I always had a thing for her, even if she was a bit of a nerd – wouldn't have done anything for my cred to go with a girl like that." He laughs and the others join in.

Kyle doesn't. "It's not about Hayley," he says. "It's about who I saw her with."

"So who was she with?" Donny says.

"Tom Rollins."

Donny frowns at this. He hasn't heard that name in such a long time. "Okay, and? They went out in high school – that was another red flag for ol' Hayley, far as I was concerned. Her taste in men."

"Yeah, but my point is," Kyle says, "Rollins is back in town. And wasn't he, like, in the Army? And wasn't he in the news a couple of times, for preventing a terrorist attack? Something like that."

"What's your point?"

"Well, my point is, was it him who attacked us?"

Donny considers this. "Rollins?" He scratches the back of his neck. As much as he hates to admit it, it makes sense. Rollins has the training to strike at them from the shadows like this. And he was always a straight arrow, not like his brother. Anthony was always a lot more laid back. Didn't have such a stick up his ass. He never went in the Army, either. Donny isn't sure what's become of Anthony. Until just now, he wasn't sure what had happened to Tom, or where he'd ended up. Didn't care, either.

"What're you thinking?" Willie says. "It sound plausible?"

"Yeah," Donny says, slowly. "It does."

Kyle sits up a little straighter. He looks pleased with himself.

"How long's he been back?" Donny says.

Shawn clears his throat. "I'd heard he's been working at

Del's place for the last couple of months. I don't know if that's when he got back, but... I didn't think anything of it at the time. I barely remembered him, truth be told."

Donny nods, considering this. Considering the timeframe.

"What we gonna do about it?" Willie says.

"We're gonna find out for sure," Donny says.

"How do we do that?"

Donny thinks again. "Fuck it – we'll grab him, and bring him in for questioning."

"And what if he didn't?" Hal says. He sits at the head of the table, leaning back in the chair.

Donny shrugs. "Then we find who did."

"Uh-huh, but if we grab this guy who's ex-Army, we rough him up and ask him some questions, and it turns out he *didn't* do anything – then what? We've just pissed off a soldier, and we're back at square one in terms of finding out who we're going up against."

Donny grins. "Whether he did or didn't, we make it so he can't come back at us. No repercussions. I don't give a shit about Rollins. Never have. He was always an asshole."

"I'll take your word for it," Hal says. He doesn't know Rollins already. He's not from Hopper Creek. He's from Santa Fe. "We assume he's working alone?"

"I guess we'll find out, won't we?"

Donny looks at the others. They don't have any protests. None of them are in disagreement. The Simmons brothers don't know Rollins either, but they don't care what they might do to him. They look down at their fidgeting hands, opening and closing their fists, perhaps thinking what they might do if they really are about to get their hands on the person who got the drop on them. They're embarrassed about it, Donny knows. Afraid they won't ever live it down, especially if it was just one guy.

Willie stands by the window with his arms folded. He looks concerned and keeps turning his head toward the glass.

"What's wrong with you?" Donny says.

Willie looks up. "Anyone else hear that?" he says.

The room falls silent. They're all listening.

"Hear what?" Donny says.

Willie straightens up, frowning now. He looks around. He looks toward the front of the house. "Like a car engine. You don't hear it?" He looks alarmed. "Shit, it sounds like it's getting closer."

Donny can hear it now, and Willie's right. It *is* getting closer. Donny turns, looking through the living room toward his front windows. It sounds like someone's driving right toward his house. The curtains are open. He sees the car coming a moment before it makes impact.

## 13

Donny lives on the outskirts of town, in a house similar in style and location to the one Tom is renting. There's no one on either side of him. This isn't a residential street. It's an isolated home, where the anti-social owner plays his music loudly through the night, and where his friends come around to get drunk, and high, and to fight and curse and fuck women they bring out here all through into the early hours.

Tonight is not one of those nights.

Tom watched Donny's house for hours before he's made his move. He didn't expect them all to be in one place, but as soon as they started to arrive he saw an opportunity. All his eggs in one basket, right where he needed them.

No doubt the destruction in Bittersweet has alarmed them.

Tom placed a brick on the accelerator, pointed it toward Donny's house, and put it in drive.

The front of the house caves in, its wooden frame splintering, its windows shattering. Tom follows the car, Beretta drawn. The car plows through the house, onto the back lawn where it finally hits a tree and stops. Tom does not follow in the wake of its wreckage. He stays at a distance, in cover, Beretta raised.

The car was not his. When he got back to town he walked along to the scrap yard and bought a Ford automatic for cheap. It was already banged and dented up. After tearing through the house, it probably doesn't look any different.

Tom is wearing the balaclava again. He can see the members of the gang rushing around inside the house. A couple of them – Willie and Shawn – are armed, waving their handguns around as they peer out into the darkness. Tom takes a couple of shots at them, to spook them. It works. They dive for cover. Shawn jumps behind a sofa. He fires blindly out into the darkness. Tom is already on the move.

He moves down to the side of the house, presses himself against it. Two sets of handguns are firing out into the dark now. Tom waits them out, edging closer to where the car crashed through, avoiding windows as he goes. He hears the voices inside, crying out in panic and confusion.

"You see them? You see anyone?"

"I can't see shit!"

"You hit anyone?"

Tom waits. It doesn't take long before he hears Donny's voice, louder than the rest. "Go and take a look," he says. "Go find them! They can't have got far!"

Tom slides away from the hole, back to the corner of the house. He counts off the bodies as they go. Six of them. Leaving Donny behind, still inside his broken home.

"I don't see anyone!" Shawn calls back into the house. "There's no one here!"

"Then get in the car and go find them!" Donny barks. "Willie, you stay with me, we'll hold it down here."

Willie heads back inside the dilapidated house, while the

others hurry off to their cars, quickly firing them up and speeding back out onto the road.

Tom heads down the side of the house, toward the back, gun raised. He can hear Donny and Willie talking inside, and then Willie steps out, inspecting the car that has crashed through the house. "I don't recognise it," he's saying as Tom comes up behind him, mistaking his approach for Donny.

Out the corner of his eye, Tom checks where Donny is. He's not looking. He's in the kitchen, staring through the house, his back turned. He's shaking his head. Tom gets up behind Willie and brings the handle of the Beretta down hard on the back of his skull. Willie collapses in a heap, similar to how Tom left him just a couple of nights ago.

He spins, checks where Donny is again. He hasn't moved. Tom moves up on him, into the house. Donny turns at his approach, but it's too late. Tom has the gun in his face.

"Holy shit," Donny says, putting up his arms in surrender. He's breathing hard. "Jesus Christ – look what you've done to my fucking house!"

"You've seen nothing yet," Tom says. He lowers his voice. Growls. He can see Donny is looking hard at him, trying to figure out who he is. "Where's the flakka?"

Donny bites his lip. He doesn't want to answer. He looks beyond Tom, to where Willie is lying prone. "Who are you, man? You know what we can do to you, you don't get the fuck outta here right now?"

Tom doesn't flinch. "Where's the flakka? Don't make me ask you again."

Donny smirks.

It's clear, despite everything Tom has already done, that Donny is not taking him seriously. Tom strikes him with the barrel of his gun, cutting open his right eyebrow. Donny goes down, bleeding hard.

Tom crouches beside him, drilling the gun into his

temple. "Have it your way," he says. "You don't have to tell me. It doesn't matter. I know it's here somewhere, and I know how I'm going to deal with it. Now, I want you to listen to me. You listening? Make sure your ears are clear."

It's not his ears Donny needs to worry about. He blinks blood out of his eyes and looks up, dazed.

"You're done in this town. All of you," Tom says. "Spread the word to your boys. You're not just done here – you're done everywhere. It's time to grow up. You can go and get some real jobs, become contributing members of society – frankly, I don't give a shit what you do next, but you're done dealing. It's over. I see you back at it, and I smash you all over again, and I'll come down harder. Now get up." Tom hauls him to his feet by his hair. "You better run." He shoves him toward the hole at the back of the house. Donny stumbles out, falling to the grass.

Tom doesn't bother looking for the flakka. Instead, he goes to the oven and turns on the gas. Rummaging through the cupboards, he finds a bottle of vodka and tears a strip off the curtains at what remains of the kitchen window. He lights it at the stove, then leaves the house through the hole at the front. The strip of curtain is burning down. From outside, Tom throws the make-shift Molotov cocktail inside, toward the kitchen. He sees the flames catch on the gas in the air. Fire spreads on the ground as the bottle shatters.

Tom walks away from the house, back toward town. He takes off the mask as he goes, stuffs it into his back pocket. Behind him, he hears the house explode. Wherever the flakka was stashed, whether upstairs or in the basement, or a drawer in the living room, Tom is confident it has been destroyed. Now, Donny and his crew have nothing left to sell.

## 14

The bus got Jim as far as Hopper Creek.

It was midday as he stepped off into what looked like the town square. There were other people milling around, going about their day. No one paid him any mind.

The first thing Jim did, he went down the road and lowered himself onto the nearest bench, his body aching. The pain in his back felt worse, like something there was tearing. Like he had an open wound.

He knew it was bleeding. He could feel it soaking into his shirt and the waistband of his jeans. Could feel a trail of it running down his left leg. His sock squelched with every step.

The bus ride here was torturous. A journey that should have only taken about an hour was extended by the bus taking a roundabout route via every small town on the way. Jim is amazed his handful of coins were able to get him so far. Having already spent the money, it became a point of determination seeing the journey through to the end, not wanting to waste a single penny. He doesn't have pennies to waste.

No one sat beside him, and he didn't blame them. He

squirmed in pain, and they probably thought he was a junkie coming down. They didn't spot the cuff on his wrist, though. He went to great pains to make sure it remained concealed. When he stood to finally get off the bus, he saw how the back of his seat was soaked through with blood. He hurried off before anyone could notice his wound.

It's getting late, now. It's dark out. Jim has spent the day hiding out down an alleyway, concealing himself behind a dumpster. He doesn't know Hopper Creek. He's never been here before. He's wondered, many times, if they have a hospital. If so, how close it is. He needs one. He's losing blood. His head feels light, but he's struggled to stay focused.

The reason for his subterfuge is the car.

It's just a regular car. A Ford. Nondescript. There's nothing special about it. But when he first arrived, and he was sitting on the bench, he spotted it coming along the road. He noticed how slow it was going. There were two men inside, both of them sitting up front. Neither of them were looking straight ahead. They were both looking to their respective sides, their heads on a swivel. Like they were searching for something in the town. Like they were looking for someone. They stopped at the side of the road, and Jim realised exactly where they'd chosen to halt – the bus stop.

Jim clings to his paranoia. He keeps his hard edges sharp. He didn't hang around to see if he was right or wrong about the men in the car. He got up and he started moving before they could see him. He slipped down the alley and peered out from behind the dumpster. Eventually, they rolled by. Still looking. Jim ducked back in as they passed. He didn't recognise them, but he hadn't seen many of the people in that hospital back in Santa Fe. The only one who stood out for him was the white-haired guy who looked like a doctor. He certainly seemed to be telling everyone else what to do.

Jim stayed where he was. The car circled the town square.

He counted the amount of times it passed by – four – and he started to wonder how long it would be before they got out and started searching by foot. Too weak to fight, or find anywhere else to hide, Jim climbed inside the dumpster, and hoped there was nothing too bad inside.

It turned out he was in luck. It was for recycling. Filled with nothing but flattened carboard boxes and shredded paper. For the first time in a long time – since he'd first met Rhonda, at least – Jim felt like some good luck had finally come his way. He buried himself under the boxes. Made himself comfortable. He slipped into a nap.

When he woke, it was dark. He found, to his dismay, that the blood has continued to seep from his back. The cardboard beneath him was red and soaked through. He climbed out of the dumpster and he hasn't moved since, still watching. Waiting. Wanting to be sure.

It's been an hour now. He hasn't seen the Ford pass by in all that time. There's only been a few cars go by. None of the occupants seemed to be looking for anyone. They just rolled on their way.

Jim knows he can't stay in one place forever. He's not bleeding hard, but it's not showing any signs of stopping, either. Eventually, he's going to run dry. He needs to do something about that, and soon. Tentatively, he moves to the end of the alleyway and peers out. The town looks clear. It's quiet. He listens to the air. The sounds of vehicles are distant.

He holds his position, scanning the area with his eyes. He knows from experience that sometimes when things are at their quietest, that's when they're at their most dangerous. He doesn't rush into anything. He's already waited so long to leave the alley, he can wait a bit longer.

Off to his right, he hears something. Footsteps. They're soft, and to anyone untrained, anyone not listening, they wouldn't be heard. Jim looks that way. It's dark and he can't see anyone. Whoever it is, they're staying close to the closed shop fronts and out of the glow of the streetlights.

Then, to his left, he hears an engine. He turns and sees its lights. Jim looks left and right, then back. There's a chain-link fence at the end of the alley. Ordinarily, Jim wouldn't see this as much of an obstacle, but not now. Not when he's already lost a litre or two of blood.

The car comes fast along the road. Its headlights strafe the alley's opening. They catch Jim in their glare. He's too tired to pull out of them. He curses himself. The exhaustion has worn him down. It's going to cost him his life.

He does the only thing he can. He moves. He turns out of the alley, and he heads right.

# 15

On foot, Tom has avoided the other members of Donny's crew on his way back and through the town. Hasn't seen any sign of them. Seems like they disappeared off down the road they thought he'd come down to attack them. He assumes they probably split up, and he wonders where their various routes have taken them. The fire rising into the night sky perhaps drew them back to Donny's.

On the way, he's heard the fire service speeding out there. It's too late for them to salvage anything. Besides, even if they could, he doubts the fire service are on the same take as the local cops. They find a stash of flakka, he doubts they're going to look for a cut. They're going to report it.

But that doesn't matter, because they won't be able to save it. It's long gone, now. It's ash.

Tom heads through the centre of town, enjoying the peaceful night air. The sounds of the fire sirens are long behind him, now. He can't hear them. Can't see the distant orange glow of Donny's burning home anymore. Can't see the smoke rising, blocking out the stars.

He checks his phone and sees he has a missed called from Hayley. He calls her back.

"Hey," she says. "I was just checking in, seeing how you're doing. I stopped by your place on my way to the hospital and your car was there but you weren't."

"I'm back in Hopper Creek now," Tom says. "Felt like taking a walk, so I left the car behind."

"How's everything going, are you all right? Did you take care of that thing you were very secretive about?"

Tom laughs. "Yeah, I did, thanks. Everything's fine. I did what I needed to do."

"That's good. I'm glad to hear it. I'm just on a break right now."

"It busy?"

"No, it's quiet. That's how I like it. You know what they say – no news is good news."

"Yeah. How was the blood drive?"

"It's going well! We've all been very pleased with it."

"That's great. You free tomorrow night?"

"I will be, after I've caught up on some sleep."

"You wanna grab dinner?"

"That sounds good to me. About eight?"

"I'll see you then."

Tom slips the phone back into his pocket. He's getting close to the store. The light for the sign is on, but other than that the storefront is in darkness. Tom can't imagine too many people are looking for DIY supplies at this time of night.

In the distance, rolling down the road, he sees headlights. Tom doesn't think anything of them, not at first. He's seen plenty of vehicles on this walk. He's checked them, sure, but he's also mostly stuck to the shadows while he's travelled. He's not easily seen.

Suddenly, a figure bursts from a nearby alley and starts

running Tom's way. Tom frowns. He sees how the car halts at the stranger's emergence, and then speeds up, as if it's following the runner. Tom watches. The runner stumbles. He clutches at his back on the left side. Tom hasn't stopped walking. He and the runner are getting closer. Tom can see now that he's a black man and he looks worse for wear. The car is pulling to the kerb, as if it intends to stop alongside the runner.

The runner is flagging. He's going down. He and Tom are close enough to touch. Tom can see his face. The whites of his eyes. He looks terrified. He's falling. His eyes are rolling back in his head. He's passing out.

The car has stopped. Its front doors are opening.

Tom reaches out. He catches the falling man. His arms go around him. Tom feels wet on his hands. He looks toward the car. The men who were getting out are hesitating. They get back inside. They close their doors. They speed off.

Tom holds the man up. "Hey," he says. "Can you hear me?" There's no response.

Tom looks down at his own hands. He moves them into the light. They're red. The man is bleeding.

## 16

As the sun rises, Donny sits and stares at the smouldering remnants of his house. He never called the fire service, or the cops, but they came anyway. He didn't want to talk to them. There was nothing to say. Instead, he roused Willie and they went elsewhere, where they could sit and watch from a distance.

Willie rubs at the back of his head and grimaces. "Shit," he says. "Shit, Donny, man, shit, I'm sorry."

Donny doesn't respond. His home has burned down to the foundations. The flakka will not have survived. He doesn't need to check to know this. There's no point in being hopeful.

Willie's phone has rung a few times, but Donny hasn't listened to the conversations he's had. He knows it's the crew calling in, checking what's happened and what to do next. Right now, they're all out of a fucking job. The stash is gone. It's all gone. They don't have any way of making money. There's nothing coming in.

Donny covers his face with his hands and rubs at his eyes. The fire service is spraying water onto the smoking embers of what's left of his house. His gas was turned off hours ago. Donny knows it was, otherwise it would all still be flaming.

"Willie," he says, letting his hands slide from his face, "I'm gonna need a place to stay."

Willie nods. "You know I've always got a room for you, brother."

Donny claps him on the shoulder.

Willie chews his lip, deliberating.

"What?" Donny says.

"Did you see who it was?"

"I saw him," Donny says. "Hell, spoke to him. Or rather, he mostly spoke to me. He was wearing a mask, though. Disguised his voice, too."

"Just the one guy?"

"That I saw."

"You know who he was?"

Donny shakes his head. "No. He disguised himself well. I can't be sure." He sucks on his bottom lip. Bites it. "We've lost everything, Willie. I don't know what the fuck we're gonna do now."

"We've got...we've got some savings, right?" Willie says.

"Not enough," Donny says.

Willie rubs at the back of his head again, picking at the scab that's formed there. He looks at his fingers, and there's blood on the tips. "This guy's put me down a couple of times now," he says, sneering. He catches Donny's eye and stares back, his gaze hard. "I don't like getting put down, and I know you don't either. So why don't you tell me, so I can tell everyone else, what it is we're going to do next."

Donny grits his teeth. He nods. "We're gonna find this motherfucker," he says. "And we're gonna kill him. And then, one way or another, we're gonna find a way to get this operation running again."

Willie grins at this. "How we gonna find who was behind it?"

"I'm open to suggestions," Donny says. "But first, we do some process of elimination. You remember who Kyle suggested? Tom Rollins. I haven't been able to get that out my head. *What if*, man, *what if*."

"You saw the guy," Willie says. "He spoke to you. You think it could be him?"

"Been too long since I saw him last. And I didn't see him move enough – didn't get a good look at his body type, or body language. Not sure seeing Rollins now would even help me work that out. Besides, like I said, he'd covered his face and disguised his voice – chances are he would've maybe disguised how he moved, too. But if someone's coming at us with military precision, makes sense to check out the ex-military guy, right?"

Willie nods.

"So we look into him. Follow him. Find out if it was him, like we planned. I don't want to pull him straight in this time, though. If it *was* him, he's gonna be uptight right now, right after doing this. We need to lull him into a false sense of security, you get me? Here's what I want you to do: call the Simmons brothers and put them on his tail. Watch what he does and where he goes. We're gonna follow him in shifts. We're gonna know his routines inside and out. And then, when he's nice and relaxed and he ain't expecting anything, we strike. We bring him in, and we find out, one way or another. It wasn't him, fine, we move on and find out who it really was, but then we don't have to worry about the possibility that it *was* him. You got all that?"

Willie is already pulling out his phone. He's grinning. "Yeah," he says. "I got all that."

## 17

T he man lies unconscious in his hospital bed. Tubes are connected to his arms, pumping fluids into his system, along with a bag of blood to replace all that he's lost. Tom and Hayley stand outside his room.

"He didn't have any ID on him," Hayley says, glancing in.

Tom nods. "I checked," he says. He holds a bag down by his side, with fresh clothes. Tom's clothes will be a little baggy on the stranger, but at least it's something. Hayley told him they'd had to cut him out of his blood-soaked jeans and shirt.

Tom has been home since he brought the stranger here. He had a shower and got changed, and then disposed of the cuff he removed from the man's wrist. He'd picked it before calling a taxi and bringing the man to the hospital. The cuff would raise questions. Ordinarily, Tom would let those questions be asked, but in this instance he doesn't think the man lying in the hospital bed is the problem. The two men in the car following him, however, are a different matter. When the stranger wakes, Tom plans on asking him about them.

"I think he might be homeless," Hayley says.

"I got that impression, too," Tom says, thinking of the

man's ragged clothes and his worn-down boots, as well as his haggard features that no doubt add a decade to whatever his actual age is.

"I've never seen him around. But also," she leans in closer, lowers her voice, "there's some bruising and scabbing on his left wrist in the shape of a handcuff. Where did you say you found him?"

"Near Del's," Tom says. "He fell into my arms." He doesn't tell her about the car that was following. He doesn't want to alarm her, and he wants to talk to the stranger himself about that first. There's a chance – a slim one, but still a chance – that the guys in the car saw he was struggling and were planning on helping. Saw that when he'd fallen into Tom's arms they didn't have to take time out of their nights after all.

A *slim* chance, but Tom likes to consider every possibility.

"So what had happened," Tom says, "why was he bleeding? Had he been stabbed?"

"Worse than that," Hayley says, shaking her head. "He's missing a kidney."

Tom frowns. "A kidney? Has someone taken it?"

"It's hard to know that. For all we know, and especially if he *is* homeless, he might have sold it. It happens. He might have sold it and he hasn't given himself the proper chance to heal, and his stitches have split and he's almost bled to death. If you hadn't got him here he *would* be dead. But we won't know until he wakes up and we can talk to him."

"Have the cops been told?"

"I asked about that," Hayley says. "Again, until we know what's happened, there's nothing to tell them. If he's wilfully sold his kidney, there's no crime." She shrugs. "There's nothing we can do, other than wait for him to wake up."

Tom nods. He checks the time. It's after midday. "I'm gonna go sit in with him."

"You sure? You don't have to do that. He's probably not going to wake up for a while. We've given him a sedative."

"That's fine," Tom says.

"Well, I guess you'll be easy enough to find later," she says, then kisses him on the cheek. "I need to go do my rounds."

Tom steps into the room. The man is in a deep sleep. He doesn't move. Doesn't so much as twitch. Tom crosses the room, goes to the window. He looks down at the street below. Thinks about the car from last night. A Ford. He can't see it down below, but that doesn't mean it isn't somewhere near, perhaps out of view. He didn't get a good look at the people inside. They could be out there. Any of the people he can see walking by. He could be looking at them right now.

Tom turns back into the room and takes a seat by the side of the bed. He looks at the sleeping man. There's something going on with him. Tom wants to know what it is. He's involved now, since last night. He has questions, and he doesn't like leaving loose ends.

It's unlikely the man is going to wake today. The drugs are going to keep him asleep, to help him heal. But Tom doesn't have anywhere else he needs to be.

# 18

Kendis's penthouse apartment has an indoor swimming pool. It's on the opposite side of the building to where his balcony is, walled in by a long window. Kendis stands by the window, feeling the warmth of the sun pouring through. He has a drink in hand. A Hennessy with two big ice cubes. He sips from it.

In the pool, Big Ron swims laps. Kendis leans against the warm glass and turns his head, watching. Big Ron does front stroke. His face comes out of the water for breath every four strokes. He's already been in the gym, and his muscles are pumped full of blood. Kendis sucks his teeth and admires the way the water runs over his striated back.

Kendis hasn't dressed yet. He slept in this morning, then took a shower. He's wearing his black silk gown, and nothing else. He has a call to make soon, a video call, but what he's wearing doesn't matter. It'll only be his head and shoulders showing on the screen.

Big Ron finishes up his laps, stopping by the ladder at the edge of the pool and wiping the water from his face and eyes. Kendis pushes himself away from the window and crouches down in front of Big Ron. "You're a machine," he says. "Up all night, then hitting the gym first thing in the day."

"It's what you pay me for," Big Ron says. His eyes flicker down between Kendis's legs, to the opening in his gown. He raises an eyebrow. "You're gonna have to give me some recovery time if you're looking to go again."

"Just enjoys seeing how you look is all," Kendis says. "It's still worn out from last night."

"I appreciate the thought," Big Ron says, pulling himself out of the pool. He reaches for his towel and starts drying himself off.

Kendis straightens, swirling his drink in its glass. His eyes never leave Big Ron. "Besides," he says, "I need to make a call soon."

"Palmer?"

"It's about that time."

Dry, Big Ron puts the towel back where he got it from. "How long's it been now? A few months? I'm amazed he's still holding on."

"We *need* him to hold on," Kendis says. "His private doctors will be pumping him full of every fancy and experimental drug they can find to keep him going while we're all racing to get him what he needs."

"All?" Big Ron says. "You think he has others looking?"

"He'd be foolish not to," Kendis says. "That's why I need Alec to stop being such an asshole and get us what we need."

Big Ron nods. He looks toward the window, looks out across Santa Fe. "Gotta be someone out there," he says.

Kendis drains his drink. "Fucking *better* be," he says, snorting.

"I'm gonna go take a shower."

Kendis nods. "I'll go get ready for my call." He kisses Big Ron. He tastes of chlorine. Then Kendis goes through the apartment toward his office. He stops at the bar on his way to put his used glass on the counter. The melting ice clinks together in the bottom. The maid will be here in an hour. She'll clean it away.

The bar is connected to the living room. It's a large room, the largest in the apartment. As well as having the bar, it also connects to the open plan kitchen, which has a marble island in the centre of it. The dining room is a separate room, and rarely used – only when Kendis has people around for meetings, or celebrations. The living room, as well as having the bar and the kitchen, has a large space with a couple of coffee tables decorated with modern art, mostly abstract sculptures that Kendis has spent hours staring at, each time finding something new in their contortions. Beyond this, there is the plush L-shaped sofa, the easy chair, and the widescreen television that covers most of the wall.

Kendis used to sell drugs, and he was good at it, until he found out organ trafficking could be much more lucrative. The shortage of healthy organs needed for transplants, not just in America but in the world at large, means he can usually name his price. He tends to cater to the wealthier end of society, those who can pay the highest *and* use their own medical teams who won't ask questions. It's also less high risk – providing, of course, he's careful about whom he gets the organs from. Kendis is always careful. He's always had to be careful. Out on the streets, he knew any day there was a bullet that could have his name on it. He also knew his crew, his contemporaries, and his rivals would come together if they found out about his sexual proclivities. It wasn't even safe for him to be gay. So Kendis knows what it is to be careful. He's *always* known.

Alec, on the other hand...

He reaches his office and takes a seat behind the desk. His computer is already turned on. He leans back and strokes his chin, thinking about Alec. For the situation Alec was in when Kendis found him, he hasn't shown much appreciation for the position Kendis has since raised him to.

Alec had just been released from prison after a five-year stretch for manslaughter. Kendis and Big Ron were there to collect him from the gate. Alec tried to stride straight past them, pretending he didn't know Kendis already, his nose in the air. His time locked up hadn't dulled his sense of self-importance.

Alec had been a surgeon. A good one. Well-respected. His work was sought after. People came from all over to go under his knife. He could do no wrong. *He* believed he could do no wrong. Believed it too much.

His workload grew and grew. It became too much for one man, but Alec refused to admit this. Would never admit that he was struggling. Instead, he turned to something that would help him get through. Something to give him a boost. He started taking amphetamines.

They worked just fine for him at first. No one could tell he was using. He felt great. More focussed. More energised. He barely needed to sleep. Alec has confided to Kendis – although to Kendis it sounded more like a brag – that he once went five days without sleep, and in that time he performed three major surgeries.

The lifestyle caught up to him eventually. It started to reflect in his work, not that Alec would ever admit this. He was missing stitches. He was giving the wrong doses. His staff covered for him, but there was only so much they could do. Eventually, tragedy struck. A young girl, twenty-two. There was concern she may have lung cancer. Alec needed to perform a biopsy – to go in and remove some tissue for further examination. A thoracotomy was performed. A complicated procedure, but he got through it. He cut through her ribs. He clamped them open. He removed the piece of lung. Everything was going smoothly. Everything was going exactly as it should.

And then he slipped.

He slipped and cut her aortic valve. She bled out almost instantly. There was nothing any of them could do to save her.

Alec admitted to Kendis, in a rare display of candidness, that he still doesn't know what happened. He's thought about it so many times, but he can't remember. It was as if he blacked out. One second he was about to close her up, and the next she was dead.

Afterward, his hands couldn't stop shaking. He's wondered if the tremors started then, at that precise moment, and that's what caused the slip.

Alec was tested. His amphetamine addiction was discovered. He was arrested. The family of the girl sued the hospital. They sued Alec. He lost everything.

And yet, what amazes Kendis is that, through it all, Alec refused to acknowledge any wrongdoing, other than for the slip. He refused to accept that his drug problem had endangered anyone. "I might have slipped up," he said, and still says, "but that was once. Think of how many lives I saved before that day. Think of how many people are still walking around, breathing, *living*, because of *me*. If I needed some help, then so be it. A sacrifice of one amidst the hundreds saved is no kind of burden at all."

Alec has never changed his tone on this. It did not, however, go down well in the courtroom. He was sentenced to ten years for manslaughter. He served five.

Kendis knew Alec before he was locked up. Kendis used to sell him the amphetamines. Alec was intrigued enough by Kendis's proposition upon his release, after Big Ron had bundled him into the back of their car.

"No one else will take you now," Kendis said.

Alec's face was defiant, but his eyes betrayed him. He knew this was true.

"You've already been struck off the medical register. What else are you supposed to do? And a man like you, what else *can* you do? You gonna get a job on the factory floor? You gonna stock shelves? Gonna become a delivery driver? C'mon, Alec. This is the best offer you're going to get and you know it."

Alec *did* know it. He shook Kendis's hand and took him up on his offer.

Alec had gone cold turkey in prison. Kendis has kept him clean since. Has told his men to keep a close eye on the surgeon, to make sure he's not using again, or even thinking about using. It's been six years now, and to Alec's credit, the men have never voiced any concerns.

Kendis checks the time. Palmer will be calling him any minute now. He straightens up and waits for it to come through.

Another minute passes and an alert sounds on Kendis's computer. An incoming video call from Palmer Elliot. Kendis accepts.

Palmer Elliot's face fills the screen, all the way from New York City. "Kendis," he says, grimacing. He looks worse for wear. His pale skin has a yellowish tinge to it. The flesh sags from his cheeks and his jaw. The loose skin on his neck looks like an empty bag. "Tell me you've got good news for me," he says, sounding like he's struggling for breath.

"If I had good news, Mr Elliot, *I'd* be calling *you*."

Palmer closes his eyes and sighs out of his nose. He nods wearily.

"I'm looking though, Mr Elliot," Kendis says. "Believe me. I've put out the word. Every day, I'm thinking of you and your liver."

Palmer nods again and opens his eyes. "AB-fucking-negative," he says. There's bitterness in his voice. "You know, before I got ill, I didn't have a fucking clue what my blood type was. Not a clue. Why should I care? And now it's all I can think about. That, and just how goddamn rare it is. That rarity's gonna fucking kill me."

"You've still got time, Mr Elliot."

"Yeah, but how long? It's getting shorter every damn day. Six months now I've been looking for this damn liver. I never thought it would take this long. Every day that goes by, it looks less and less likely I'm gonna get it." He shakes his head and looks off to the side. He chuckles suddenly. "I've picked out my headstone, Kendis. You should see it, though, it's real handsome. If I'm gonna be the richest man in the graveyard, I damn well want people to know it."

"I'll get you your liver, Mr Elliot," Kendis says. "I haven't given up faith, and neither should you. That's what keeps us going. You keep that in mind. Last thing I want is to get you an AB-negative liver, call you up all excited to share the good news, and it turns out you've gone and given up on me."

Palmer smirks. He runs a hand down his face. He looks tired. Kendis tells him so. "I *am* tired," Palmer says. "I'm in pain all the fucking time. I move, it feels like I'm being stabbed. I feel like I'm gonna throw up all the time. I can't even eat. You see how much weight I've lost? Look at this shit, man." He jiggles the baggy skin of his neck. "It's fucking disgusting. I can't even look in the mirror no more." He purses his lips, is silent for a moment. He's thinking. "You know what I think about, Kendis? You know what I think about more than anything else? What if you *do* come through – what if you *do* find me a liver, an honest-to-God AB-negative liver, and what if it doesn't take? What if my body rejects it?"

"That's sounding hopeless, Mr Elliot," Kendis says. "You've gotta keep the faith, like I told you. Positive thoughts."

"I'm through my positive phase," Palmer says. "These

days, all I have are negative thoughts, and the knowledge that death is creeping closer and closer. All my fucking money, and what can I do about it? I can't do shit, all because of this stupid fucking blood I've got running through my veins."

Kendis gives him a sympathetic look. "I'm sorry, Mr Elliot. It's truly terrible."

"The worst of it is, I was never that heavy a drinker. At least, I never thought I was. Sociable, that's what I always thought. Just a drink here and there, when out with friends. Maybe I was out with friends more often than I kept track of." He shrugs. "Maybe too many glasses of wine on an evening. But I was never an alcoholic. It was never a problem."

"I believe you," Kendis says. He doesn't. A person doesn't catch such a serious alcohol-related liver disease if they're not putting away the sauce.

"I haven't touched a drop since the diagnosis," Palmer says.

Kendis doesn't believe this either, but he nods along. "Keep it up," he says. "You're doing great, Mr Elliot." Once Kendis gets him a new liver, he doesn't care what Palmer does with it next. He can drink himself into another bout of jaundice for all he cares. By then, Kendis and Big Ron will have been handsomely rewarded for their troubles and they'll be long gone.

"Well," Palmer says. "I've got other calls to make. And you need to find me a liver."

"We're all busy," Kendis says. "Hopefully I'll talk to you again soon, with good news."

"Here's hoping." Palmer ends the call.

---

## 19

The stranger was still asleep in his hospital bed when Hayley came to collect Tom for their date. "Whatever he's going through, he's in the best place here. It's the safest place for him, too."

They've come to a bar. It's not one of the two in the town square. It's a little deeper into town, and it serves food. They've got burgers. "How'd you sleep?" Tom says.

Hayley went home shortly after talking to Tom earlier in the day, after she'd finished her rounds. She'd hung around a little longer than she'd needed to after Tom had turned up with the bleeding stranger. "I slept like a log," she says, her burger poised before her mouth. "Were you in the room all day?"

Tom nods, chewing.

"I know I already asked you, but why? You brought him in – you've done more than you needed to."

Tom takes another bite of burger before he answers. Thinks about what he's going to say. He doesn't want to alarm Hayley by telling her about the two men in the car. "A man fell bleeding into my arms in the dead of night," Tom says. "It seems like he could be in trouble. And then you've told me he's missing a kidney. That raises questions."

"And you're a curious guy."

"Always have been."

Hayley puts down her burger and picks at fries, dipping them into ketchup. "If he *is* in trouble, what then?"

"I guess that depends on the kind of trouble," Tom says. "And the kind of help he might need."

Hayley falls silent, thinking about this while she eats. "How long ago did you say you left the Army?"

"I didn't," Tom says. "And it's...complicated."

"Okay, well, you told me you'd been travelling before you came back to Hopper Creek. How long were you travelling for?"

"A few years."

"How often did you help people in trouble, while you were travelling?"

"Once or twice."

She looks at him, considering him and everything he may have been through during the last few years. "Do you...do you get into a lot of trouble, Tom? I've noticed the scars... And I've seen stab wounds before, too, and I know what they look like when they heal."

Tom takes a drink of water.

"Where've you been the last couple of days, Tom?"

Tom puts down his burger. He looks at her. He doesn't answer, because he doesn't want to lie. He doesn't want to put her in danger, either.

Hayley wipes her fingers on a napkin. She sighs. "Before I came back to the hospital to get you, I was listening to the radio while I got ready. It played the local news. There was a fire last night. Right before you came into the hospital with the bleeding stranger. They didn't say whose house it was, but they said where it was, and I know who lives there.

Donny Bradshaw. They say it was a gas leak. His home blew up." She looks at Tom. "Have you heard about it?"

Tom looks into her expectant blue eyes. "I did it," he says. "I blew it up."

Hayley blinks. This isn't the answer she anticipated.

"I've seen what unchecked dealing can do to a town," Tom says. "You've seen the effects it was already having. It's a cancer, and it was just going to continue to spread and grow. I've cut it out."

"You could have killed someone," Hayley says, making sure to lower her voice.

"I made sure they were clear."

"*You* could have been killed."

"They weren't a risk. Donny and his crew are just boys looking to make fast money. Nothing more."

"Do they know it was you?"

Tom shakes his head. "I've been careful."

A thought occurs to Hayley. "The other night, when I invited you in, where did you go?"

"I've been watching them for a while, Hayley," he says. "It was time to make my first move. I would have liked nothing more than to go inside your home, to have a drink and sit and talk – and maybe more – but I needed to act. So I did."

"What did you do, exactly?"

"I beat up the Simmons brothers and took their stash. Then I did the same to Willie Shaw. It was to spook them, and it worked. When I went out of town, that was to find the source. The lab where they were getting the flakka from. I destroyed that, too."

Hayley is silent for a while, likely stunned. She glances around the room, as if worried Donny or one of his boys is nearby. She picks up her burger, then puts it down again. She picks it back up and takes a bite, chews mechanically while staring off to the side. Tom watches her. It's a lot for her to process.

Finally, she swallows and turns to him. "Why didn't you tell me?" she says.

"I didn't want to put you in any danger. If I slipped up and they found out it was me, they'd come for you. The less you knew the better. It was safer for you this way."

"That's bullshit," Hayley says, shaking her head. "You could've told me. What, did you think I was too delicate to handle it? Or did you think I wouldn't understand?"

"I suppose a little of both," Tom says. "But more of the latter."

"Are you kidding me?" She leans forward. "When we saw Kyle Hobbs the other night, you think I *didn't* want to slap the taste out of his mouth? You think I haven't thought about beating on Donny Bradshaw? Believe me, if I thought I could, I would. I've got to admit, I've never thought about blowing up his house, but I guess that's where we differ."

"You think it was too extreme?"

"I assume you probably have a good reason."

"I have a few," Tom says. "First, he had flakka in his house, and he wouldn't say where it was. Secondly, I'd already trashed it when I drove the car through–"

Hayley's eyes go wide. "You drove a car through? They didn't mention that on the radio."

"–and thirdly, and I guess this was the most important, it was to scare him. To scare all of them. A show of power that would frighten them off. Tell them I meant business. I wasn't joking around."

"Make it so they'd be too scared to attempt anything back?"

"That's the plan. The hope, I guess. Machiavelli said if you're going to do people harm, make sure you do enough you don't have to worry about their reaction."

"Well, if a long-dead Italian philosopher says it's all right..."

Tom can't tell if she's being sarcastic, but then she grins. She reaches across the table and takes his hand.

"I'm not going to lie and say I'm not concerned," she says. She bites her lip. "I...I understand – at least I *think* I understand – why you've done what you've done. You took matters into your own hands. You did something most people would only fantasise about. To paraphrase another long-dead philosopher, German this time, you had the will to power to get things done."

"Nietzsche," Tom says.

Hayley grins and winks at him. "You're not the only one who reads, Tom."

"I remember you were a real bookworm in high school," Tom says. "That's one of the things I always liked about you. First time I was in your room, I spent most of the time looking at your bookshelves."

"Even though I was right there, ready and willing to spend the evening making out," Hayley says. "Are you trying to change the subject?"

"No. Just remembering. In amongst all the Phillip K. Dick and Isaac Asimov and Octavia E. Butler, you had Dostoevsky. I was impressed. I was impressed by all of it, but I've always had a soft spot for Dostoevsky."

"Well, I remember you eventually *did* stop looking at my books and joined me on the bed. But when was that, the third or fourth visit?" She smiles playfully.

"I don't remember it taking so long."

"I do," Hayley laughs. "I remember it was the first time we had the house to ourselves, and we–" She stops, but Tom knows what she was about to say. He remembers. It was the first time they were intimate. Their first time together, and the first time for both of them. "Now we really *are* getting off subject," Hayley says. "Listen, I think I'm done eating. Do you wanna get out of here? I think a walk would do me some good."

"Sure," Tom says, then he goes to the bar to pay.

The night sky is clear and dotted with stars. Hayley links her arm through Tom's as they walk. Neither of them speaks for a long while. They walk in silence, and breathe in the cool night air.

It's Hayley who speaks first. "Are you worried about them finding out it was you?"

Tom thinks how to answer. "They don't worry me," he says. "If they found out it was me, if they came after me, or you, I'd just have to do what old Machiavelli said and smash them harder."

"I have to admit, it concerns me a little that that's how you live your life."

"I'm not always looking for trouble," Tom says, though even as the words leave his mouth he's wondering if it's true. He's been thinking about this a lot lately.

When he got back to Hopper Creek and he saw what was happening, he could have turned a blind eye to it, just like everyone else. Instead, he chose to make it his business. He chose, once again, to go to war. Sometimes, he wants peace. He wants quiet and solitude. Other times, most of the time, he doesn't. He wants outside noise to drown the noise that's within his head. It feels like an addiction.

"Let me ask you something," Hayley says.

"Sure."

"It's something I've always wondered. And I've wanted to ask since we first got back in touch, but I keep putting it off and putting it off, and I guess I just need to come out and ask it."

"Sounds serious," Tom says.

"Maybe I'm bigging it up more than it needs to be. I guess,

I just... I've always wanted to know, ever since you disappeared – well, I guess that's just it. *Why* did you disappear? Why did you join the Army?"

Tom doesn't answer straight away. He thinks. "Why did I join the Army?"

"Yeah. I mean... We'd broken up not long before that, and I was with someone else, and then you just disappeared and I never saw you again... I've always worried that...that it was my fault."

Tom shakes his head. "It wasn't your fault," he says. "I didn't leave because of you. That's not why I joined the Army. Our break-up was cordial, as I recall. We stayed friendly."

"Yeah, we did, but then I started to doubt that, and I started to worry, and when you came back and we've been hanging out and dating again, all those old worries started to come back too."

"Well, I hope I can assure you that our break-up had nothing to do with my joining the Army."

"Okay. I suppose that's a relief. So, why did you, then?"

"I'm going to have to think on that."

"You don't know?"

"I have...I have reasons. But I'm going to need to straighten them out first."

Hayley squeezes his arm. They're not far from her house now. They don't speak again until they reach the bottom of her porch. Hayley takes her arm from his and turns to him when they stop walking. "Do you have anywhere else you need to be tonight?" she says.

"Not tonight," Tom says.

"Do you want to come in?"

Tom looks to her front door. "Yes," he says. "I do."

## 20

Donny checks his phone, reads the message from Max Simmons. He turns to Willie. "They say Rollins still hasn't come home yet."

Willie looks at the time. It's almost midnight. "It's late," he says. "Maybe he's split?"

They sit in Willie's kitchen, drinking beers. In between mouthfuls, Willie presses the cold bottle to the back of his head, and runs it across his cracked lips. Donny takes a long drink. "Maybe he has, but I don't want anyone slacking off. We all stay vigilant, until we know where he is and what he's doing."

Willie plays with his phone on the tabletop. "What do you want me to tell everyone else? They've been combing the town, but no one's checked in yet."

"Tell the rest they can go home," Donny says. "But I want the Simmons brothers to stay on Rollins's home. Soon as he turns up, I wanna know about it."

"I'll call around," Willie says, getting to his feet. He presses a button on his phone and puts it to his ear as he leaves the room.

Donny sits alone in the kitchen. Willie lives on a street. He has neighbours. It's quiet, but Donny doesn't like it. It's not quiet enough. He misses the isolation he had in his own home, where he could do whatever he wanted and there wasn't anyone nearby to bitch or complain. Sometimes, just because he could, he'd walk naked around the property. He'd piss off the back porch.

He presses the cold beer bottle to his temple and closes his eyes. His house is gone. Completely gone. He grinds his jaw. When he finds out who it was, when he knows for sure, there's going to be hell to pay.

There's a knock at the front door. Donny turns at the sound but doesn't move from the table. Willie steps into view in the hallway, slipping his phone back into his pocket. It's clear from the look on his face, as he turns back to Donny, that he's not expecting any visitors. "Let me go see who it is," he says. "But be ready in case it's nothing good."

Donny nods and braces himself, ready to run out the back door if he needs to.

Willie goes into the living room to look out the front window, and returns a moment later, waving his hand in the air to show it's nothing to worry about. "It's cops," he says. "One of ours."

"Who?" Donny says, getting to his feet.

"Duncan." Willie goes to the front door, opens it up. "Evening, Officer," he says, grinning. Donny joins him.

Duncan Mather is only a couple of years younger than them, but he looks much younger. Even now, nearly thirty, he can't grow a full beard, and his face remains child-smooth and soft. In his police uniform, he gives the impression of a young boy playing dress-up. He looks them both over and seems relieved. "Just checking in," he says. "Wanted to make sure the two of you were okay – especially *you*." He nods at Donny.

"Why wouldn't I be?" Donny says. "It's not like I haven't just lost everything I've ever worked for *and* my house has been burned to ash."

"We couldn't find any sign of you there," Duncan says. "I was worried something bad might've happened. *To* you, I mean. Obviously, your house burning down is really bad."

Donny steps outside, onto the porch, with the cop. Willie remains in the house, stepping away to resume the calls he was making when Duncan turned up. Donny looks up the dark, empty street, and to the houses opposite. Only a few of them still have their lights on. Most of them look like they've bedded down for the night. "Don't suppose you all have any ideas who might've done it?"

"We'll look into it," Duncan says, "but we don't have anything right now. You don't know who it was?"

Donny shakes his head bitterly. "Wish I did."

"A gang?"

"I don't know," Donny says, his voice getting harsher, wanting Duncan to understand that he doesn't have a fucking clue who's coming after him, and repeating the same stupid questions over and over again isn't going to help work it out.

Duncan picks up on his tone and raises his hands apologetically. "Didn't meant to upset you."

Donny leans on the porch railing, his back to Duncan. As far as he's concerned, they don't have much more to talk about.

Duncan stands next to him, leaning his back against the railing, trying to look into Donny's face. "I'm glad you're not hurt," he says. "But whoever it is that's coming after you, you know we need you to deal with it quietly, right?"

Donny doesn't answer.

"Another gang, whatever, you know we'd all love to help out any way we can, but we can't get involved. We let you do your thing on the assurance it's all gonna be kept quiet."

Donny turns his head a little, raises an eyebrow. "And let's not forget the pay-offs."

"Hey, hey, we're all friends here," Duncan says. "I'm not looking to fall out with you, man. I'm just wanting it to be clear why we can't help you with this. You know I'm sorry for that. I just want you to understand."

"Uh-huh," Donny says, straightening up. "Don't worry, I understand. I understand perfectly. But I don't need your help anyway, Duncan. Not from any of you. Never have. We'll deal with it ourselves. Of course we will. We never expected to do it any other way. And we'll keep it quiet, you don't have to worry about that. Hell, we're not the ones who've made any of the noise in the first place."

Duncan nods. "Okay. You know I'm sorry, though, right?"

"Sure," Donny says, and slaps him on the arm harder than he needs to.

Duncan doesn't say anything to this. He starts to step down off the porch, his visit concluded.

Donny stops him. "Just one thing," he says, holding up a finger. "Oh, and make sure your buddies know about this, too. The flakka is gone. All gone – from here and Bittersweet. There might be some of it left lying around between here and there, but I can't do nothing about that. My point is this – I'm not making any money. And when I'm not making any money, well, I don't have anything I need to pay you all off *for*. You get me?"

Duncan has frozen at this, his eyes darting to the side as his mind races, calculating how much he's about to lose out on.

"Yeah, that's right," Donny says. "We're all gonna be hurting for a while. Make sure all your buddies know about that too, won't you? Thanks, Duncan." Donny returns to the railing. Duncan eventually tears himself away and gets back into his cruiser. He drives off, slowly. Donny watches him go, his lights fading down the road.

If he's going to hurt, he's going to make sure everyone else does, too.

## 21

Tom wakes before Hayley. She's all tangled up in his arms, the blanket between them. Her bare left leg is thrown over him, and her right is stretched out across the mattress. She breathes softly into his ear.

Tom disentangles himself and slides out of the bed, not wanting to disturb her. He has to scour the floor for his clothes. His underwear and socks are at the bottom of the bed, along with Hayley's, but his jeans are out in the hall, and his shirt is close to the front door. After they'd gotten inside, it didn't take long for them to pounce on each other. Just like old times, when either of them had an empty home, though it was usually at Hayley's place. Her parents went away together quite often, for quiet weekends that they used to take Hayley along on when she was younger but which she opted out of when she became a teenager. It was very rare that Tom would take her along to his home. For a start, his father was usually there. Secondly, he wasn't sure she'd enjoy, or feel comfortable within the confines of their fortified house. Jeffrey, his father, would probably try to get her to take part in some drills or survivalist training. Tom wasn't going to expose her to that.

As he goes, he gathers up Hayley's dropped clothes, too. He folds them and piles them neatly on a chair in the corner of her bedroom. She's still sleeping. He has a quick shower and then goes through to the kitchen and starts making breakfast. Hayley's refrigerator and pantry are well stocked. Tom decides to make eggs. He scrambles them, and serves them on toast.

Hayley is drawn by the smell. She comes through to the kitchen, rubbing at her eyes, wearing only a baggy T-shirt that hangs halfway down her thighs. "You wake up too early," she says, yawning and taking a seat at the table.

"I tried to be quiet," Tom says.

"You weren't exactly banging around," Hayley says. "I'm just a light sleeper is all."

"I should've remembered."

"Can't remember everything." She yawns again and sits with her right knee drawn up to her chest.

Tom places a plate of scrambled eggs before her and then sits down opposite. "I've put some coffee on," he says. "I don't really drink it myself, but I thought you might like a cup."

"That's very considerate," Hayley says, leaning over her plate and scooping up a forkful of eggs. Her hair is a mess, but Tom likes how it looks. While she chews, she starts pulling it back from her face, then ties it back into a loose ponytail. "I'll wake up soon," she says. "It won't be long and I'll be back to my usual shiny, radiant self."

"You're already shining and radiant," Tom says.

She waves him off playfully. "Do you have plans for today?"

"You know I do."

Hayley looks at him, confused, and then she realises. "The hospital," she says.

Tom nods. "He'll probably wake up today. I want to be there when he does."

"You know, I'm heading there later. I could always just call you when he does."

"I don't have anywhere else I need to be."

"What about Del's? At this point he's probably wondering if he still employs you."

"I'll call him later. And I don't *need* to be there. He manages just fine by himself. He appreciates the company is all."

Hayley finishes eating. "I'm gonna go take a shower," she says. "I'll have the coffee when I come back."

Tom stands with her, gathering up their empty plates. "Hey," he says, and motions her closer to him.

Hayley steps to him, smiling. "I haven't brushed my teeth yet."

"I don't care," Tom says, kissing her.

She strokes his cheek and then leaves the kitchen, heading through to the bathroom.

Tom clears up, then pours Hayley a coffee. He knows how she takes it – cream and two sugars. He carries the steaming cup through to the bedroom, places it on top of her bedside cabinet.

He can hear the shower running. He takes a seat on the edge of the bed. Soon after, the shower tapers off. He hears Hayley get out and dry herself off. Hears her brush her teeth. He smiles.

Hayley comes back through to the bedroom naked, with her drying hair tied up. She pulls on some underwear. Tom watches her, admiring the shape of her body. Remembers it last night, beneath him and on top of him. She sees him watching and winks.

"As good as you remember?" she says.

"Better."

Hayley pulls on a pair of jeans and a vest.

"What're you going to do before you head to the hospital?" Tom says.

"I've got some chores I need to do," Hayley says. "Some errands I need to run. When I get there, I'll be sure to stop by the room and check in, see how our patient's doing."

Tom nods. "Take a seat a second," he says.

She frowns at him. "That sounds serious."

"I was thinking about what you asked last night."

"What I asked?"

"About why I joined the Army."

"Oh. Yeah." Hayley rounds the bed and sits down beside him, her knee brushing his.

Tom clears his throat. "I said I wasn't running away, but I don't think that's entirely true. When I think about it, I'd been trying to run away for a long time, the same way my father was, in his own way. My brother, too. We were all trying to run away in our own ways, ever since my mom died. We were all trying to find a way to cope with her death." Tom purses his lips, remembering that time. It was so long ago now. "From the time I was nine, when she died, I just remembered having this...this *weight* bearing down on me, on my chest, crushing me. I thought it would go away, but it never did. I told my dad, and he said it would go away in time."

"Did it?" Hayley says.

"Not by itself."

Hayley strokes his arm. "I'm sorry, Tom. I remember when your mom died. You missed school for about three weeks."

"I wasn't sure Dad was ever going to send us back."

"How did Anthony take it?"

"He took it bad, but he was barely five. He didn't always understand what was happening. He fluctuated between uncontrollable crying, and asking when Mom was going to come home. I think long term it affected him more than any of us realised."

"It's a kind of grief that doesn't go away."

"No, it doesn't, but I found ways to outrun that grief. To distract myself from it. To forget about it, if just for little bursts at a time."

"What was it?"

"It began when our dad started drilling us in survivalism, and in doomsday prepping. He'd teach us how to live off the land. He'd set us tasks. Drop us off in the desert and we had to find our way home."

Hayley frowns. "I know he was grieving, but that doesn't sound like great parenting."

"Maybe not, but it was what I needed. Living off my wits like that, it took the weight away. I finally felt like I could breathe again. Whether it was what Anthony needed, I'm not so sure.

"Me, I was always chasing that feeling – or rather, that lack of feeling. Not needing to think, just *do*. Not being able to grieve because I was too busy surviving. At eighteen, I needed to start thinking about what I was going to do with my life, and there was nothing here that called to me. And then I started thinking about the Army. It was like I'd already been training for it most of my life. It just made sense."

"Did you talk to anyone about it, before you joined up?"

Tom shakes his head. "No. I knew my dad would try to dissuade me. He wouldn't agree with me working for the government in any capacity." He grins.

"How did he take it when he found out?"

Tom thinks. "Since I joined the Army, I can probably count on both hands the number of times I've seen my father. It hasn't been many. We don't tend to talk about anything like the Army or the government on the rare occasions we see each other."

Hayley nods. "I'm sorry you felt that way, Tom," she says. "That you felt like you needed to run away and put yourself in danger just to try and make yourself feel better. You need to remember you were just a child when your mom died, and that was a lot to process. Have you ever thought about going to therapy?"

"No."

"Maybe you should."

"Maybe I should."

She looks at him like she knows he won't. "There's nothing wrong with getting help. It's very rare that self-diagnosing works for people, especially in such a destructive manner."

"It's healthier than drugs and alcohol."

She laughs at this. "I mean, I guess that depends on the situations you find yourself in. Most drunks and junkies aren't getting shot at."

Tom smiles. He takes her hands and kisses her. "I'm going to go to the hospital."

Hayley stands with him and embraces him. She squeezes him tight. "I'm glad you've come back here, Tom," she says, her face in his chest. "It's good to have you back here."

Tom holds her back, then kisses the top of her head. Her still-damp hair smells like her shampoo. Hayley starts to pull away. Tom pulls her back, holds her a moment longer. She doesn't protest. She kisses him on the neck and keeps her arms wrapped around him as the early morning light streams through her bedroom window and bathes them both in its glow.

## 22

K endis wasn't planning on going to the hospital today – he was planning on staying away from the ghastly place as long as he could manage, or at least until an AB-negative liver showed up – but that was until he was told about the donor who escaped.

He's already railed at Big Ron on the drive over, and Big Ron has taken it with all his usual stoicism, nodding along and never taking his eyes from the road.

He finds Alec in his office. "What the fuck happened?" Kendis says, bursting into the room.

Alec is sitting at his desk, opening a package. Kendis can see that it contains new scalpels. Kendis leaves Alec in charge of ordering all of the medical equipment he needs. He still has some contacts within the medical industry, and he's able to get them at a discount, and quietly. Alec turns and looks up at him, slowly, raising an eyebrow. There's no rush about him. There never is. "What are you referring to?"

"What do you *think* I'm referring to, damn it?"

Alec shrugs.

"The escape!" Kendis clenches his fists. He has to hold

himself back. He wants to launch himself at the smug son of a bitch.

"There was an escape," Alec says.

Kendis tilts his head and raises a fist. "Don't get smart with me, motherfucker."

Alec shrugs again. "You seem to already know, so if you're going to state the obvious, then why shouldn't I?"

"You think I didn't need to know?"

"You *do* know. Why would I waste time reaching out when I know one of your goons will already have done so?"

"I thought I'd made myself clear, Alec – anything that happens *here*, you're responsible for it. If it's something I need to know about, I want *you* to be the one to tell me."

Alec leans back in his chair and waves a dismissive hand in the air. He takes a moment to look Kendis up and down, and then to do the same to Big Ron. He smirks a little. "It's all in hand."

"What's that supposed to mean?" Kendis says.

"The escapee," Alec says. "I sent men after him."

Kendis waits a moment. "*And?*"

"And nothing. Not yet, anyway."

Kendis has to take a deep breath. He reminds himself it's important not to let Alec get under his skin. That's what he's trying to do. It's all about power with this motherfucker. He's always looking for an angle. "Who is he?"

"Who?" Alec says.

"The escapee."

"How should I know?" Alec says, lacing his fingers. "Just another homeless nigger, same as all the others your goons bring me."

Big Ron bristles at this. He takes a step forward. "You wanna run that one by me again?"

Alec smirks.

Kendis puts his arm across Big Ron's chest to restrain him.

Turning back to Alec, he says, "He didn't have a name? No ID?"

"I'm sure he has a name, but I don't know what it was. I doubt anyone else in this building does either, and frankly, I don't think they care. I know I certainly don't. If he hadn't managed to slip away, you wouldn't be asking me right now, either."

"How did he get out?"

Alec tells him what happened, so far as he can surmise.

"Was he sedated?" Kendis says.

"Of course he was," Alec says. "The problem is, most of these people are homeless because they got hooked on something they found to be more important to them than shelter. I have no way of knowing how high their tolerance is, and so I have to do my best to guess. I'm usually so accurate. You're frankly lucky no one has pulled something like this before."

Kendis glances up at Big Ron. Big Ron is still glaring at Alec, but he's not straining against Kendis's arm any longer. Kendis thinks it's safe for him to lower it. "You said you sent men after him."

"I did."

"And? Have they found him?"

"They know where he is. He got on a bus, got off in some little town called Hopper Creek. Do you know it?"

"It sounds familiar," Kendis says.

"It's where Hal went," Big Ron says. "It's where he works now."

Kendis remembers. Hal went to work for some drug operation going on out there. "That's right," he says. "I've never *been*, but I've heard of it."

"Yes, well, I haven't," Alec says. "But that's where he is. Apparently he managed to give them the slip when he first got off the bus, and when they next caught sight of him it was dark. They almost had him, but they say someone emerged from the shadows and caught our falling escapee."

"Falling?"

"He's just undergone major surgery, Kendis, and he hasn't given himself any time to heal. No doubt he's losing blood. Anyway, they thought it best not to engage with the stranger, considering they had no idea who he was and he hadn't seen their faces. They thought it was best to keep it that way."

Kendis feels uncomfortable with all of this. "Where is he now?"

"His mysterious benefactor took him to a local hospital."

"*Hospital*?" Kendis says. "Shit. Are you for fucking real? A *hospital*?"

Alec doesn't look concerned. "You don't need to worry yourself."

"I *am* fucking worried! He's in a hospital, missing some fucking organs – questions are going to be asked!"

"And what answers can he give them? Relax, Kendis. You're getting too worked up. Think of your blood pressure."

"My blood pressure is fine until I'm anywhere near you, you son of a bitch!"

Alec doesn't appear offended by this. If anything, he looks pleased. "He was full of drugs," he says. "Even if they weren't enough to keep him unconscious, they likely fried his brain. He wouldn't have been thinking straight. He was able to escape from here, but chances are he couldn't see straight. He might not even remember where it was."

"That's not good enough."

"I agree," Alec says. "Your men are still on him, Kendis. They're outside the hospital right now. Hell, I've even sent some more men over there. They're watching all four corners of the place. He won't slip by us again."

"Where's the hospital?"

"It's in Hopper Creek. I think it's fairly new. It's certainly not anywhere I've ever attended."

Kendis feels himself calming, but only a little. "They know where he is?"

"They know he's in the building," Alec says. "They're trying to find out which room, but I'm sure you'll understand such a matter needs to be handled with some delicacy. They don't want to arouse any suspicions."

Kendis is nodding at this. "Okay. All right. This isn't the worst thing. This can be salvageable. What about cops? Have they been called?"

"No cops," Alec says. "The men have been watching out for them. Most likely, if he's split his stitches, the doctors there probably have him under heavy sedation to keep him asleep. To keep him calm, and to help him heal. He's more than likely unconscious still now, as we speak. They'll want to talk to him before they contact the local law enforcement. It's not like he's been stabbed, or shot, or poisoned. He's had surgery, that's all."

"But when he wakes up," Kendis says, "after they speak to him, they *will* call the cops."

"We hope to have him dealt with by then," Alec says.

Kendis bites his lip. "I don't like this." He looks up at Big Ron.

Big Ron shakes his head, agreeing. "We should go out there," he says. "Deal with this ourselves. It's too important to leave it with anyone else. We need to oversee this, hands-on."

He's right. Kendis turns back to Alec. "That's exactly what we're going to do."

Alec shrugs. "Suit yourselves."

"You're in charge while we're gone, Alec," Kendis says, with more than a little reticence. "But don't think I won't have eyes on you."

Alec scoffs. "You always do."

"Try not to let anyone else escape."

"I'll do my best."

Kendis and Big Ron leave him in his office. Kendis doesn't have time to respond to his flippant comment. There's too much on his mind. Too much stress suddenly weighing down on his shoulders.

"What are we going to do when we get there?" Big Ron says as they exit the hospital. He unlocks the Lexus but neither of them gets straight in.

Kendis leans on the roof and shakes his head. "I'm not sure, but we can think about that on the way. We get a good look at the place, and I'm sure something will occur to us."

"That's not much of a plan."

"I know it's not, but my mind is fucking racing right now. I need some time to think."

Big Ron nods. He starts to get into the car. Kendis opens the door and goes to join him, then realises he can feel a buzzing in his pocket. He pulls out his phone. It's ringing. It's not a number he recognises. Whoever it is, he spots he already has three missed calls from them. He never felt it ringing. No doubt it was while he was trying to deal with Alec. He answers the call.

"Kendis Dukes?" the voice on the other end says.

It sounds familiar to Kendis, but he can't quite place it. "Who's asking?"

"This is Hal Redford. I hope you remember me."

"Hal," Kendis says, slipping into the car and raising his eyebrows at Big Ron. "What a surprise. And what a coincidence. We were just talking about you."

Hal sounds surprised, and confused. "Oh really?"

"Uh-huh. We were talking about that town you left Santa Fe to go work in. Hopper Creek, that right?"

"That's right," Hal says. "Why – why were you talking about Hopper Creek?"

"We'll get to that. Why are you calling, Hal?"

"I, uh, I need a job, Mr Dukes."

"You can call me Kendis, Hal, you know that. And I don't have a problem hiring you back. We never fell out. We had a very amicable parting. You got a good offer and you were looking to make more money – I can respect that. I *am* curious, though, why you're looking to leave your current employer?"

Hal snorts. "There's no employment to be had, Mr Dukes – I mean, Kendis."

"What do you mean by that?"

"I mean we were selling flakka, and the flakka is all gone. It's been destroyed. Donny, who I was working for, he's trying to find out who was behind it, but even if he manages that, what then? The lab's destroyed. I've gotta be realistic about all of this. I need money, and I'm not gonna get it hanging around here and hoping for the best."

"This Donny, he a local boy?"

"Whole crew are," Hal says. "I'm the only outsider."

Kendis exchanges a look with Big Ron again. They could use these locals to their advantage. "As luck would have it, Hal, I'm heading over to Hopper Creek soon. Very soon. We should meet up, later today. Let's talk business. We might all be able to help each other out."

"Okay," Hal says, sounding intrigued. "Well, now you've got my number. When you get to town give me a call, name the time and place, and I'll be there."

"I'll see you real soon, Hal." Kendis hangs up, turns to Big Ron. "This could work in our favour. Let's go."

## 23

I t's not visiting hours, but no one hassles Tom. They know Hayley, and they know who he is to her. They leave him alone to sit in the room with the bloodied stranger he brought in last night.

He hasn't woken yet, but Tom notices he's moving more. Twitching. He can see activity under his eyelids. It shouldn't be too long now.

Hayley started her shift a couple of hours ago. She stopped by to say hello when she arrived, and to check on the patient. Tom has been alone since. Just he and the sleeper.

It doesn't take too much longer before he starts to wake. His eyes flutter open. He looks confused at first, and then alarmed. Tom leaves the room and finds Hayley, tells her the patient is awake. She comes back with him to check the guy over.

They keep him calm. Make sure he's all right. Let him know where he is, and how he got here. Stress that he needs to stay calm so as not to tear his stitches open again. Hayley doesn't tell him yet about his missing kidney.

Before she leaves the room, Hayley turns to Tom. "Don't

push him," she says. "He needs to rest. I'm letting you talk to him first before anyone else does, and I could get in big trouble for that."

Tom nods. He understands this, and he appreciates it. Hayley leaves the room. He's left with the guy, who regards him with suspicion.

The man has to clear his throat before he speaks. "Who are you?"

"Tom Rollins."

"You brought me here?"

"Yeah. You remember that?"

"I don't remember much. I rolled into town, and then... Then I'm here. It's now. And I'm sitting with Tom Rollins."

"I'm sitting," Tom says. "You're lying down. You remember your name?"

The guy looks at him, but doesn't answer directly. "Of course I do."

"You wanna share it with the class?"

"Well, since you showed me yours... It's Jim. Jim Belafonte."

"Good to meet you, Jim. Just to give you a little perspective on time, you came into the hospital here the night before last."

"Shit, for real?"

Tom nods. "Like Hayley said when she was in here, you needed to rest. You nearly bled out."

Jim runs a hand down his face. He rubs at his eyes. "It's been a while since I last lost a day like that."

"Why don't you tell me a little about yourself, Jim."

Jim looks at him. "I told you my name because you gave me yours. You wanna hear my story, then I'm gonna need to know more about you first. This is a quid pro quo situation."

Tom holds out his hands. "I've got nothing to hide."

"Yeah, well, not all of us are so proud. Let me ask you this – you a military man, Tom?"

Tom smiles. "Army," he says. "You can tell?"

"Uh-huh. Like recognises like, my man. You can have that one for free."

"Appreciate it. How long ago did you leave?"

"How long ago did *you* leave?" Jim says.

"Four years," Tom says. This was when he left the CIA, not the Army, but it was when he decided he wouldn't work for the government anymore.

"Four years, huh? You're still just a pup, ain't you?"

"Thirty-two."

"Thirty-two, goddamn. I left the Army fifteen years ago, give or take. *Shit.*" He shakes his head. "Fifteen years. Where does the time go?"

"Why'd you leave?"

"Honourable discharge," Jim says. "I had PTSD."

"I'm sorry to hear that."

Jim waves a hand in the air. "I'm over it. I've had bigger problems since."

"You're homeless," Tom says.

Jim raises an eyebrow. "You can tell?"

"Probably the same way you could tell I'd been in the Army."

Jim grins. "You're a military man, and you always will be."

Tom cocks his head. "I told you I left."

"I know you did, but that's not what I mean."

"Then what do you mean?"

"I mean it'll always be a part of you. Maybe it's the duty, the routine – maybe it's the action. Some guys, it becomes like an addiction to them." Tom grits his jaw at this, but he doesn't think it shows. "I've been around a lot of ex-service men and women while I've been on the streets, and I know what I'm talking about. I've seen it in their eyes, and in their body language. The way y'all hold yourselves. Hell, I used to be the same. I think, for you, I think it's the latter – I think you're addicted to the action."

"Why's that?"

"Like I said, the way you hold yourself. You have that prison look – shoulders hunched, always ready for an attack. Always checking over your shoulder, aren't you? Check every room you enter, looking for points of escape, points of entrapment. Never feel more comfortable than when there's a gun in your hand. Everywhere you go, you've got your eyes wide, just looking for trouble. You're always ready to step in, offer a helping hand if it means you're gonna get to see some action. I ain't wrong, am I?"

Tom doesn't answer.

"I know I'm right," Jim says. "I'm here, ain't I? And *you* brought me here."

"Why were those men following you?"

Jim smiles, like this question proves his point. He shrugs. "I don't know."

"Do you know you're missing a kidney?"

"Figured I was missing something, once I started bleeding so much."

"When Hayley was in here and she told you you had stitches, you didn't seem surprised."

"Hayley?"

"The nurse."

Jim smiles. "She your girlfriend?"

"I suppose she is."

"That's real sweet. I had someone. Not even all that long ago, now."

"You're changing the subject."

"You a cop or something? You're asking an awful lot of questions. Or could it just be that addiction you have, wanting to know where the action could be?" Jim grins.

Tom allows a moment of silence to pass before he speaks again. "I've heard that a few times now," he says. "From people who care about me. At least, I think they do, anyway. And I think they're worried about me." He takes a deep breath. "I don't know how it was for you, but when I was in the Army, we were told to look out for one another. We had no one to rely on but the men to our left and the men to our right. Those ahead of us were the enemy. Those behind us, barking the orders – well, they were almost as bad. The grunts, us, we were brothers. We had to take care of each other because no one else would."

Jim listens. He turns his head to the side and looks out the window. "I miss that," he says finally, his voice low.

"I do, too," Tom says. "Maybe that brotherhood wasn't there to help you in the past, when things started going wrong for you, but I'm here now. We're brothers, Jim, you and I. We didn't serve together, or at the same time, but we're brothers. If you need help, I can give it to you. If you need money, I'll give you my last dollar. If you need a ride somewhere, I'm right there paying for gas and taking you door to door. You can trust me, Jim."

Jim chews his lip. He turns back to Tom. "Before you knew I was Army, why'd you hang around? You say you brought me to this room, and then I wake up a couple days later and yours is the first face I see. Why?"

"Because before I had questions," Tom says. "Now, I have concerns. I want you to talk to me, Jim. But I want you to feel like you *can*, not like you have to. If you don't want to tell me what's going on, then fine. I won't press it. But if you think you can trust me, then I'm right here for you."

Both men are silent. Jim is thinking. He stares off into a corner of the room. It's clear he's battling with doubts. He's probably been let down before. Disappointed. Betrayed. He looks up finally. "Why'd you leave?"

"I got an offer to do something else," Tom says. "It seemed like a good idea at the time, but I came to regret it. Government work. Black ops. *That's* what I left four years ago."

"Shit," Jim says. "Sounds like you've been around."

"More than I ever expected."

Jim clears his throat. He takes a long breath. "You think you can get me a cup of water?"

"Sure," Tom says. He leaves the room and goes down the hall to where the water cooler is. He takes his time, giving Jim space to think. He gets back and hands the plastic cup to Jim, who takes it gratefully and drinks. Tom returns to his seat. He glances out the window as he passes, subtly so Jim doesn't notice. It's a quick look, but he doesn't see the Ford from the other night.

Jim finishes drinking and puts the plastic cup to one side. He rests his head back on his propped-up pillows. "All right," he says, turning back to Tom. "Let's talk."

## 24

"The PTSD hit, and I couldn't hold my gun straight," Jim says. "I'd freeze in the field. Well, when you're in an Afghani warzone, you keep that up and it's just a matter of time before you catch a bullet. That was the end of that. They sent me on my way. So I came back home, back to my wife, and my kid, and..." He stops, looking down at his hands. He balls them up. He grits his teeth.

"Boy or girl?" Tom says.

"Boy," Jim says. "Well, a man. He'll be twenty-three, now. Like I said, where's all the time go? I haven't seen him...I haven't seen him in thirteen years. Thirteen damn years." He closes his eyes and shakes his head. "I'm not sure...if we passed each other in the street, I'm not sure we'd even recognise each other. I don't know if he's still in New Mexico. Once his mom kicked me out, I don't know what they did next. At that time, I didn't care. I wasn't thinking about anyone else. Just myself. When I eventually thought to check in on them, they didn't live there no more. They'd moved. I don't know where. Doubt I ever will.

"I don't blame her if she did. I don't blame her for sending me on my way. Someone needed to. I got back, and I tried to keep it together. I got a job. It was just at a gas station but it was something. I couldn't hold it down, though. I went through a whole load of jobs, and I couldn't hold any of them down, because the PTSD would catch up with me. A noise too loud – a car backfiring, or a box being dropped – and I was a wreck. I'd freeze, and no one could get through to me. No one could move me. I was a fucking mess. You know I said I'd been with a lot of ex-military out on the streets? Same thing had happened to a lot of them. And they all said the same thing, too – this government doesn't take care of its own. It doesn't take care of the men and women who risked their lives and their limbs and their mental stability to uphold peace and security in this country. We were cast out and forgotten about, like we never even existed."

"That's why we have to be brothers," Tom says. "Out there in the trenches, we can't rely on anyone else."

Jim nods. "I needed to try and calm myself. I didn't have any addiction to combat. Hell, if anything, I had a fear of it. I needed to calm the noises. The screaming and the explosions and all that other shit. I needed to get it out of my head, out of my system. I needed it gone. I'd wake up screaming in the middle of the night, and it went on and on for years. None of us in that house slept, and it was all my fault. I needed to find something that would stop it. Something that would bring me peace.

"Alcohol didn't do it. Neither did weed. They weren't strong enough. I was getting desperate. I tried the hard stuff. *That* did it. Heroin. Hell, I've snorted it, smoked it, and injected it by now. I've taken it all ways. *That's* what helped. And at first, it really did help. I was calm, man. I was everything I needed to be. I was working in a store at that point, and it was the longest I was able to keep a job. I was sleeping through the night. I wasn't screaming no more, or freezing, or shaking. Nothing was getting to me. I'd finally found that peace I needed. In our house, we were all sleeping.

"It didn't last. Of course it didn't. I traded one battle for another. The drugs got the better of me. Got so they were all that mattered. Lost my job. Lost my home. Lost my family. I had nothing left but the streets and my heroin, and it stayed that way for a long, long time."

Jim falls silent. He looks pained, and it has nothing to do with his stitches. Dredging up these memories rekindles a deep-rooted pain he forgot he had. "I thought I'd never quit the drugs," he says. "I was ready to let them kill me. What else did I have? I was happy to fade away into them. I lost those years, man. All those years I was high, I don't remember them. They just drifted by in a haze. The only things I *do* remember are the times I didn't have the money to get high. The fucking *pain*, man. I *wished* I was dead when that happened. But I always managed to find the cash for that. I always managed to find a way to get what I needed. I've done things, man, things I'm not proud of." He shakes his head.

"It's not your fault," Tom says. "We've all done things we're not proud of."

"I was gonna die in the gutter," Jim continues, "and I was ready for that. Day to day, I was just waiting for it to happen, knowing that every time I passed out high, staring up at the stars, I probably wasn't gonna wake up. And I was fine with that. Truth be told, I *wanted* it. I was sick and tired of being alive. I'd fucked up so much. Then I met Rhonda." He smiles, thinking of her. "You ever found someone like that? Someone who just saves your whole fucking life? Maybe Hayley out there."

"I'm not sure I've ever been so low," Tom says. He thinks of Alejandra, his right hand moving unconsciously to his left shoulder and the Santa Muerte tattoo there. Even she didn't save his life. It hadn't needed saving. She just gave him a reason to live.

"I hope you never are," Jim says. "But I have been, and it was Rhonda who pulled me out of it. Rhonda who helped me get clean, and gave me a reason to stay that way. And I'm not gonna lie, it wasn't pretty, kicking the drugs. You think you're a mess when you're on them, or when you need them, but when you're trying to stop taking them is a whole different ball game. Your own body, your brain, it all rebels against you. Suddenly, nothing else matters more than cooking that shit up and getting it into your veins.

"Rhonda stayed with me the whole while. She never gave up on me. All the way through, she was by my side." He smiles, remembering. "Do you like the Beach Boys?"

Tom blinks at the sudden question. "Sure, I like the Beach Boys."

"I always used to think of that song, 'Help Me, Rhonda', when I was with her." He grins, and adds, "I'd sing it to her sometimes."

"That song's about getting over an ex as I recall," Tom says. "How'd she take that?"

"Well, it was accurate. She was getting that heroin out of my heart."

"She sounds very special."

"She is. Except...except now I'm worried she's dead."

"I'm sorry to hear that. What happened?"

"I don't know yet, but I haven't seen her in nearly three weeks now. That's too long." Jim purses his lips. He looks at Tom and tells him what happened to him in Santa Fe. How he was knocked out and woke up in a hospital room. He tells him every detail he can remember. "They took my kidney. That guy in the bed next to me, it looked like they'd taken a lot more from him than just a kidney. I don't know why they were keeping him alive." He takes a deep breath and grimaces, steeling himself before he says, "I'm worried that's where Rhonda ended up. And if they got hold of her..."

He doesn't need to finish. Tom knows what he's thinking. If they got hold of Rhonda, she's most likely dead now. If they were through harvesting her organs, what further use would they have for her? Jim doesn't want to say this. He doesn't want it to be true.

"Are you going to contact the police?" Tom says.

"I don't trust cops," Jim says.

"In this case you might not have a choice."

"You think they're gonna believe me?"

"They're beholden to at least look."

Jim sighs, but he's considering.

"If you've escaped, they might have already moved their operation."

"I don't want to talk to cops," Jim says. He looks at Tom. "But if *you* wanna call them, give them an anonymous tip..."

Tom nods. "You remember where it was?"

Jim tells him. Tom memorises the address.

"The men that were following you when you fell on me," Tom says, "did you recognise them? From the hospital maybe?"

"I didn't get a good look at them, but I know they were looking for me," Jim says. He tells Tom of how he hid away, and they circled the town square. "Did you see their faces?" he asks.

Tom shakes his head. "It was dark, and their headlights were shining into my eyes."

"I don't like being followed," Jim says. "And I like not knowing what they look like even less."

There's a knock on the room door, and then Hayley slips inside. "Do we have a name for the patient yet?" she says, striding across the room and stopping next to the bed. She's smiling at Jim. He tells her his name. "Nice to finally meet you, Mr Belafonte."

"Please, call me Jim."

"I hope Tom here hasn't kept you talking too long," Hayley says. "I told him you need to rest."

"Nah, Tom's all right," Jim says. "He's a good one." He turns to Tom. "I can see she's a good one, too. If you've got hold of her, you better never let go. A beautiful woman, *and* she's a medical professional? You've hit the jackpot, my man."

"See, that's what I've wanted to tell him," Hayley says, "but, y'know, I think he admires my modesty the most."

Jim laughs at this.

Hayley turns to Tom. "I'm going to have to tell Dr Oswald that Jim's awake now," she says. "He's been asking. He's going to want to check him over. I thought I should give you a heads-up."

Tom nods and stands. "Thanks." He steps closer to Jim's bed, places a hand on his arm. "I'll be back to check in on you," he says. "In the meantime, you do what Hayley says. You start bleeding out like you were the other night, I might not be around to catch you again."

"Sometimes a man's just gotta keep moving," Jim says.

"And sometimes he's gotta *heal*," Tom says.

Jim grins and holds a fist out to Tom. Tom bumps it and then leaves the room. Hayley follows him out. "Did he tell you what happened?" she says once the door is closed, keeping her voice low.

Tom makes sure no one is nearby, then gives her a quick rundown.

"Oh, my God," Hayley says. "That's awful. Has he called the cops?"

"Not yet, and he says he's not going to. He doesn't want to deal with them."

"That's insane! It sounds like there's other people there and–"

"I'm going to call them," Tom says.

Hayley nods. "Okay. Are you doing that now?"

"Yeah. I'll let you know how it goes." They say their good-byes and Tom kisses her before he leaves, then Hayley goes off to find Dr Oswald.

## 25

A lec reclines in his chair, eyes closed, Mozart on the stereo.

His days and his nights are in this hospital. For six years now, this is how it's been. In a way, that's how Alec has always wanted it. It's how he likes it. When he still had his license, there was nowhere he'd rather be than the hospital, blood up to his elbows while he worked away in someone's chest cavity. There was nothing for him beyond the hospital walls. There still isn't.

Down the hall from his office, he's converted a patient room into his living quarters. There isn't much in there. He doesn't need much. Just a cot and a hot plate and a rail to hang his clothes on. Kendis's men do his washing, and they bring his meals. All his needs are catered for.

Still, as much as Alec enjoys this set-up, as little as he wants for anything, there is still *one* thing he'd like more of: *power*. Some could argue he has enough, but at the end of the day these men will always be *Kendis's* men, not his own.

If he were running things, they'd be a lot smoother. He'd be cutting into a higher class of person, too. Not these dirty, degenerate, homeless people he's brought on a daily basis, and most of them junkies to boot. What good are their organs, really, when they've been ravaged with alcohol and drugs?

Alec opens his eyes and sighs. This used to be enough for him. But six years is a long time. He stands and starts stretching, keeping himself limber. He should be going into surgery soon, but Kendis has halted it. He's put a halt to the pick-ups, too. He's nervous. Is worried their runaway might start talking, and that he'll talk to the police and send them here to look around. He wants them all ready to run, should the need occur. He's called all his men in, and posted them in and around the building on lookout. If Alec has to flee this place, he'll miss it. He's become accustomed to it. It reminds him a little of his prison cell. He grew to be comfortable there, too. He's found ways to be comfortable everywhere. It's easy enough to do when he's more than confident enough in himself and his abilities to know that no matter where he goes, he has worth. If the medical board couldn't see that, and look past one little mistake, then that's their problem.

But if there's one thing he wants more, it's everything Kendis has. His position. His power. The extra cut of the money that Alec himself is doing all the work for in the first place.

Kendis has been useful for some things, of course. He set this all up. He bought this old hospital, and listed it as a commercial building, ostensibly under construction. The men that Kendis has filled it with to guard it, to watch and handle Alec's patients, they pass as security guards. An empty building filled with men would raise too many questions if Kendis hadn't had the foresight to do this all properly.

Kendis isn't stupid. He isn't an idiot, Alec has to commend him for this at least. It does, of course, make him curious as to why Kendis is so desperate to find an AB-negative liver. It's specific. There has to be a buyer lined up. If a buyer needs a liver, they don't have much time left. Alec runs his hands back through his hair and laces his fingers atop his head, wondering. Wondering who the buyer is, and how much they're worth. Wondering how much they're offering for this liver.

Alec thinks it might be worth his trying to find out the answers to these questions.

Alec goes to his door. He pokes his head out into the hall, turning left and right. He spots one of Kendis's men down the hall to his right, and waves him over. Alec can't remember his name. He never bothers to learn them. They're not important enough to matter to him. They're Kendis's men – he can take the trouble to find out their names.

"I've been thinking," Alec says, when the man is close enough. "Our patient who got away... We should probably take some precautions in case he tries to talk to anyone." Alec was blasé when Kendis voiced these same concerns to him, but that was just to undermine him. To get under his skin. Truthfully, Alec knows Kendis was right to be concerned.

"What were you thinking?" the man says.

"Clear the lower floors," Alec says. "That goes for the basement, too. If anyone comes looking, I doubt they're going to search the whole building." He strokes the corner of his mouth. "And if they do, we'll have to think of a way to deter them."

The man nods. "So, move all the patients to the upper floors?"

"Yes. Do it now."

"And the bodies?"

"Get rid of them. Take them where you usually do and bury them there."

"I'll gather up some of the others and we'll get right on it," the man says.

Alec slips back into his office without a word, and closes the door. He returns to his chair and leans back in it, lacing his fingers. Returns to his thoughts. It's time for him to start making moves of his own. It's time for him to take over this whole operation, the way it should have always been. Alec looks to the near future. It won't be long now. First, he starts with the liver buyer. Finding out who he or she is. After that, everything will fall into place. He smiles to himself.

## 26

Tom calls the cops in Santa Fe before he drives home. Sends them, anonymously, to the abandoned hospital. Tells them he's concerned about some of the things he's seen and heard happening there. Tells them he's seen armed men around the grounds. That he's seen a man running away, being chased. He hangs up before they can press him, before they can ask too many questions.

Tom gets home. He doesn't go straight inside. Circles the perimeter first, checks his windows, and his front and rear doors. Everything's untouched. No one's tried to break in. Tom goes inside. It's not a big house, but it's more than enough for what he needs. It's all on one floor, and has a living room, a kitchenette, and a bedroom. There is storage space in the attic, but Tom doesn't need it. He doesn't have enough things.

He goes through to the bedroom, and pauses by the window. In the distance, in the trees, something has caught his attention. Movement there. Slight, but more than wind rustling the branches. Tom stays loose. Casual. Acts like he hasn't spotted anything at all. Like there's just something wrong with the window and he's trying to fix it. He pushes it open, but makes like it's stuck. He works at it. All the while, his eyes are on the trees. Watching.

He picks out the figures. Two of them. They're trying to be still, but they're not used to stakeouts. Not used to staying in one place for long periods of time. They keep shifting and twitching. Tom gets a good look at them. Kyle Hobbs and Shawn Stark. Kyle keeps shifting his weight, and Shawn swats at him to stay still.

Tom finishes his pretend fixing of the window and moves away from it, closing it. He steps back into the doorway, out of Kyle and Shawn's view. Tom considers them watching his house and everything this means. Presumably, they've figured out he's the one behind the destruction of the flakka, as well as Donny's home. Or at least that they suspect he had something to do with it.

He wonders how long they've been out there. He wasn't home last night, so he has no idea when they first arrived.

He thinks about Hayley. Her home. They know he's with her. Kyle saw them together. Are they watching her place, too? Tom grits his teeth. He needs to know.

He gets low and crawls back into his room, grabbing his bag. He knows everything should be inside, but he checks it anyway, just to be sure. His burner phones, his Beretta, KA-BAR, his picture of Alejandra – they're all there. Zipping the bag closed again, he slips it onto his back and leaves the room. Goes to a window at the back of the house, on the other side of the living room. He looks out, scans the distance. It's clear here. There aren't trees for anyone to conceal themselves behind. Just fields of long grass. Tom watches for a while. He doesn't see anyone. Donny's boys aren't professionals. They don't know what they're doing. They're watching the front of the house, nothing more. Two of them together, waiting for him to return and not having the sense to spread out, watch his escape routes. When he checked, before he came inside, he saw no evidence anyone had been up close to his home. They haven't looked at it closely.

Tom opens the back window and jumps outside. He'll have to leave his car behind, but that's fine. It's not far to go to Hayley's house. He can travel everywhere in Hopper Creek with ease on foot.

Staying low, he starts running. Deeper into the field, and into the long grass, concealing himself in it. He circles back, to his left, through the trees that line the side of the road there. He gets to the main road and keeps running, breathing through his nose, keeping it calm and level, his heartbeat at a steady rate. He's not straining himself.

He passes by parallel to where Kyle and Shawn are concealing themselves. He could ambush them if he wanted. He could find their vehicle hidden somewhere in these trees, and he could sabotage it. That's not what he wants to do, not right now. He doesn't want them to know he's seen them. Instead, he keeps moving. Clears the area and gets off the road. He doesn't know how long Kyle and Shawn have been there, or what kind of cycle they're working on. Another two from the crew could be on their way to relieve them. Tom doesn't want to pass them on the road. Doesn't want them to see him. Right now, he knows they're watching him – that gives him the upper hand. He's not going to give that away.

As he nears Hayley's street, he slows. Starts walking. Looks around. Looks into every vehicle he sees, parked and moving. None of them are familiar to him, but that doesn't mean anything.

When he reaches Hayley's, he goes in through the back door. It's locked. He has to pick it. He's very careful. Doesn't want to damage her home. He gets in and moves quietly, listening to the house. It's very still. He goes to the windows and peers out, keeping himself concealed. The street looks clear. He goes upstairs to be sure, looks down on the road from this vantage point. Grows more and more confident that Hayley's home is not being watched. Just his.

Tom doesn't relax straight away. He heads outside, looks around. Checks in the flowerbeds for footprints. There aren't any. Checks the windows and their frames. No one has been here. No one has tried to get in, other than himself. He returns inside. He needs to keep moving, to get to the hospital and make sure Hayley is all right, but first he needs to check something.

He turns on the television and puts it to the local news. While it plays, he fires up Hayley's laptop and searches online to see if anything has happened at the abandoned hospital in Santa Fe that Jim told him about. He sits on the edge of the sofa, the laptop on the low coffee table. His eyes flicker toward the television. The bag remains on his back. He's not planning on being here long. Except, he can't find anything. He remembers when he made the call, checking the time. It's been a couple of hours, now. Long enough. More than.

Tom hits refresh on the laptop a few times, and on the television watches as the news runs through its cycle of local interest stories without change. No updates, no breaking revelations. Nothing.

It doesn't mean anything. Not yet. The cops may not have been by. It was an anonymous call, and an outlandish, if vague, story that he presented them with. If they're already busy, they're not going to prioritise driving by. If they think it's a prank, they might not go at all. Tom blows air. He'll give them until night, check again then. He might have to call again, press the matter. Perhaps tell a more attention-grabbing story. He's already said he saw a man running away, being chased. Perhaps he should add blood into the mix. Tell them he saw that the runaway was bleeding, and he left a trail on the road behind him. Would that be enough? He could maybe throw in a gunshot or two.

Tom turns off the television and shuts down the laptop. He looks out the windows one more time, and makes sure the street remains clear. It is. He slips out the back door again, and relocks it after himself. Outside, he starts running again. To the hospital, now. To Hayley.

## 27

Hal's face lights up when he sees Kendis, as if he didn't expect he'd be here, despite Kendis having called and arranging the meet when he arrived in town. "Tell me where's good to eat, Hal," Kendis said on the phone. "And that's where we'll go."

Kendis and Big Ron have already eaten when Hal reaches them. The waitress is busy clearing their table. Big Ron stands and Kendis motions for Hal to slide into the booth. Once he's in, Big Ron sits back down beside him, boxing him in opposite Kendis. Hal isn't alarmed by this. He still looks too relieved to see Kendis. Still smiling like a child. "Mr Dukes," he says, "it's very good to see you again."

"I'm sure it is," Kendis says. "Hopper Creek, huh?" he says, looking out the window. "It's quite a place. I can see why you'd leave Santa Fe for it."

"It seemed like a good idea at the time, Mr Dukes."

"Well, we're all trying to scrabble upwards, aren't we? Sometimes we make mistakes and end up tumbling back way further than where we came from." He looks back at Hal.

"But I didn't come all this way just to catch up and exchange pleasantries. Let's talk business."

"I don't have much business to speak of, Mr Dukes," Hal says.

"I told you on the phone, call me Kendis."

"Okay, sure. But like I told you on the phone, I *need* business. Anything you've got for me, I'll take it."

Kendis rests his head on a hand, his index finger pressed into his cheekbone and the rest of his fingers curled in front of his mouth. Slowly, he takes a sip from his soda and watches Hal. Keeps him waiting. He lowers his glass. Wipes condensation from the side of it. "I could be able to do you one better, Hal," he says. "*All* of you."

Hal tilts his head. "All of us?"

"Who do you work for here, Hal?"

"Uh, he's called Donny. Donny Bradshaw."

"Tell me about him."

"Well..." Hal looks side to side, thinking how best to answer. "Until – until not that long ago he had this town locked down *tight*. Everything was running smooth. He knew what he was doing. Nobody was coming at us, trying to touch us – nobody would dare."

"So what happened?"

Hal holds out his hands. He blows air and shakes his head. "I don't know, man. Not a clue. *Someone* came at us, and hard. Destroyed all the flakka. It'll take years to get this thing up and running again, if they ever do."

"This Donny Bradshaw – he know who it was?"

"They're all suspicious of this guy they used to go to high school with, and he usedta be in the Army or something, but I don't know anything about that."

"What was he like to work for?" Kendis says.

Hal frowns. "He was all right. I didn't have any problems

with him. Like I said, he kept things running smooth here, right up until they weren't."

"He'd have to be a good leader to do that, right?"

Hal glances up at Big Ron, who is looking back down at him. "Sure, sure, I guess so," Hal says. "Although..."

Kendis raises his chin. "What?"

"Well, he's *local*. He's lived here his whole life. In high school, he was a big deal. A jock, y'know. Kind of a bully. That kinda thing. He could throw his weight around and people would jump to do what he said, and I don't think that's ever really changed. He's kept a lot of that sway. He parlayed it into a way to make money."

"So things were smooth because he knew everybody?"

"Pretty much. He knows the cops here – *that* made things *very* smooth."

"*All* the cops?"

"Enough of them to matter."

Kendis nods at this.

"And everyone else was too scared of him to try anything."

"Apart from this soldier they knew in high school."

"*If* it was really him," Hal says.

"You have doubts?"

Hal shrugs. "It doesn't really matter to me."

Kendis grunts. "It could matter to *me*, though," he says.

Hal raises an eyebrow.

"You need work, Hal, and I can use the hands. But I need more than just your one pair. This Donny, do you think he'd be open to bringing his crew into my fold?"

Hal grimaces. "I mean, he's desperate, but I don't think he's the kind that likes being told what to do, so..."

Big Ron speaks up. "You could always present it as a partnership," he says. "At first."

Kendis nods. He smiles. Looks at Hal. "Maybe I need to meet Donny for myself, and then we can gauge how things are going to be presented, and how they're going to *be*. Can you facilitate that, Hal?"

"Yeah, of course."

"Good. I need it as soon as possible. I'm talking today. Hell, within the hour."

"Okay," Hal says. He looks at Big Ron, wanting to stand. "I'll tell you what – you just stay here. Get some coffee. Make yourself comfortable – but not too comfortable. I'll go see him, let him know you've got a business proposal, and then I'll bring him right back here with me."

"Sounds good, Hal." Kendis nods for Big Ron to let him out the booth.

Hal hurries off and Big Ron slides back in. "If they're having a problem with some soldier," Big Ron says, "are you sure you want to make that trouble ours?"

Kendis waves a hand. "If it takes us a day out of our way, so what? It's nothing for us to be concerned about. We'll show these hicks how it should be done. And long term, this is a good investment for us. We deal with our runaway, and we get some more men. More men means we can increase our operation. Maybe put our fingers in a few more pies."

"I'm gonna trust you know what you're doing," Big Ron says, "because I *always* trust that you know what you're doing. Now, I'm gonna get some coffee. You want some?"

Kendis nods. "You know how I like it," he says.

As Big Ron slips out the booth, Kendis watches the window. He can see Hal out there, in the parking lot. He's on his phone as he rushes to his car. If Donny and his crew are no good to Kendis long term, then fine. They can stay and rot in Hopper Creek. So long as they can help him deal with his own problem, that's all that really matters to him.

He leans back and rolls his neck, hearing it pop, and waits for Hal's return, and his meeting with Donny Bradshaw.

## 28

Tom gets to the hospital a couple of hours before the end of Hayley's shift. He checks in on her, and lets her know what's happening. Hayley's eyes go wide as he tells her. "They're not watching my place?" she says.

"No."

"But they're watching yours?"

"Yeah."

"If they get bored at yours, it's probably just a matter of time before they come to mine," Hayley says.

"I know that, and that's why I'm not letting you out of my sight," Tom says. "Because you work long shifts, Hayley, and if they're watching your empty house it's just gonna be a short matter of time before they get bored of *that*, too. They know you, and they know where you work, and they're gonna come looking for you here soon enough."

"You can't come here with me every day, Tom."

"It won't be every day," Tom says. "It'll just be until I can either get them off the trail, or throw them off forcefully if need be."

Hayley grits her teeth. "Fine," she says. "But you're not going to be able to follow me on my rounds."

"I'll be in the lobby," Tom says. "Or else in the car. I'll be very discreet. You won't even know I'm here, and neither will anyone else."

They agree to meet in the lobby at the end of Hayley's shift. Tom goes to Jim's room. He knocks but doesn't wait for a response. Jim is standing by the window. He spins at Tom's entrance, but calms when he sees him. "Tom," he says. "Can't keep away, huh?"

"You're supposed to be horizontal," Tom says, swinging off his backpack and placing it on the bed. "And healing."

Jim turns from the window, his left hand clutching the metal bar holding his various drips. "Hard to get comfortable when you're too busy worrying."

"You see anyone out there?" Tom says, joining him at the window and looking down.

"No," Jim says, moving away. "If they *are* out there, they're doing a good ass job of hiding themselves."

"That's what I came to see you about, anyway," Tom says, grabbing his bag as Jim gets back into the bed, wincing as he pulls up the blankets. Tom reaches into his bag and pulls out a burner phone. He checks it doesn't have a name already attributed to it, and then holds it out to Jim.

"A phone?" Jim says, taking it.

"With one number saved to it," Tom says. "Mine. I'm gonna be at and around the hospital a lot, but I can't always be here. If something happens – anything's worrying you, or you happen to spot someone on the road outside – then I want you to give me a call straight away. Any time."

Jim nods and places the phone within easy reach on the bedside table. "I appreciate that, Tom. I'm not exactly in the best state to defend myself."

"Well, if anyone gets close enough, I'm sure you'll give them hell until I can get here."

Jim laughs. "You know I will."

Tom goes to the window and looks down again. He sees a couple of Fords, but they're not the same as the one from the other night. One is white and one is red, and the other was black, Tom is sure. It was dark and hard to tell, and the lights were in his eyes, but he's sure it was black. He checks the time as he turns back to Jim. "You up for some company? I've got a couple of hours."

"I'd appreciate that," Jim says. "I'm not gonna get any other visitors. None I'll be happy to see, anyway."

Tom takes a seat. "So," he says. "How do you like Hopper Creek so far?"

## 29

Kendis sees them arrive, pulling into the parking lot and getting out the car together. Three of them altogether – Hal, and two men Kendis doesn't know. He's watching through the window. He assumes one of these two strangers must be Donny. "Here they come," he says to Big Ron. "And they've brought a friend. You come here, sit beside me."

Big Ron does as he's told, and they're both facing the entrance as the three men enter the diner. Hal nods at them and then brings the two over. The three slide into the booth without exchanging pleasantries. The one opposite Kendis starts speaking. "All right," he says, "what's this about?" He sits hunched, his shoulders up. His hands are clasped together on the table.

Kendis smiles at him. He assumes this is Donny. "Maybe we should swap names," he says, "before we get down to business."

"I already know your name," Donny says, then adds, "*Kendis*. And this big motherfucker must be Big Ron. There. Now we all know each other."

"Not quite," Kendis says, and he tilts his head toward the man in the middle. "I can guess who you are, Donny, and I know who Hal is, but *this* man's a mystery to me."

Hal opens his mouth, presumably to tell Kendis the man's name, but Donny cuts him off.

"This is Willie," he says. "He's *my* Big Ron – my right-hand man. You think I was gonna come here and meet you without backup?"

"You'd be a fool if you did," Kendis says, still smiling.

"And I ain't a fool. Now, Hal said you had some kind of proposition."

"I have jobs," Kendis says, "and I understand you need them."

Donny shoots a look at Hal, but Hal pretends not to notice. Donny turns back to Kendis. Kendis keeps smiling. He stays loose. Casual. Takes a slow sip of his lukewarm coffee.

Donny is a long time speaking. He's measuring Kendis. He runs his tongue around the inside of his mouth while he thinks. Kendis reckons they could be here a while before he formulates a thought. He leans forward across the table, takes the lead. "Let me tell you what I need," he says, "and what I can offer in return."

Donny looks like he has a bad taste in his mouth. This is difficult for him. As Hal warned, he doesn't want to take a step back from leadership. "Fine," he says finally.

"I'm looking for a man," Kendis says, "a homeless black man who escaped from me in Santa Fe. I don't know his name, and I only vaguely know what he looks like, but I do know that he rolled into your town here a couple of nights ago and he's currently holed up in the Hopper Creek Medical Centre. Now, I understand you're a local boy. Getting in and out of the hospital shouldn't be too much of an issue for men like yourselves. Finding the man I'm looking for shouldn't be too much trouble either, should it?"

Donny frowns. "And then what?"

"And then you kill him, and you keep it quiet. Is that a problem for you?"

Donny smirks. "No."

"Good. I'm glad to hear that. Now, if you can get in and out of the hospital as ably and capably as I believe you can, then I need you to check the records there and find something else out for me, too."

"What?" Donny says.

Kendis smiles. He looks around the room. It's quiet in the diner. There's no one nearby. He notices how the staff avoid coming over or looking their way since Donny and Willie have arrived. "How much has Hal told you about what I do?"

"He's not told me shit," Donny says. "Just says you're a big deal in Santa Fe, and that he used to work for you before he came to work for me."

Kendis leans in closer. "I'm in the organ business, Donny," he says.

"What's that supposed to mean?"

"It means I sell human organs to the highest bidders."

Donny's brow is deeply furrowed. "Shit," he says. "That's hardcore."

"Uh-huh. I need a very specific organ, Donny, and I'm having trouble tracking one down in Santa Fe. While I'm here in Hopper Creek, I figure I may as well see if there's one on offer."

"What do you need?"

"I need a liver," Kendis says. "And it needs to be from an AB-negative blood-type donor. What I need you to do, Donny, is get into the hospital's medical records and find me someone in Hopper Creek, or nearby, with the blood type AB-negative. Can you do that for me, Donny?"

"Why can't you just do that in Santa Fe?"

"You think we haven't *tried*?" Kendis says. "We came close, once – we came *so close*." He holds up his hand, index and thumb mere millimetres apart to show how close they came. "But he was an old man, and he died before we could get to him. This is a *rare* blood type we're looking for. And also, hospitals in the city are busy, and there's security, and the cops are nearly always there for some reason or another. It's no easy thing for us to get in and check the records. But here, in a small town like this, it's not going to be so busy, is it? And this is *your* town, isn't that right? No one's going to bat an eye if they see you around."

Donny thinks for a moment. "You're asking a lot," he says, "and you still haven't said what we get in return."

"I told you," Kendis says. "I have jobs to offer. But, of course, if you can find me someone AB-negative, you'll be handsomely rewarded for that. And you'll be rewarded for dealing with my runaway problem, too. And Hal told me you've been having an issue with someone you used to go to school with, is that right? A soldier? I'll help you deal with him."

Donny glances at Willie while he considers this. They lean in close and speak in whispers. Hal watches them, then looks at Kendis and raises his eyebrows, nodding his head. Kendis can't tell if Hal can overhear what they're saying, or if he's just hopeful it's positive. Hal gives a thumbs up. Kendis ignores him.

Donny turns back to Kendis. "All right," he says. "It feels like we can help each other out. Getting in and dealing with your runaway ain't gonna be a problem. The liver, though – Willie here seems to think that's a rare blood type."

"One of the rarest," Kendis says.

"Then we'll check, but you probably shouldn't get too hopeful."

"I keep my expectations tampered, but it's always worth checking. If you don't look, you'll never find."

"They've had the blood drive recently," Willie says, loud enough for Kendis to hear. "So it sounds like you've come asking at a good time, at least. That's probably put a few more names and bloods on record that the hospital might not have had before."

"That *is* lucky," Kendis says. "Let's hope one of them can give us what we need."

Donny thrusts his arm across the table suddenly. Kendis looks down. Donny wants to shake. "Sounds like we have ourselves an arrangement," Donny says.

Kendis takes his hand and they shake. "Sounds like we do," he says. They smile at each other, and Kendis can see he's going to have trouble with Donny. Hal was right – Donny isn't a follower. He wants to lead. It doesn't matter though, not long term. So long as Donny and his men can deal with the runaway – and more importantly, if they're able to find him a liver – then Kendis won't have much to do with Donny for very long.

They break their grip. Donny begins to stand. "Then let's get to it," he says.

## 30

Tom checks in and around Hayley's house when they get back. Hayley waits in her car. Tom, once again, finds no sign of any attempted break-ins. He lets Hayley go inside, and then he circles the block, checking the street and the parked vehicles, and the windows of the houses opposite and neighbouring. They're not watching Hayley's home. Tom wonders if they're still sitting around watching his empty house.

Inside, he finds Hayley in the bathroom. She's in the shower. She turns to him when he reaches the doorway, the water running down her body. She squeezes it out of her hair and places it over her shoulder, out of her face. "Find anything?" she says.

Tom shakes his head. "No."

"You happy?"

"For now."

She grins. "But you're going to stay vigilant, I'm sure."

Tom leans into the doorway, his arms folded. "Always do."

Hayley massages shampoo into her scalp. She grins at him. "Are you enjoying the view?"

He winks at her.

"You look like you could do with a shower yourself."

Tom considers this.

"Don't keep me hanging too long," Hayley says. "I'm nearly clean. I'm not gonna be in here forever."

"Let me go check the locks, and I'll be right back," Tom says.

Hayley puts her head back under the water, rinsing the shampoo from her hair. "Be quick," she says. "If you're lucky, I'll be here waiting."

Tom moves quickly around the house, checking that the doors are locked, and looking out the windows to make sure the street remains clear. It is. He hurries back upstairs, to the bathroom. Hayley is still in the shower, leaning on the glass with both hands. She smiles as he appears. "Almost missed me," she says, but Tom knows this isn't true. She's been waiting.

## 31

There's a knock at Alec's office door. It's getting late. It's dark outside. Alec looks toward the sound and smirks to himself, not answering. Waiting.

The knocking comes again. Harder, more frantic now. "Damn it, Alec, you in there? You awake? This is an emergency!"

Alec waits a beat, then says, "Come in."

One of Kendis's nameless men bursts in, looking panicked.

"What is it?" Alec says.

"Cops are here, man!"

Alec straightens a little. "Are they inside? At the door?"

"Not yet," the man says. "But we've spotted their car. They've circled a couple of times and now they've parked up. They're watching."

"They're still in the car?"

"Last I checked, but they're probably gonna come up close real soon."

"Who's going to deal with them?"

"Shit, I dunno, man – I will, I guess–"

"No, no, not you, you're too jittery," Alec says.

"I can keep it together."

"I can't trust that. If they try to get past the cleared levels, what will you tell them? *Well?* I'm asking."

The man stammers. He doesn't have a quick enough excuse as to why the hypothetical police officers cannot leave the ground floors.

Alec is not impressed. He starts clicking his fingers to emphasise the passage of time. "Not good enough," he says. "Not fast enough. How's that going to deter them?"

"Well, who else is gonna speak to them? *You?*"

Alec grins. "Give me your jacket," he says.

The man starts to protest, but he gives up before he gets going and gives Alec the jacket. The man looks him over. "Those are some fancy slacks for a security guard, man."

Alec zips up the jacket. With the flat of his hand he brushes his hair forward and presses it down against his forehead. "Stay up here, out the way," he says. "And make sure everyone else knows to do the same. I'll deal with this." He turns to leave, to head downstairs, but then pauses and turns back. "I'll be sure to let you all know how it goes. And listen closely when I tell you – you could all learn a thing or two."

Alec takes the stairs down. He checks a window as he goes, searching out the cop car. He spots it, and the two cops that have driven it here. They're walking toward the hospital.

Alec doesn't speed up. Maintains the same casual pace on his way down to the lobby. The front doors are locked. The cops aren't going to try and bust it down before he gets there.

When he reaches the lobby, he makes like he's about to walk straight by, then doubles back like he's just realised there are two men at the door. He goes to them, pulling out his keys. He clears his throat on the way, preparing himself to talk, to lower his tone and drop his diction. He gets the door open and leans into it once it's open. "Evening, Officers," he says, plastering a sloppy, down-home smile on his face. "Can I help y'all?"

"You work here?" one of them says.

"Certainly do," Alec says. "There a problem?"

The cop looks past him. "We're not sure. You mind if we come in, take a look around?"

Alec holds the door open for them. "Be my guest."

Both cops stroll inside. Alec follows them, but he keeps a leisurely distance. He picks at his teeth, making himself look bored. The cop who's done all the talking so far turns to him. "What's your name?"

"Bud," Alec says.

"How long you worked here, Bud?"

"Not too long. About, oh, six months now."

"Uh-huh. How is it?"

"It's fine. It's quiet. I work nights and I've got the place to myself mostly. There's a couple of other guys I'm usually on shift with, but we all take different wings. We barely see each other."

The cops are still looking around. The one who isn't talking is going room to room, glancing into each one. Alec watches him but isn't obvious about it. There's nothing to find down here. They've never kept anyone on the ground floor. It's the next floor up where they used to keep people. That was the lowest they went. He's prepared for the cops to want to go up there. Maybe down to the basement, too.

"You ever get any trouble here?" the cop says.

"Trouble?" Alec says. "What kind of trouble?"

The cop shrugs. "I dunno – kids, homeless people trying to break in looking for a place to stay. Stuff like that."

"Not while I've been here," Alec says. "I've heard stories from some of the other guys that it used to be bad like that, when people thought this was just a derelict building and there weren't any plans for it, but they say it's quietened down a lot."

"Speaking of," the cop says, turning to him fully now, "I've wondered – what *are* the plans for this place? I heard it was gonna be a hotel."

Alec blows air and holds out his arms, his best country bumpkin pose. "Search me, man," he says. "I haven't been told anything, and I don't even know who I'm supposed to ask." He laughs. "Hell, I'm not so sure they know themselves."

The cop grins. "Ain't that always the way?" He calls to his partner. "You about done here?"

"Yeah," the other cop says, walking back to them.

Alec looks between them both, his expression plain and servile. Unthreatening. "Were the two of you looking for anything specific?"

"No, nothing specific," the cop says. "We got a call, someone saying they'd seen armed men here."

"Well, some of the guys carry weapons," Alec says. "But they're all fully licensed. As you can see, I don't, myself." He shows off his bare hips.

"I think there was something about seeing a guy being chased, too. You know anything about that?"

Alec laughs. "No, I don't. I ain't heard anything – but, I mean, that *is* our job. So it wouldn't surprise me none if that *had* happened."

The cop laughs too. "Ah, probably just some prank call, you know how it is. You know they're bullshit but you've gotta at least make a show of turning up, right?"

"Ah, okay," Alec says, his mouth slack as he nods slowly, making out like he doesn't know what the cop's talking about at all but he wants to act like he does. It's important for him to keep up the act here. It's kept the two of them from wanting to go upstairs, or down into the basement. "Well, I sure hope you don't feel like you've wasted your time too much."

The cop waves. "There's always something to waste our time," he says, chuckling. "May as well be here as anywhere else."

Alec sees them to the door then waves them off. He locks the door and heads back upstairs, stripping off the jacket as he goes. He finger-combs his hair back into place. On the way, he stops by a window and looks down at the cop car. It's already leaving.

The man is waiting for Alec near his office. "I saw them leave already," he says, sounding impressed. "What did you tell them?" He holds out his hand for his jacket.

Alec drops the jacket short, so the man has to pick it up from the ground. "Stick with me and I'll tell you all about it sometime," he says, striding straight through to his office. He pauses, turning back in the doorway. "Like I said, you and the others could learn a few things." He closes the door.

Donny heads to the Hopper Creek Medical Centre with Willie, Kyle, Shawn, and Hal. Willie drives. Donny sits up front with him. The other three are squeezed into the back. Kyle has the worst position, squeezed between the other two.

Behind, a couple of cars are following. Kendis and Big Ron are in a Lexus, and there's a black Ford behind them with two of Kendis's men in.

The Simmons brothers are out at Rollins's place. Donny calls them. "Anything?" he says.

"Nothing exciting," Micky says. "He's still in there. Looks like he's probably asleep. Place is in darkness."

"Anyone been to see him?"

"No, no one."

"Okay. Keep an eye on him. Let me know if anything happens. Anyone comes or goes, I wanna know."

"Got it."

Donny slides his phone back into his pocket. To Willie he says, "We deal with this thing for Kendis, and we could have this business with Rollins all wrapped up by this time tomorrow."

Willie nods. The hospital is in view ahead. Donny turns, speaks to the men in the back. "Everyone clear on what they're doing?"

The three heads nod in unison.

"Good," Donny says.

Donny will stay outside with Kendis and Big Ron. Willie knows the janitor, Jack Cooper. They're drinking buddies. Willie got in touch with him earlier, gave the description of the man they're looking for and the story of his arrival in town, in case that helped. Asked him to find out what room he's in. Once Willie has spoken to Jack and paid him off, he and the rest of the crew present will go and deal with the runaway.

Apart from Kyle, who will take in Kendis's men. He'll direct the two men toward where the records are kept (information which will also be provided by Jack the janitor), while Kyle himself will distract the receptionists. Cause enough of a distraction, enough chaos, for Donny's boys and Kendis's to slip by and do what they need to.

"What kind of distraction?" Kyle had asked while they were gathered around Willie's kitchen table, planning.

Donny shrugged. "Just pitch a fit," he said. "You look ill most of the damn time anyway."

"Charming," Kyle said. "What kind of fit are we talking? Like, an overdose, an epileptic fit, a–"

"Jesus Christ, Kyle," Donny said, exasperated. "Use your fucking brains, huh? Work it out. Do a junkie fit for all I care – hell, looking at you, that one would make most sense. And besides, before long they're gonna get real used to the sight, once all the junkies realise their flakka ain't coming back."

Willie stops the car. The Lexus and the Ford pull up behind them. Donny watches the building. It looks quiet. It's late, and Hopper Creek isn't the kind of place that gets a lot of emergencies.

Willie undoes his seatbelt. "Right," he says, "I'll go find Jack." He checks the time. "We're on schedule. He said he'll be at the back door. I won't be long."

Donny turns to the others in the back as Willie gets out of the car. "You all ready?" he says.

"Sure," Kyle says, rubbing under his eyes, getting himself ready for his big performance.

"Good," Donny says, then turns back and waits for Willie to return with their information.

## 33

Tom sleeps light. He's already woken at least once every hour to check the doors and the windows, and look out onto the street. It's stayed quiet. Nothing to get alarmed about.

But this time he wakes at a nearby sound, right here in the room with him.

He twists, recognising it. His phone, buzzing on the bedside table. Next to him, Hayley groans in her sleep and turns over, but doesn't wake. Tom checks the caller ID. It's Jim. He answers fast. "Jim," he says, getting to his feet and stepping outside the bedroom. He goes to the nearest window and looks down. "Everything all right?"

"I'm not too sure," Jim says, his voice low, whispering. Tom can hear him moving around his room. "There was this janitor lurking around my room earlier, after lights out. I dunno, maybe it was nothing, but I felt like he kept looking in. I was lying back. It was easy enough for me to pretend I was asleep. I slit my eyes and watched him out the corner. The motherfucker got me uncomfortable, you know? Made it so I couldn't settle for the night, and I think it was a good thing – I've been checking the road, and Tom, the Ford that followed me to town is out there."

"You're sure it's the same one?"

"I can't see the plates, but it's the same model and colour," Jim says. "It looks like there's a couple of other cars with it, but it's hard to tell. They could just be parked there and have nothing to do with each other, y'know? One of them's real fancy. But whatever, I ain't taking any chances. First the janitor hanging around, and now the Ford out on the road? No, man, I'm not gonna lie here and wait for them."

"No, that's good," Tom says. "I'll get dressed and I'll come and get you, fast as I can."

"I'm pulling on my clothes now," Jim says, and Tom can hear the way he struggles. "They ain't gonna catch me with my pants down."

"Just hold out. I'll be right there," Tom says, heading back into the bedroom. "And keep the phone on you. I won't be long."

He wakes Hayley and tells her what's happening. She needs to come with him. He doesn't want to leave her here alone.

Hayley doesn't protest. She pulls on some clothes while Tom does the same, then they hurry from her house and to her car. Tom drives. He puts his foot down and screeches through the night.

## 34

J im winces as he gets dressed. The fresh stitches in his back tug against his flesh. He moves carefully, as carefully as he can, but right now his true priority is speed. He's already plucked the various drips from his arms, and their fluids leak across the ground. His forearms sting where they were inserted, and leak a little blood. They soak into the sleeves of the shirt he's pulled on.

The clothes are Tom's, and clean, but the boots are his own. They still squelch a little with the blood – his blood – that has soaked into them. He checks the soles are dry and leave no marks on the linoleum. They don't. He goes to the door and looks out the window, peering into the hall. The overhead lights are off, and it's lit only by the dim night-time lamps. There aren't any nurses or doctors moving about. No janitors, either.

Gently, Jim opens the door. He hurts all over, and wishes he'd been able to sleep in peace. To recover. To heal. He grits his teeth and forgets about how he wishes it could have been. This is how it is. They could be coming for him. They could have found him. They could know exactly which room he's in.

He doesn't leave the room straight away. He checks the way. Leans forward and peers out, checking down the corridor. He pulls back into the doorway almost instantly. Three dark shapes coming his way, striding with intent. Jim bites his lip. They certainly didn't look like doctors or nurses. He slips back into the room and carefully clicks the door back into place. He keeps moving. Can't afford to stay still. They're getting closer.

Feeling like his stitches are going to pop, he drags a dresser in front of the door, not caring how much noise it makes now. The door blocked, he crosses the room to the window. It has a safety latch. He pushes against it, using all the strength he has – remembering his escape from the abandoned hospital in Santa Fe – and manages to break the latch. Part of him hoped this might set off an alarm, but it does not. Jim doesn't waste breath cursing. He leans out the window and looks down. There's nowhere to drop, except all the way to the flowerbeds. However, off to his left, there's a fire escape. If he were to lean out far enough, he could reach it. Use it to get down, or into another room. When the men coming for him get into the room and see the open window, when they investigate further and see the fire escape, this is what he needs them to think.

Jim has no intention of risking his life reaching for the escape. Instead, he drops to the floor and rolls under the bed, and he waits.

The men outside reach his door. They try the handle. They're quiet about it at first. They don't want to wake the sleeping patient. But then they realise the door isn't opening as easily as it should. Maybe they're looking really closely through the window of the door, and seeing that the bed is empty and the window is open.

They're throwing their weight into the door now. Jim hears the dresser scraping along the ground.

"Get it fucking open, come on!" he hears one of them barking. He sounds desperate.

They manage to push the dresser far enough back they can squeeze through. Jim lies as still as he can. Holds his breath. Watches as three pairs of boots come racing into his room, straight to the open window. They're peering out. He can hear them talking, but can't make out what they say.

They turn. They're rushing from the room. Except, one of them halts. His feet turn toward the bed. Jim freezes. He feels a cold trickle of sweat run down his spine. His stitches twinge and itch. He stares at the legs.

The legs begin to bend. A face comes into view. His lips are split and scabbed. The man is heavyset. He looks strong. "He's here!" he shouts, showing off chipped teeth, and then he starts reaching under the bed.

Jim rolls the other way, out of his grip, out from the other side of the bed. It's too late as he pushes himself up – the other two have returned at the bellow from the man who stayed behind. One of them slams into Jim from behind and wraps his arms around him. Jim uses the attacker's momentum against him, rolls over the bed and throws him off the other side. The other man is quick to follow up, diving at Jim on the bed and pinning him.

"Keep him down, Hal," the man who found him says. He seems to have the most authority. "Hold him still. Shawn, get your ass up and get over here. Keep him quiet – keep him quiet!" He noticed how Jim was filling his lungs, getting ready to scream.

Jim struggles, but he's weak and outnumbered. The one called Hal keeps him pinned, while Shawn covers his mouth, prevents him from making noise. The bigger man, the one who found him, is taking a pillow off the bed.

"It's already been noisy, Willie," Hal says. "And look at the mess he made before we got here. Is the fucking pillow gonna make any difference?"

"We'll tidy up once he's dead," Willie says.

"And the window?"

"Fuck the window. They can wonder about it. They'll think he was in some kinda crazed state before he died, the fuck do I care? Now hold him down so I can get at him – there, that's it. Keep him right there."

Willie moves in, the pillow held in both hands. Jim struggles, kicks at him.

"Grab his legs – Shawn, grab his legs!" Willie says.

"What about his mouth? What if he screams?"

"Fuck his screams – I'm about to cover his damn face."

Jim's mouth is uncovered. His legs are clamped down. His mouth is clear, but he can't scream. Hal is pressing down on him too hard. He's squeezing the air from him.

Willie is moving in. He's bringing the pillow close.

To Jim's right, the door is thrown open, banging hard into the dresser. The noise gets everyone's attention. Willie, Shawn, and Hal all look toward the sound. Jim turns, too, and he feels something he wasn't expecting – relief.

It's Rollins.

---

## 35

**D**onny straightens at the sight of Tom rushing into the hospital.

"*Shit.*"

Kendis notices. Donny is in the back of his Lexus. Kendis looks at Big Ron, then turns to Donny. "That doesn't sound promising."

"You see that guy that just ran in?" Donny says.

"I saw him."

"That was Tom Rollins – the soldier you're gonna help us out with. This could be trouble."

"Why should it be trouble?" Kendis says. "Do we have evidence he knows Jim Belafonte?" They learned the runaway's name from the janitor Willie spoke to.

"I dunno, man," Donny says. "I've just got a bad feeling with this fucking guy. Why's he here? Why's he running in?" Donny shakes his head. He pulls out his phone and calls the Simmons brothers. Micky answers. Donny isn't patient with them. He's straight to the point. "The two of you asleep over there?"

"What do – what do you mean?" Micky says.

"Anything you wanna fucking tell me? I told you to get in touch as soon as you saw anything – *anything*, motherfucker."

"Donny, what're you talking about?" Micky says.

"Rollins is *here*."

"What? At the hospital?"

"That's what I said. I told you to watch the fucking place – how'd you miss it?"

"We've been watching his place, Donny, I swear to God. We've barely even taken piss breaks. We haven't seen him leave, not since we got here. Kyle and Shawn said they saw him come back. Maybe they missed him–"

"Or else he fucking made you and he's slipped out," Donny says. He sneers. "*Fuck.*"

Kendis is watching him. "I don't like the sound of any of this, Donny."

Donny ignores him. "Micky, I'm sick of this shit. If this son of a bitch wants to go to war with us, then we'll take him to fucking war."

"What do you want us to do, Donny?"

"You and your brother are gonna burn his fucking house down. His car's still there? Burn that, too. Fuck it all up. I'll let you know where we are when you're done, then haul your asses to us." Donny hangs up the phone and turns to Kendis and Big Ron. "You need to let your men know he's gone in there. Send them to Jim's room to cut him off."

"We don't know that's where he's gone," Kendis says. "He was in a hurry – maybe someone he knows has had an accident."

"You wanna take that risk?" Donny says. "This nosey motherfucker stuck his nose into my business and ruined it. What makes you think he's not gonna do the same to you? What's to say he's not up there right now and he's getting Jim out? I'm done with him. Fuck him. I want his fucking heart."

Kendis deliberates, then turns to Big Ron. "Call them," he

says. "If this Rollins *is* interfering, we wanna make sure they're there to cut him short."

Donny is getting out of the Lexus. He leans on the roof and runs a hand down his mouth, watching the hospital and wishing he could see inside, wishing he knew what was happening in there.

## 36

Tom is surprised to find that he recognises these men. Willie Shaw, Shawn Stark, and Hal Redford. He was expecting strangers, not members of Donny's crew. This is concerning. Has Donny's crew joined up with the organ harvesters from Santa Fe? Did they always have some kind of arrangement? Tom doesn't believe this latter – he watched them for too long and never saw any evidence of this before he made his first move. Has their desperation at losing their flakka, and their flakka manufacturers, driven them to seek out new employment? There's no other reason for them to be here in the room with Jim, Willie with a pillow in his hands, clearly about to smother him.

There are too many questions. Whatever the reasons, they don't matter right now. What matters is getting Jim out of here.

Willie makes the first step toward Tom, throwing the pillow to one side. He swings his heavy fists, but he's slow. Tom is able to duck through easily and come face to face with Shawn. Tom kicks him square in the chest and drives him back into the wall, knocking the air out of him. He spins back as Willie strikes at him again, and again Tom ducks through, this time reaching Hal. Hal quickly lets go of Jim in order to defend himself, but it doesn't do him much good. He can't get his hands up to his face fast enough before Tom has punched him on the bridge of the nose. Hal stumbles back, clutching at his face.

As Tom turns, Willie moves faster now. He drives himself into Tom's midsection and drives him back into the door, slamming it shut. Tom throws his elbow back and connects with the rear of Willie's skull, loosening his grip. He repeats the blow and Willie lets go. Tom grabs him around the skull with both hands and slams his forehead into the door's window. He does it twice more and on the third blow the glass shatters. Willie collapses to the ground, blood streaming down his face.

Hal makes a lunge for Tom, but Tom easily grabs him by the wrist and spins with him, throwing him over his shoulder. He hits the ground hard, and groans as he squirms there.

On the other side of the room, Jim has rolled off the bed. He's wincing, but he drives his knee into Shawn's face as he passes. Tom goes to him and takes him by the arm, slinging it over his shoulder. "You good?" he says.

"Better than I could be right now," Jim says, "if you hadn't turned up when you did."

They step over the fallen bodies and exit the room. The sounds of the battle and the shattering glass in the door have brought some of the other patients to their doorways, and a couple of nurses are hurrying toward them. All of a sudden, there's a lot of life in the corridors. It was quiet as Tom made his way here. There was a gathering of people in the lobby, but he didn't pay it much attention as he hurried through.

"Hayley's outside," he says to Jim, low enough so only he can hear. "She's got the car running."

The corridor is now busier than Tom would like. If he

sees a member of Donny's crew, then fine, easy, he knows it's an enemy. But if they *have* teamed up with the harvesters from Santa Fe, and if they're here too, then he's fighting blind. He doesn't know how many of them there are, nor what any of them look like. Even the men that were trying to pick up Jim the other night – it was a fleeting glimpse, and their headlights were shining right in Tom's eyes.

Tom doesn't like not knowing who his enemies are. Every person they pass in the corridor, most of them rushing the other way, he eyes with suspicion. Even the doctors can't be trusted. Anyone could have pulled on a white coat and be pretending to work here.

As they round a corner, heading for the fire stairs, Tom feels someone slam into him from behind. He manages to roll through, but Jim is sent sprawling. As Tom comes up, turning, he sees two men. He doesn't recognise either of them. Nearby, someone screams. Tom sees why – one of the men is carrying a hunter's knife, held low down by his side. The other man is unarmed, but he's circling, attempting to get behind Tom. On the ground, Jim crawls. Tom grabs the back of his shirt and drags him closer, putting himself between Jim and the two men. He glances back down the corridor behind him, but even if these two had back-up coming, he wouldn't know who they were. He needs to deal with this quick and get out of here. The corridor is too busy and cramped, and there's too much risk of sudden ambush.

Tom goes straight for the one with the knife, surprising him, putting him off balance. He slashes through the air, but it's desperate and sloppy and Tom easily avoids it. As the man slashes again, Tom catches him, hooking his striking arm under his left and holding it against himself, pinning it. With his right hand, Tom delivers a palm strike to the man's throat. He gags.

The other man attempts to intervene. Tom spins the body

he's holding and knocks them into each other. The unarmed man doesn't go down. He struggles to get close. Tom uses the man with the knife as a shield to keep the other at bay. By now, though, Jim is on his feet. He spins the unarmed man around and drives a fist into his stomach, doubling him up. Jim shoves him aside. With him dealt with, Tom finishes off the man he's restraining, driving a headbutt into the centre of his gasping face and putting him down.

Tom and Jim keep moving. They reach the door for the fire stairs and slip through it. They wait a moment to see if anyone follows them. From here, they'll have the blind advantage. No one comes, though.

"Let's keep moving," Tom says.

They head down the stairs. Jim holds at his back and breathes hard. Tom checks his shirt, but he hasn't bled through. His stitches are holding.

"We're nearly there," Tom says. "One more level to go."

They get to the bottom and head out a fire escape, which sets off an alarm inside the building. Tom takes Jim's weight again, his arm over his shoulder. They head around to the side of the hospital where Hayley waits. The engine is running. She must see them coming. She gets out of the car and opens the back door. Together, they put Jim inside and then dive back into the front. Tom gets behind the steering wheel.

Hayley can hear the fire alarm sounding from inside the hospital. "What the hell happened in there?" she says, looking them both over.

"I'll tell you later," Tom says, and speeds away into the night.

## 37

Willie, Shawn, Hal, and Kendis's two men are looking beat-up. Willie has taken the worst of it. They each nurse their various ailments from the beating Rollins and Jim gave them. Willie presses ice wrapped in a dish cloth to the back of his neck. He moves it around his head and presses it to his face. "I'm getting real sick of this shit, man," he mumbles, his face twisted.

They're at Willie's house. The Simmons brothers are here, too. They arrived about ten minutes ago. They assured Donny that Rollins's house had been dealt with – they'd watched it burn to the ground.

Back at the hospital, Donny, Kendis, and Big Ron saw Rollins make his escape with Hayley and Jim, their car tearing out from around the corner of the hospital and disappearing off into the dark. They'd hurried inside and retrieved their men from the chaotic hospital before the cops and the fire service could arrive. They were all pulling away in their three vehicles as the flashing lights of the services arrived.

"Where the hell were you while all this was happening?" Donny says to Kyle, motioning toward the wounded men.

Kyle holds up his hands. "I was doing what I was told," he says. "I was distracting the receptionists."

"Uh-huh, and what about when we sent word Rollins was there, and everyone was to go and cut him off?"

"No one's ever accused me of being a fighter," Kyle says. "And I never got the message. I was too busy rolling around on the floor and causing a scene."

Willie waves a hand. "It doesn't matter now, Donny," he says, wiping dried blood from under his eyes. "What's done is done. They got away this time, but they won't next."

Donny laces his hands atop his head. He looks to Kendis, who is on the sofa and looking over the scene with a nonplussed expression.

"So, did we get anything worthwhile from that trip?" Kendis says, feeling Donny's eyes and looking back at him. "Or did we just waste all of our times?"

It's one of Kendis's men who speaks up. "It wasn't a total waste," he says. He's rubbing at his stomach like he has an ache there. All eyes turn to him.

"Well?" Kendis says. "What is it?"

"Someone in town has AB-negative blood," the man says. He reaches into his pocket and pulls out his phone. "I took a picture of the details."

Kendis's face lights up. Any concerns he may have had earlier seem to have melted away. "I swear to God, if you're joking right now I'll fucking kill you." But he's smiling as he says it. He knows the man isn't joking. Kendis is inching forward on his seat, practically bouncing.

Donny glances at Big Ron, who stands near to where Kendis sits. He notices how the big guy is suppressing his own relieved smile. "This is all good, right?" Donny says, seeing a chance to salvage something from their earlier disasters. "Not a complete bust, right?"

Kendis is waving at his man to bring him his phone. "Show me," he says. "Come on, quicker. Show me."

The man holds at his stomach like he's worried his guts are going to fall out. He crosses the room, phone held out in front of him. Kendis takes it in both hands and studies the screen. "Name and address," he says, almost laughing. "This is gold – this is fucking *gold*."

Donny moves closer to see for himself. "Who is it?" he says.

"How should I know?" Kendis says, laughing giddily as he turns the phone to show him the details.

Donny feels his eyes go wide. He looks around the room. "*Is* this a joke?"

Kendis sees the look on his face, hears the tone in his voice, and he's not so giddy anymore. "What is it?"

Donny ignores him and looks to everyone else. They're all confused. "What's the problem?" Willie says.

Donny shakes his head. He can't help himself – he starts to laugh. He looks at Kendis. "You ain't gonna fucking believe this."

Kendis frowns. "Try me."

Donny doesn't answer him straight away. He turns to the man who took the picture. "Did you check everyone, or stop at the first person you came to?"

"It was on a computer," the man says. "All we had to do was put in the blood type."

"And *this* was the only AB-negative person that showed up? The only person in Hopper Creek? The only person in the surrounding areas, who has their bloods on record at least?"

"Jesus Christ, that's what I said," the man says.

Grinning, Donny turns back to Kendis and holds out the phone. "You wanna know what's so hard to believe? What's so damn *funny* about this? The one person in this area with AB-negative blood, the one person who has what you need, is Hayley Teller."

The nonplussed expression has returned to Kendis's face. "And who is Hayley Teller?"

"She's Tom Rollins's girlfriend," Donny says, and he starts laughing again.

Kendis raises an eyebrow, digesting this. He exchanges a glance with Big Ron, and then turns back to Donny. He smirks. It turns into a smile. His shoulders begin to bounce. Before long, he's laughing too.

## 38

A lec's phone begins to ring. He's listening to music, Rachmaninoff, loud, and he barely hears it at first. Checking the caller ID, he sees it's Kendis. He sighs and considers letting it ring out. Kendis will no doubt ring again, and again, until Alec finally answers. He picks up before it can ring out to get it over and done with. "What can I do for you, Kendis?"

"I hear the cops have been by," Kendis says.

"I'm sure you have."

"And that you dealt with it."

"Don't sound so surprised."

"I'm very impressed, Alec."

"I don't need to be patronised, either."

Kendis chuckles.

Alec is surprised by the sound. It confuses him. Makes him curious. "You sound like you're in a good mood," he says.

"I've had good news," Kendis says. "We have the liver. You need to get yourself to Hopper Creek and cut it out of her. I'm staying in a motel just outside of town. I'll send you the details. This is where you'll meet up with us."

"You have someone? You have her now, with you?"

"Not yet," Kendis says, and Alec rolls his eyes. "We're working on it."

"Then it sounds like there's not too much of a rush."

"There's a rush," Kendis says. "Just get your ass over here. It's hot where you are. I don't like that the cops have been by. That's too close. We deal with this liver away from the hospital, and we can think where we set up next after that, when things have cooled."

Alec leans back in his chair. He runs a finger down the side of his face, thinking. Thinking about the liver. Thinking about Kendis's desperation to get his hands on it. The fact that he seems eager to leave the hospital, despite Alec having dealt with the cops.

"Are you still there, Alec?" Kendis says. "I know you are. I can hear that classical shit playing."

"Don't call Rachmaninoff shit. What would you rather I was listening to? NWA? The Wu-Tang Clan?"

"When have you ever heard me listening to rap, Alec? Though I'm impressed you know at least two names. They're probably the only two, right?"

Alec sighs. "What do you expect me to do with the patients? Leave them here?"

"No, I want everyone in Hopper Creek. Get rid of the patients, but keep it clean. Clear the whole place out."

"Don't you have buyers lined up?"

"They're nothing major – kidneys, retinas, bone marrow, and they're all common blood types. It's nothing we can't easily replace."

"If you say so."

"I do say so. And you've heard what else I've said, too – clear out the hospital and get over here ASAP."

"Very well. I'll get right on it." He hangs up the phone. Taps it against his chin. He puts the phone down and then opens the top drawer of his desk. He brings out the container holding his scalpels. He takes one out, and spins it around his fingers. It's sharp. Alec's movements are deft. One slip, he could slice through his valuable hands. But he doesn't slip.

He remembers when he was in prison. They only thing he missed, truly missed, while he was locked away was the feel of a scalpel in his hands. At night, while everyone else slept, Alec would stand with his eyes closed, holding a stick or a twig or anything he could find that was a similar enough shape, and imagine he was holding one. Imagine he was cutting open a patient. It kept his skills sharp. Kept his fingers dextrous. He'd stand there in the dark, making imaginary incisions, and he'd feel like an orchestra conductor.

He stops twirling the scalpel and pushes himself to his feet. A quick rack of his brains brings forth zero names, so instead he opens his office door and calls, "Boys! Boys, to me!"

One of them appears. The same one who earlier told Alec the cops had turned up.

"Go get the rest," Alec tells him. "Go and get everyone. Chop, chop!" He claps his hands together, avoiding the scalpel.

As the man hurries away, Alec strolls to the end of the corridor and down the stairs, heading for the furthest room holding a patient. He'll start there and work his way back. While he goes, he can hear the man calling to the others, gathering them up, and then he's wondering where Alec has gone, and they're all searching for him. Alec could have waited where he was – there weren't many men to be gathered. About five of them in total. They can come find him. He hasn't gone far. Alec starts to whistle. A jaunty tune to himself.

He reaches the furthest room. From behind, he can hear the men hurrying to catch him up.

"Alec!" the man he spoke to, told to gather up the others, calls to him. "Hold up! What are you doing?"

Alec stops whistling as he reaches the room and turns back to the men. They come to a halt in front of him. There are six of them altogether. Alec was off by one. "I've just spoken to Kendis," Alec says. He tells them what their boss said. Tells them word for word.

"So we need to get rid of the bodies?" Kendis's man says. "There's about a dozen people in these rooms. What are we supposed to do with them? Dig a mass grave? We just had to get rid of all the bodies in the basement, for Christ's sake. We're gonna have to find a *new* burial site. Or do we put all of *these* bodies in the basement and cover them in lye, come back and deal with them after we've been to Hopper Creek?"

Alec shrugs. "I'll leave that up to you." He winks, and then turns into the room. He recognises the patient on the bed. Black female, early thirties. Alec removed one of her lungs, and she's currently hooked up to a ventilator. He wanted to keep her alive, what with her still being so young and healthy. Her organs would fetch pretty numbers. Now, though, according to Kendis, she's worthless. Expendable, and easily replaced. Alec goes to the head of her bed and strokes her hair. It hasn't been washed in a while. It's matted together. He looks at her taped-shut eyes. He takes the scalpel and reaches around to the other side of her neck, away from his body, and cuts her carotid artery. Blood sprays violently, and her cardiogram goes wild.

"What are you doing!" the man behind him says. He rushes forward, next to Alec. "What the fuck, man? Look at this blood! We're gonna have to clean this up!"

Alec chuckles. "Yes. Yes, you are." He turns on his heel and heads out of the room, on to the next one. The group of men scatter before him.

"Stop!" The man is chasing him, but he won't get too

close. He's scared of Alec, and of his scalpel. "Stop, damn it! It's too much mess! We can do this carefully, we can do it clean. All we've gotta do is put a pillow over their damn faces!"

Alec turns his head a little to see him. He winks. "Perhaps, but this is far quicker." He reaches the next patient and almost skips up to him, repeating the same process as earlier, but without the preamble this time. No looking him over, remembering him and what has been taken from him. No stroking of his hair. Just a quick cut of his carotid, and Alec is on his way.

The men are panicking now. They're rushing around. The one who Alec has been talking to is barking orders. He's trying to get the men out ahead of Alec, to smother the patients, to keep the mess he's making to a minimum. Alec laughs on his way, jauntily moving from room to room like the angel of death, cutting carotids as he goes and leaving pools and sprays of blood on the floor and the walls in his wake. He realises he's grinning as he goes, grinning like a maniac, and then he's laughing, laughing all the way, and he can't stop. He doesn't want to stop.

## 39

Tom decided against returning to Hayley's house. After fighting with Donny's crew and the men from Santa Fe, Hayley's would be the first place they'd go looking for him. For them. If Donny and his men don't already know where she lives, they'll easily find out.

Instead, he heads to a motel on the outskirts of town. He leaves Hayley and Jim in the car while he checks the place out. Again, like back at the hospital, he's not sure who the danger is, but he keeps his eyes peeled. He's vigilant. He doesn't find anything out of place. So far as he can see, the motel isn't busy. It looks like there's only a few rooms being occupied. Of course, people come and go all the time. Some of the rooms could be taken and their users not be currently present.

Tom gets back to the car. Hayley has moved to the backseat with Jim. Jim has raised up his shirt and Hayley is inspecting his wound. "It looks all right," she says when Tom returns. "It hasn't burst. The stitches are all still in place. There's just a little bleeding, is all, but that'll wipe right off."

"Feels like it's on fire," Jim says, putting his shirt back into place.

"I've got some painkillers in my bag," Hayley says. "Never leave home without them."

"I hope they're strong."

"They're as strong as you need."

Jim laughs.

"It looks clear," Tom says. "I'll go get us a room. Just the one. We're going to share. I'll be on watch, so I'm not planning on doing much sleeping."

"We'll take shifts," Jim says.

"You need to rest."

"So do *you*," Jim says. "We all do. I'm well enough to keep an eye on things for a couple of hours."

"You want me to take a shift?" Hayley says.

"Don't take this the wrong way," Tom says, "but you're not trained like we are."

"I think I can spot if someone's planning on attacking us," Hayley says.

"There's more to it than that."

"I mean, I'll happily sleep through," Hayley says. "I just wanted a moment to feel as gung-ho as everyone else here."

Tom grins at her and then heads to reception to book them a room. He gets one with two single beds. The three of them go to the room. Tom takes the car and parks it out the way, down the side of the building. He checks it's concealed from view, then returns to the others. Hayley catches him at the door, indicates she wants to speak to him quickly outside.

Tom signals to give him a minute, then he sticks his head into the room. "Jim, put the news on. Local stations. I called the cops about Santa Fe. See if anything comes up about it."

Jim gives him a thumbs up and reaches for the TV.

Tom steps back outside, to Hayley. "What's up?" he says.

"I'm worried about the hospital, Tom," she says. "Not the one in Santa Fe – *mine*. Where I work."

"It's fine," Tom says. "Any damage it sustained was localised to Jim's room."

"The fire alarm was going off."

"There wasn't any fire. Jim and I tripped it when we left via the fire escape."

Hayley looks off into the dark. She rubs her arms like she's cold, but it's a warm night. "I guess I'll see it for myself," she says. "I'm on shift tomorrow." She checks the time. "*Today.*"

"You're still going in?" Tom says.

"Of course I am," Hayley says. "It's my job, and they need me. They probably need me more than ever, after tonight."

Tom deliberates. He doesn't want to tell her what she can and can't do. Also, the hospital might be the safest place for her to be, especially after tonight. It's unlikely they'll go back there. "All right," he says, nodding. "We lay low tonight, get some rest, but tomorrow I'll accompany you on your shift."

"I'm getting used to that now."

"This is serious."

Hayley sighs. "I know it is. I'm just trying to – to inject some levity into the situation. If I stop to think about what's going on here too long it'll drive me crazy. I mean, organ harvesting? Drug dealers? And now, from what you say, the two of them seem to be working together? Have they *always* been working together? It's insane." She shakes her head and rubs her arms again.

Tom reaches out and pulls her close, hugging her tight. She returns it, wrapping her arms around him. "I'm sorry I got you involved in this," he says.

"It's not your fault," she says, pulling back. "Things like this, if you turn a blind eye to them they have a tendency to fester until they affect everyone. It was just a matter of time."

They stand outside a moment longer, in each other's arms, taking in the night air. Tom watches the road. Cars and trucks pass by, but none of them pull into the motel's parking lot. They go into the room and Tom locks the door. Jim is sitting on the end of one of the beds, watching the television.

"Has there been anything?" Tom says.

Jim shakes his head. "Nothing yet."

Tom folds his arms and stares at the screen. The discovery of an organ harvesting operation in an abandoned hospital should reach the news. Should be all over it. The top story. It should be national. If there's nothing showing, the cops either didn't go, or they didn't find anything.

Whatever the case may be, he knows he can't dwell on it. It doesn't matter. It's time to move on and deal with the battle that has come to his town. He doesn't like to rely on cops anyway. He doesn't like to rely on anyone but himself and a select few he trusts completely.

"All right," he says. "It's time to get some rest. I'll take first watch."

## 40

Tom takes first watch, but Jim struggles to get to sleep.

The room is in darkness. Tom sits by the window and watches the outside. After an hour, Jim sighs and gets out of the bed. He joins Tom by the window.

"Can't sleep?" Tom says.

"Too pumped," Jim says. They speak in whispers so as not to disturb Hayley. She went out like a light. "I'm happy enough to take over if you wanna get some shuteye."

"I'm not tired," Tom says. "But I'd appreciate the company if you don't wanna go back to bed."

Jim pulls up a chair and sits near to him. Tom isn't surprised Jim can't sleep. They're both paranoid, and vigilant.

"This sure takes me back," Jim says, grinning. "Like being back in the Army. Keeping watch."

Tom nods. "I think the same thing every time I need to do this."

Jim raises an eyebrow. "You have to keep watch often?"

"More than you'd expect."

"We talked about this in the hospital already, didn't we?"

Jim grunts. "I was gonna say I suppose it's better than turning to drugs, but I'm not so sure. Probably just as dangerous."

"That's debateable."

Jim chuckles. He looks back toward the bed where Hayley sleeps. Tom looks, too. She's lying on her side, the blankets wrapped tight around her. She looks peaceful.

"She looks like an angel," Jim says, smiling, turning back to Tom.

Tom agrees.

"I usedta watch Rhonda sleep," Jim says, looking off to the side. "When we were together, I felt like I had to stay awake, to watch over her. I guess like we're doing now, for Hayley. A lot of the time, though, I wasn't watching out. I was just watching *her*." He laughs. "She didn't look peaceful when she slept. She slept frowning, and I don't blame her. She had to be ready to wake and run at any moment. I probably look the same when I sleep. Hell, you probably do, too. But, you know what I would do sometimes? When Rhonda was sleeping, and she was frowning like that, I'd reach over, very carefully, and I'd stroke her forehead. The first couple of times, she jolted awake, looking ready to either run or claw my eyes out. But I got it so my touch was *very* gentle, and she didn't wake anymore. And you know what would happen when I stroked her forehead, and her hair, and her scalp? All her worry lines, they smoothed out. They went away. It wasn't for long – it would be for like five minutes, ten max – but for that brief time, she was soothed. She was calm. She was at peace. Because of *me*. I did that. Asleep, she knew I was there for her, caring for her, keeping her safe." He smiles, sadly, and Tom sees how he's twisted up inside, remembering. His lower lip trembles a little, but he bites down on it from the inside, controlling it.

Jim sits back and runs his hands down his face. "I know it doesn't do any good to dwell on things like this, or to think about what could have been, but I *do*. We all do. And what I wonder about most is how different things could have been if Rhonda and I had met in a different life. If we weren't homeless. If I wasn't on drugs. If we'd met like normal people do, and we'd gone on dates, and we'd got married, had a home, had kids."

"There's very little that's normal about people," Tom says. "You got what you got, and however it happened, it was yours. It didn't have to be normal."

"Maybe, but I wish it had been. Normal and boring. Just like everyone else." Jim sighs. "I miss her, Tom. I miss her so much. I know she's dead. I'm never gonna see her again. I'll never even see her body. I'll never get to bury her, and visit her grave. She's just..." He waves fingers in the air. "She's gone. All I know for sure – all I *think* I know for sure – is that they took her in Santa Fe, and they killed her there, too. So some part of her's still gotta be there, right? Her atoms, her dust, her essence, her spirit – her *whatever*, that's where it has to be."

Tom doesn't answer. He thinks of when he went down to Mexico to scatter Alejandra's ashes. He didn't go there to reconnect with her essence. He went there because it was what she wanted. He looks at Hayley and grits his teeth. He can't let anything happen to her. He needs to be here for her in case any danger comes, the way he wasn't for Alejandra. The way Jim wasn't for Rhonda. He turns back to the window and checks the parking lot. There are a few extra cars there now that weren't present when they first arrived, which doesn't surprise him or worry him. He expected this.

"What do you think, soldier?" Jim says. "You think you're gonna settle here?"

Tom turns back to him. "Why do you ask?"

"You got everything you need here, right? A job, a beautiful girl – a *future*. What more could you need, man?"

Tom looks at him.

"You'd miss the action, wouldn't you?" Jim says.

"There's more to me than that," Tom says.

"I sure hope so, man. Because you deserve happiness, Tom. And so does she." He motions toward Hayley. "I ain't seen much of the two of you together, but it looks to me like you make each other happy. You don't wanna throw that away because you're always looking for a war. Men looking for war can't settle down, Tom."

"What about men running from it?"

"Well, so long as you stay off the drugs, you should be all right." Jim winks.

Tom doesn't respond. He watches Hayley while she sleeps. She turns, her back to them now.

A long moment stretches out in silence. "You all right, man?" Jim says. "I didn't mean to upset you."

"I'm not upset."

"You're sitting there with your brow all furrowed like that."

Tom leans back in his chair and looks out the window again. It's still clear out there. "If you're awake, I might try and get some sleep," he says.

"Sure," Jim says. "I ain't gonna be able to get any for a while yet."

Tom stands and pats him on the shoulder as he passes. "Give me a few hours," he says. He goes to the other bed while Jim takes his position by the window. Tom lies down. He doesn't close his eyes straight away. He looks toward Hayley, her body turned toward his. Her face turned to him, too. She's close enough to touch. Tom reaches out, his arm bridging the gap between their beds. Gently, he strokes her forehead, her hair, her scalp. In her sleep, she smiles.

## 41

A lec leaves the hospital, but he doesn't go straight to Hopper Creek. He slips out while Kendis's men are still distracted clearing up the mess he's made, scrubbing at the blood and carrying out the bodies. Knowing Kendis isn't home, Alec takes a car and drives to his apartment.

Alec has packed. Everything that's important to him is in the trunk of the car. There isn't much. A couple of changes of clothes and his scalpels. He doesn't need much else. He'll go to Hopper Creek, as Kendis has said, and he'll get the liver, but he'll do it on his terms. Right now, he's still deciding what those terms are going to be. He's hoping the trip to Kendis's home will provide him with the answers he needs and help him make his decision.

No doubt one of Kendis's men has already informed him as to Alec's disappearance. Alec doesn't care. It won't matter for long. He's turned off his cell-phone. If Kendis is trying to contact him and is unable to get through, he's likely panicking right now.

Alec reaches Kendis's apartment building. It takes a while

for him to get inside. He has to wait for someone to eventually leave, at which point he slips in through the closing door. He makes his way up to the penthouse via the stairs. Alec is in good shape, and it barely raises his heartrate.

He's been to Kendis's apartment before, but only a couple of times, and it was long ago now. Both occasions were shortly after he'd been released from prison, once Kendis was making money from the organs Alec was providing him and he could afford a place like this. He brought Alec out to talk business and expansion. Back then, Alec was still playing ball. It's hard to believe it's been six years now. The memories of visiting the penthouse, and thinking how he was staying at the hospital for all his hard work, were what started to put his back up. He was putting in all those hours, all that work, just for Kendis to reap the rewards.

It's easy enough for Alec to get into the penthouse. He uses brute force, kicking through the lock. There's no one else on this level. No one to hear the noise he makes. Alec gets inside and takes a stroll around, looking the place over. It looks the same as the last time he was here. He runs the tip of his finger along the L-shaped leather sofa and the mahogany dining table. He inspects the pieces of art dotted around the place. He looks in on the pool. Enters it, and smells the chlorine in the air. He goes to the window that looks out over Santa Fe. Thinks how he could make himself very comfortable here.

He smirks. This isn't why he came. There's something he needs to do. He needs to stop allowing himself to get distracted by the opulence.

He finds Kendis's office. Goes to the computer. It's sleeping. Alec boots it up. He's surprised to find it doesn't need a password. Kendis probably thought he didn't need one. Not here, safely tucked away, at the top of this secure building. All of this wealth, it's made him soft and careless.

Alec takes a look around the computer. Checks the various files. It doesn't take him long to find a spreadsheet. It details where, and to whom, the organs Alec has harvested have gone. Next to them all, it says how much they have paid. Alec bites his lip. He's barely seen a fraction of these figures. There's another document that holds names of people looking for organs, and what they're willing to pay. Alec can see the desperation in some of the figures offered.

Finally, at the bottom of this document, he finds what he's looking for. The AB-negative liver. The details are provided in bold, the text font bigger than all the rest. This is the most important organ of all, and yet there is no monetary figure beside it. This makes Alec more curious than he already is. He checks the details. Palmer Elliot, in New York City.

Alec sits back. He looks through Kendis's recent call log. He's in communication with Palmer Elliot once, sometimes twice, a week. He hits dial, and he waits.

It takes a while for Palmer Elliot to answer. When he does, he looks tired, and there is a yellowed, jaundiced tinge to his flesh. He frowns, seeing the face looking back at him. "Who are you?" he says.

Alec puts on his best smile. "Hello, Mr Elliot," he says. "You were probably expecting Kendis?"

"Damn right I was expecting Kendis – who the fuck are you and why are you calling me? Do you know what time it is? I'm trying to sleep here!"

Alec doesn't let his smile falter. "My name's Alec Hill, Mr Elliot," he says. "Have you heard of me?"

"Why the fuck should I have?"

"That surprises me," Alec says. "Maybe I should give my full title – *Doctor* Alec Hill."

Palmer takes notice of this. He cocks his head a little. "You're Kendis's surgeon."

"That's right."

"Then why didn't you say so?" Palmer's tone, his whole demeanour, changes. "But what are you calling for?"

"Oh, I'd assumed Kendis had already been in touch."

"I spoke to him a few days ago," Palmer says.

"Then I'm calling with good news, Mr Elliot. We've found you a liver."

Palmer Elliot's relief is palpable. He starts laughing. There are happy tears in his eyes. "Holy shit," he says. "Holy *shit*. You got one? Oh my God, you finally got one!"

"We certainly have," Alec says. "That's why I was calling – to introduce myself. Going forward, you're probably not going to see much more of Kendis."

"Why's that?"

"Between you and me, I think he's already spending the money you're about to pay us."

Palmer laughs at this. "I'm sure he is."

"It's a very generous amount," Alec says, choosing his words carefully. "I know I certainly wanted to thank you for *my* half of that money."

"Well, 2.5 million is worth thanking a man for!"

Alec digests this. Five million total. That son of a bitch. "It certainly is," he says. "It's been a pleasure talking with you, Mr Elliot, but I should get going now. That liver isn't going to extract itself. I'll be back in touch very soon, and we can exchange delivery and transfer details then."

Palmer nods eagerly. "Sure thing," he says. "Don't keep me waiting!" He laughs again.

Alec hangs up the call and sits back, lacing his fingers. Five million dollars. Five million, for an AB-negative liver. Kendis kept this from him. That no good motherfucker – the only person he was going to share that with was his fag bodyguard.

Alec takes a deep breath and keeps his cool. It's no good getting worked up. He needs to stay calm. To think straight.

To plot his next steps, although deep down, he already knows what he's going to do.

First, he goes back into Kendis's folders and prints off the spreadsheet of all the potential buyers. He folds it up and stuffs it into his pocket. If he wants to, he'll work his way through it in the future. Right now, he needs to focus on the liver. That precious, valuable liver. Nothing else matters but that, and the five million dollars attached to it.

He leaves Kendis's penthouse. Leaves his building, and returns to the car. He needs to get to Hopper Creek. He can think on how to address this, how to hold this against Kendis and Big Ron, on the way.

## 42

E arly in the morning, a few hours before Hayley needs to start her shift, the three of them drive to Santa Fe. Tom takes the wheel. Hayley sits in the back. Jim sits up front.

On their way out of Hopper Creek, they notice activity in the direction of Tom's place. He and Hayley exchange a look, and then he makes a quick detour to drive by it. They find his home burnt to the ground, its remains still smouldering. The fire service is there, picking through the wreckage. The Chevy has been burnt out, too. A couple of cop cars sit nearby. Tom turns the car around and they continue on their way.

"Donny," Hayley says, leaning forward.

"Has to be," Tom says. "Either him or his new friends."

They head to Santa Fe, and they go to the abandoned hospital Jim escaped from. Tom knows his way around Santa Fe, but Jim directs him anyway. Tom parks down the road from the hospital, near the bus station, and they watch.

"They picked an interesting location," Hayley says,

looking around. "It's not city centre, but it's not exactly secluded, either."

"Hiding in plain sight," Tom says. "If they're quiet and if they're careful, it doesn't matter where they are. If they own the building in an official capacity, then no one's going to think they're doing anything unofficially."

"But when someone like Jim here escapes," Hayley says, "they don't exactly have to run far."

Jim chuckles. "I went *straight* for that bus," he says. "Although, I gotta admit, when I got out the building, the last thing I was expecting to see so close was a bus stop."

Tom has been watching the building all the while they spoke. "I'm gonna have to get a closer look," he says. "It's too big to see anything from here."

"You want me to come with?" Jim says.

Tom shakes his head. "Stay here with Hayley. I'll come back and get you if needs be."

Tom gets out of the car and crosses the road, approaching the abandoned hospital carefully. As he goes, he thinks about his rented home in Hopper Creek. Of its smouldering remains. He doesn't feel any real sense of loss. He wasn't attached to it. It was just a place to lay his head. If Donny was hoping to send a message, he succeeded in doing that, but it probably wasn't as personal as he was hoping.

Tom peers through the chain-link fence and through the bushes and looks into the hospital's windows as he passes by, but most of the ones on the ground floor have been blacked out or covered over. He can see it's the same for ones on higher floors, too. He heads around to the entrance. It's locked. He can't see anyone inside. He circles the building, finding places he can look in. He finds a good spot with a view of a corridor and the stairs, and watches for a while. No one appears. He can't hear anything inside. He thinks it's empty. He goes back to the car and lets Hayley and Jim know.

"So what do we do?" Hayley says, shielding her eyes from the early morning sun as she leans out the open window.

Tom reaches out without thinking and brushes a lock of her hair behind her ear. "We go inside and take a look around," he says. "See if there's anything there."

The three of them go around the back of the building. Tom finds a rock on the ground, and wraps it in his jacket. He smashes a window with it, his jacket dulling the sound. He climbs through first, smashing out the rest of the glass shards, and then Jim helps Hayley through before climbing in himself. They listen to the building before they move any further. It's deathly quiet.

"Should we split up?" Hayley says. "Look around?"

Tom shakes his head. "We stick together."

They search the ground floor first. There's nothing to find. The place is empty. All the while they look, they don't hear anything else in the building. It seems truly abandoned. A strange, familiar smell permeates the air, only occasionally drifting into their nostrils. It's faint, but instantly recognisable as bleach. They exchange glances at the smell.

They go down into the basement next. Tom checks the light switch. It works. The space is illuminated by the harsh glow of strip lights. The basement, like the ground floor, is empty. Tom walks the space, looking around. He spots something on the ground, and kneels for a closer look. A sprinkling of powder. Hayley sees it too and crouches beside him. They avoid touching it. "Lye?" she says.

"Looks that way," Tom says. He looks around the basement. "They could have been bringing the bodies down here and covering them in lye to disguise the smell."

"It looks like they've scrubbed the place," Jim says.

"Smelled like it upstairs," Tom says.

"If there were bodies down here, makes you wonder what they've done with them."

Tom nods. They go back upstairs, and up another level. The smell of bleach grows stronger the higher they go. They check each floor room by room. They're all empty.

"There were beds when I was here," Jim says. "At least, there was in my room. There was equipment, too. And now everything's gone, and the place smells like bleach."

"If the cops *did* come," Tom says, "it doesn't look like there was anything for them to find."

"They could have left here after Jim escaped," Hayley says. "They didn't know where he was going, or who he could talk to."

Tom goes to a window and looks down at the bus stop.

"Man, I hate it in here," Jim says. "I dunno, maybe it's because I've been here, and I lost a part of me here, and I know what was being done here – but this place just feels evil. It gives me the creeps." He shivers.

"No," Hayley says, "it's more than that. I feel it, too. It's like it's seeped into the walls. Do you feel it, Tom?"

Tom has turned back from the window to watch them. "No," he says, shaking his head. "I don't feel anything. But I see the size of the place, and get an idea of the scale of the operation they were running. There's a lot of rooms, and a lot of space for a lot of beds. That all adds up to a whole lot of organs being harvested and sold on the black market, or however else they might be selling them."

They move through the rest of the rooms, but at this point it feels perfunctory. In a few of them they find faint speckles and smears of blood that haven't been properly cleared up.

"Did they kill the people they had here when they were clearing out?" Hayley says, looking sick.

"I don't know," Tom says, inspecting a couple of the droplets closer. They're very dry. "But it looks like they have." He stands back up. "There's not really any other reason for there to be blood in these rooms. We've seen the operating theatre, and it was spotless. About the only place here that doesn't smell like bleach. This blood, it looks like they've had to scrub it. They've gone room to room, and they've killed the people they had here. Shot them or slit their throats, it's hard to tell."

Hayley is pale. She covers her mouth with her hand.

"Why..." Jim says. "Why couldn't they just...*smother* them? Like they were gonna do to me. Why not keep it clean? Especially if they knew they were gonna have to tidy up after themselves."

"I don't know," Tom says.

"Evil," Hayley says, uncovering her mouth. "They're murderous, evil butchers."

Jim nods at her. "You're right. And now they're on the move. We don't know where they are anymore."

"They could be in Hopper Creek," Tom says. "They certainly seemed to be last night."

"And we're going back there?" Jim says.

"You don't have to," Tom says. "You can split now if you want. We won't hold it against you. But Hopper Creek is Hayley's home. We're not going to resolve this by running from it. We have to run *to* it. Hell, if we're lucky they might have given up on us and moved on."

"Except you don't really believe that."

"No, I don't, but it's still an option."

"But even if they have," Jim says, eyeing Tom levelly, "if they *have* given up and moved on, you're still going to go after them, aren't you?"

Tom doesn't answer.

Jim takes a deep breath. "I'm coming back with you," he says. "Best thing we can all do is stick together, right? You've helped me out, and I'm gonna return the favour as best I can."

"Then let's go," Tom says. "There's nothing else for us here."

They leave the room they're in. Jim goes first. Hayley holds onto Tom's arm before he can go, and he pauses, turns back to her.

"Hopper Creek is *your* home too, Tom," she says. "You know that, don't you?"

"Yeah," he says. "Of course. But I've only just returned to it. You've been there a lot longer than I have."

There's a sad look on her face that he doesn't understand, and he doesn't question, either. She squeezes his arm, then quickly kisses him, and they follow Jim out of the room.

## 43

Duncan Mather comes by Willie's house. Kyle is sitting out on the porch as he approaches, and comes inside to let Donny know. Donny isn't surprised he's turned up. He goes out to meet him, standing at the top of the stairs on the porch with his arms folded. Duncan parks his cruiser and comes over. Donny doesn't move. Doesn't let him come up the steps.

Duncan shifts his weight from foot to foot, feeling awkward at the foot of the porch. "Morning, Donny," he says, craning his neck to look up.

Donny grunts.

Duncan clears his throat. "Listen, uh, you wouldn't know anything about Rollins's place burning down, would you?"

Donny shrugs. "Why would I know anything about that?"

Duncan has to clear his throat again. Before he can speak up, Willie leaves the house. Silently, he steps up next to Donny. There's a scab at the top of his forehead from when Rollins smashed his head through glass. Duncan sees the scab and grimaces. He takes a step back.

"What do you want, Duncan?" Willie says, his voice gruff.

"I was just, uh, I was telling Donny about Rollins' place burning down–"

"You were asking if we did it," Donny says.

"Now what kind of a stupid fucking question is that?" Willie says.

Duncan's mouth gapes like he's a fish.

"Duncan, stop wasting our time," Willie says. "And stop bringing your cruiser by my house. What do you reckon the neighbours are gonna think when they see you coming here all the damn time? Get your ass back to work and maybe you'll find who *is* responsible."

"Arson ain't never been our style," Donny says, with a smirk. "You know that."

Duncan holds up his hands in surrender. "I just needed to check," he says. "All I came out here to do, to say – look, last time I saw you, I begged you – keep things quiet. Okay? That's all I'm asking. Just keep things quiet. The louder things get, the less I can–"

Donny waves him off. "You've said all this before," he says. "We heard you the first time."

Willie tilts his head toward the cruiser. "Get out of here, Duncan."

Duncan hesitates. He swallows, and Donny can hear the dry click in his throat. Duncan nods and starts to back off finally, his hands still raised. He gets back into his cruiser and turns it around in the road. Donny and Willie watch him go back the way he came.

When he's gone, Donny snorts. "Asshole," he says.

Willie laughs.

---

## 44

Tom, Hayley, and Jim get back into Hopper Creek and swing by the motel. Hayley needs to start her shift soon. They'll drop Jim off at the motel, and then Tom and Hayley will head straight to the hospital. Hayley isn't thrilled about Tom having to hang around the hospital, but she understands why he needs to do it. Things are dangerous. The visit to the abandoned hospital in Santa Fe has further compounded this for her. And, worse than that, they don't know who all of their enemies are.

They pull into the parking lot for the motel. Tom scans the area. It's quiet. He sees only one person around. A tall black guy, well-built, at the vending machine. He's not paying them any attention.

Tom pulls to a stop in front of their room. "Keep this hidden," he says, handing his Beretta to Jim. Jim nods and tucks it into the back of his jeans, under his shirt. "Lie low here," Tom continues. "You've got my number. Any issues, call me."

"Got it," Jim says, getting out of the car.

Hayley gets out of the back and into the front, taking Jim's place. She strokes Jim's arm as she passes. "And make sure you *rest*," she says. "I know I keep saying it, but you've *got* to do it."

Jim grins. "I'll rest," he says, "I promise. Cross my heart, and my one remaining kidney."

"You know I'll be checking later," Hayley says.

"I know you will," Jim says. "Have a good shift. I hope the place isn't in too much of a mess for you after last night."

"Me too, Jim, me too."

Jim pats the top of the car and then turns, heading to the motel and their room. He passes the tall black guy as he goes, who doesn't turn his head as he continues on to his own room with an armful of snacks and soda cans.

Tom and Hayley watch Jim as he goes. Watch until he's inside the room and waving them off before he closes and locks the door.

"All right," Hayley says, nodding. "He's in. Get me to work."

# 45

Kendis looks up as Big Ron returns to the room, his arms loaded with snacks and soda cans from the vending machine. It all looks a little too sugary to Kendis, but he's starving and doesn't care. He's lying on his stomach watching television, and turns as Big Ron returns. Before he can say anything, Big Ron cuts him off.

"They're here," he says.

Kendis blinks. "What? Who's here?" He thinks of the men coming from Santa Fe. Of Alec.

Instead, Big Ron says, "Jim Belafonte, Rollins, and Hayley – the liver. I've just seen them."

Kendis pushes himself bolt upright. "*What?*"

Big Ron goes to the window and peers out around the curtains, signalling for Kendis to stay where he is. "Rollins and Hayley are leaving, but Jim's stayed behind. I know what room he's in."

"You're sure it was them?" They'd looked them up online last night, after they'd found out Hayley Teller's blood type. Images of them had been easy enough to find – Rollins and Jim in their Army uniforms, and Hayley in her nurse's scrubs.

"I'm sure," Big Ron says.

"And you were careful when you saw them, right?"

Big Ron turns back around, nodding. "I didn't give anything away. I saw them out the corner of my eye and I just kept walking. I passed close by to Jim as he was going to the room, and I got a good enough look at him."

Kendis is practically bouncing on the edge of the bed. He forces himself to calm down. "All right," he says. "This is good news for us. We know where one third of them are right now. The other two – the girl has become more important to us. We need to know where they're going. She works at the hospital, right?" He knows she does, but he's excitable.

Big Ron has remained calm. He nods. "That's right."

"Okay. I'm gonna call Donny and see if he can get there ahead of them, check that that's where they're going." He scrambles for his phone. "But we've gotta be careful about this. They've fallen into our laps. We've gotten lucky and we can't let that slip away from us. We have them lined up, so we've got to stay cool." Kendis finds Donny's number and hits dial. While it's ringing, he speaks to Big Ron. "Keep an eye on Jim, but be subtle about it. Just watch his door or something. Make sure he doesn't go anywhere."

Big Ron turns back to the window and looks out, and Kendis assumes he can see the door from where he stands. "It doesn't get much more subtle than that," Kendis says, and then Donny answers his call.

## 46

D onny and Willie race straight to the hospital after Kendis's call. Donny tells the rest of the crew to stay behind, to wait at Willie's house until they hear anything further from him. Kendis emphasised that they need to be careful. They need to be subtle. Donny figures having everyone here would be too obvious. Rollins would see them. So just the two of them have come. They've parked in the furthest row of the hospital's parking lot, and they've come the rest of the way on foot. They stand under trees, out of view. They look around for Hayley's car.

"What's she drive, a Prius?" Willie says. "I don't see it."

Donny doesn't either.

"We could've beat them here," Willie says.

"If here *is* where they're coming," Donny says.

They wait and they watch. Donny looks to the building. Remembers the chaos they caused last night. He wonders what it's like inside. Wonders if they've cleared up all the mess. "You spoke to your janitor buddy about last night?" he says.

"We've messaged," Willie says. "He's said it all calmed

down after a couple of hours. It's a hospital – they need to know how to operate under stressful conditions. That's how he put it. He said they've had worse things happen."

"Yeah? Like what?"

"Drunks looking for fights. Jonesing junkies running wild. Says they just clear it all up and get back to business. Says the cops weren't even here all that long."

"Duncan never mentioned the hospital," Donny says.

"We might not have given him the chance."

"Or else nobody realised it was us. You said most of what happened was on an upper floor. Not as many staff around. And even the ones that were, they're not all gonna be from Hopper Creek."

"That's all true."

Donny looks down the road. There are plenty of vehicles coming and going, but none of them are Rollins and Hayley. He shakes his head and pulls out his phone, turning away. He's about to call Kendis, to tell him that this is a bust, when Willie nudges him.

"Not so fast," he says, stepping back behind a tree and making sure Donny does the same. "Here they are."

Donny peers out, and sure enough he sees Hayley's Prius. Rollins is driving. They watch as he pulls around the side of the building and pulls up into the staff parking. Donny keeps his phone in his hand. He grips it tight, watching. Hayley and Rollins both get out of the car and go inside. Rollins looks around on the way. Donny and Willie both duck back, hide behind the thick trunk of the tree. They peer out a moment later. They're both gone. Donny scans the area, makes sure Rollins hasn't spotted him and is creeping up. There's no sign. It looks like they're both inside the building. They wait to see if either of them come out. Ten minutes pass by. Fifteen. Neither of them do.

Donny calls Kendis. He answers promptly. "They're here," Donny says.

Kendis sounds relieved. "That's good, that's great."

"So, what do you want me to do?" Donny says. "Get the crew here, then go in and get the girl?"

"No, *no*! Don't do that. We don't want a repeat of last night. Like I said, we've got to be careful. We don't want them to slip away again. If Rollins is there, and he sees you, things are gonna get loud, just like last night. Louder even, if you're trying to grab his girl."

"Then what do you want us to do – just sit here and watch the fucking place?"

"I want you to get the girl," Kendis says. "But I want you to use your brains about it. You think you can do that? Big Ron and I are gonna deal with Jim. *You* get the girl. We can deal with Rollins later. The girl is what's important right now. And make sure she's unharmed – a little bruising here and there, that's fine, but I don't want her dead, or bleeding out. Her blood, her organs, they're too valuable, all of them. I don't want any serious harm done to her."

"What do you take us for? Thugs?"

Kendis doesn't answer straight away, and Donny takes this to mean that this is *exactly* how Kendis sees them. "Listen, just be careful, all right? Distract Rollins or something. Find a way to get him out of there, and then snatch the girl. You think you can do that?"

"Yeah, we can do that. We're not inept."

"Good. I'm sure you're not. Contact me when you've got her. We're not going to stick around."

Willie looks at him as he hangs up the phone. "How much did you hear?" Donny says.

"All of it," Willie says.

Donny nods.

"You got a plan?" Willie says.

Donny is silent for a moment, thinking. Then he starts to smile, an idea occurring to him. "Yeah," he says, "I do. And I'm gonna go see to it myself. You wait here, keep an eye on things, but make sure Rollins doesn't see you. Call Kyle and Hal, get them to meet you here and help you out with grabbing Hayley."

"What're you gonna do?" Willie says, frowning.

"I'm gonna call the others, and get them to meet me somewhere else."

"Where?"

Donny smiles. It's filled with malice. He has bad thoughts running through his head. Bad, vengeful thoughts, and he just doesn't care anymore. Fuck Duncan Mather and fuck Kendis Dukes – things *are* going to get loud and they *are* going to get messy. Most of all, fuck Tom Rollins – he has taken from Donny, and now Donny is looking to earn back what has been taken from him with blood.

## 47

Tom sits in the hospital lobby and pretends to read a magazine, but really he watches everyone who comes and goes. Occasionally he heads outside and walks the perimeter, keeping an eye out for anyone he might recognise – from Donny's crew, or whoever their new enemies are. He doesn't see anyone.

The hospital is active, and there are a lot of people moving at all times, and Tom doesn't like it. Makes it harder to keep track of everyone and everything they're doing.

Tom sees how the women on the reception notice him. They don't approach or question him, though. They know who he is to Hayley. They know he brought Jim in, too, and he's surprised they don't at least ask about Jim, and if Tom knows where he's gone or how he is. He wonders what they think he's doing sitting here for so long.

Hayley comes down to him on her break and they have lunch together. "Have you seen anything you don't like the look of?" she asks. They have sandwiches. She tears the plastic off hers and Tom does the same to his own.

He shakes his head. "No. Hopefully it stays that way."

"If it does, what then?"

"Then tonight I go hunting. We can't just wait for them to come and find us."

Hayley takes a bite out of her sandwich and nods thoughtfully. "Okay," she says. She looks like she wants to say more, to *ask* more, but she doesn't.

"What's it like around here?" Tom says. "After last night."

"Business as usual," Hayley says. "No one got a good look at who it was, and no one really understands what it was all about. The cops came and took some statements, but that's all. No one's expecting anything further to come of it."

"Have they said anything about Jim?"

"They're worried, naturally, but they saw him escape. He came here under suspicious circumstances, and he's leaving the same way. No one's going to ask too many questions. They're already busy enough."

Tom nods. They eat in silence for a while. He glances around the cafeteria at Hayley's colleagues. She distracts him by reaching across the table and squeezing his arm.

"It's nice," she says, "having lunch together. I know the circumstances aren't ideal, but it feels like it's been a while since we were last able to go on a date."

"It hasn't actually been that long," Tom says.

"I know, but it feels a lot longer, what with everything happening."

"That's true."

"When this is all over," Hayley says, "you're gonna have to really treat me – you're gonna have to take me somewhere special."

"But we've already been to the best motel in town."

Hayley has to cover her mouth when she laughs. "Something even more special than that," she manages to say when she's done laughing.

"I'll have to really put my thinking cap on."

"You certainly will. I feel like I've been very understanding throughout all of this."

Tom takes her hand and holds it. "And I appreciate that."

They finish eating and Hayley has to get back to work. Tom returns to the lobby. He takes his time on the way, looking the place over. He doesn't see anything that raises alarm, but he doesn't allow himself to settle. In the lobby, he picks up another magazine to pretend not to read and he resumes his lookout.

## 48

S hawn and the Simmons brothers meet Donny at the town square. He's sitting on a bench, awaiting their arrival and looking toward the supermarket. Remembering how much simpler things used to be. How he used to run this town. How easy it all was.

Things will get back to that, he's sure. He just needs to deal with all of this shit first. Things might not be exactly how they were, and it's unlikely they'll be selling flakka again any time soon, but he'll figure a way through. They'll work for Kendis until they find how to stand on their own feet again. Kendis is just a means to an end.

Shawn and the Simmons brothers join him on the bench. "What're we doing here?" Shawn says.

Donny nods to the top of the square. Shawn and the brothers look. They see the hardware store. Del's Supplies. "That's where Rollins was working," Donny says. "Just him and the old man. They woulda spent a lot of time together, the two of them."

Shawn turns back to Donny. It's clear he doesn't understand.

"I'm sure they got friendly," Donny says, "or at least friendly enough that Rollins wouldn't want anything bad happening to the old man."

Shawn understands now. The Simmons brothers already did. The four of them rise from the bench and cross the square to the store. Donny checks the inside is empty of customers first. It is. The only person he can see is Del himself, behind the counter, reading a newspaper. The four go inside. Donny locks the door after them, and flips the Open sign to Closed.

Del looks up from his newspaper as they enter, and his back stiffens. He's seen what Donny has done. He puts the newspaper to one side. "Help you boys with something?" he says.

Donny strides to the front. "You sure can," he says. He presses his hands on the counter and leans his face into Del's. "Call Tom Rollins, and tell him you need him here."

Del doesn't back down. "Why would I want to go and do a thing like that?"

"You're gonna find out soon enough," Donny says. "And if you don't do this the easy way and just fucking call him, you're gonna find out the *hard* way."

Del doesn't move. He stands his ground. His eyes flicker left and right, and Donny knows he sees how the Simmons brothers are encircling him.

Del clears his throat. "I'm not gonna be intimidated by the likes of you punks," he says. "I know you. I know you all. Some of you used to be good kids, before you started hanging around with *this* asshole." He indicates Donny, and he looks straight at Shawn when he says it. Shawn, who used to have a Saturday job here so long ago.

Donny shakes his head. "Come on now, Del, there's no need for name calling."

"Get the hell out of my store, all of you."

Donny takes a deep breath. He looks at Del. "I gave you the choice," he says. "I want you to remember that. I gave you the choice, and you chose the hard way, you stupid old man. You're gonna make that fucking call – I swear to Christ, you're gonna call him, and you're gonna tell him to come here, and you're gonna tell him to come *alone*."

"The hell I am," Del says, firm.

"We'll see about that," he says, and takes a step back. "Shawn, maybe you're a little soft on the old man from when you worked here. You go and stand by the door and make sure no one interrupts us." Donny motions to the Simmons brothers. He looks into Del's face and he smirks as he says, "Get him."

## 49

Tom receives a call. He's surprised to see it's from Del, though he supposes it shouldn't be too much of a shock. He should have contacted Del a while ago, let him know what was going on, but he's been busy. His mind has been on too many other things.

"Hey, Del," he says, answering. "Listen, I'm sorry, I should've been in touch with you days ago and–"

Tom isn't greeted with a voice. Instead, it's a wet gurgle, and a groan. He feels his blood run cold. He presses the phone hard against the side of his head.

He hears the phone move, and a voice comes on the line. He recognises it. It's Donny Bradshaw. "Rollins," he says, "you hear that? You hear what we've done to your buddy here? He's spitting up his own teeth right now, all on account of how he couldn't play nice. Just like you, huh?"

"What do you want, Donny?" Tom says, speaking through gritted teeth.

"Hell, you fucked up my business, I figure I can see fit to fuck up *yours*. Now, before we do anything else to old Del here, and before we burn *this* building to the ground, here's what I want *you* to do – get your ass down here, Rollins. Get your ass here, and come alone. If you ain't alone, I swear to Christ I'll kill him."

Tom clenches his jaw. His mind races. "Where are you?"

"Where do you *think* we are, you dumb fuck? We're in Del's Supplies. Your old workplace, ain't that right? Don't keep us waiting. You got fifteen minutes." Donny hangs up.

Fifteen minutes isn't long. It'll take Tom that long just to drive there.

He gets up from his seat and starts moving without thinking. Before he can grow too frantic, he goes looking for Hayley, to tell her what has happened. It's hard to think straight. He manages to find her at the nurse's station two floors up. She joins him off to one side and he tells her about Del.

"Holy shit," she says, eyes wide. "What are you gonna do?"

"I don't know," Tom says. "But I can't just leave him with them. It sounded like they'd already beat him pretty bad."

"Tom, just call the cops."

"I've told you, Donny is friends with the cops," Tom says. "They're no good to us. They can't help us."

Hayley bites her lip. She hesitates before she speaks again. "Can you – can you handle them?"

"It's not an ideal situation," Tom says. "But I don't have a choice. For Del."

Hayley nods. "Go and get him," she says. "You have to help Del."

"You need to come with me."

"No, Tom. Listen, I'm safer here. Go to Del. I'll be right here when you're done."

Tom is torn. He doesn't want to leave her, but he can't keep Del waiting. He thinks of how Jim was almost taken – how he would have been killed if Tom hadn't turned up when he did. But this is different, he thinks. It's daytime, and Hayley is surrounded by co-workers. People who know her, and who would know if she were in trouble. At least, he hopes they would. He thinks she's right – she's more secure here than anywhere else. She's as safe as she can be without him around, though he doesn't like it. "All right," he says. "Just...be careful while I'm gone. You see anyone who looks suspicious, you *run*. All right?"

Hayley nods.

"You've got my number."

"I've got your number, you know I do. Now *go* – go to Del."

Tom has to move. He has to move *now*, or else he won't go at all. Del is in danger. Del needs him.

He turns and he runs.

## 50

Jim hasn't rested, as he promised Hayley he would. He hasn't been able to. He's been too busy being careful. Watching his exits. Keeping an eye on the front. He's moved between windows, seemingly at all times. He can't remember the last time he stopped.

He keeps Tom's Beretta close. Keeps it in his hand. It's been a long, long time since he last fired a gun, but it's like riding a bike. He knows he hasn't forgotten. He never could. Even at his lowest moments, when all he could think about was his next fix, he never forgot how to field strip an M4, or how to clean and oil his sidearm.

He takes a seat briefly on the edge of one of the beds, his back aching. His stitches are burning. He's sick of them but knows he still has a while to go before they heal. He takes deep breaths. He forces himself up to his feet, and to keep moving. Can't get too comfortable. He goes to the back window. The escape route, if needed. There's woodland out there. It provides cover if he needs it. Places to hide.

Halfway back to the front window, he hears voices outside. A car door closing. Jim freezes. Tightens his grip on the gun. He doesn't go straight to the window. He circles around, staying out of easy view of anyone looking in. Raises the gun. He gets to the side of the window. Peers out. There's a group of guys gathering in the parking lot. Jim watches them. Counts six. He notices some of them are carrying weapons, keeping them concealed.

Jim doesn't overthink it. He starts moving again. Heads to the back of the room, to the bathroom window. Gets it open and climbs out, not wanting to waste time. The gathering of armed men in the parking lot is more than enough to set off mental alarms. He'll get clear of the room, find a place to hide out, then call Tom and let him know – but getting somewhere safe first is his main priority.

He drops to the ground outside, but hears noise off to his left. He looks, then checks the right, too. There are more men. They're circling the motel. They see him. They call to the others. They have guns. Jim doesn't hesitate. He raises the Beretta and fires, twice left and twice right. He doesn't expect to hit anything. The shots are to back them up, to scare them off. To make them hesitate. To buy him time while he starts running. They're not going to get his other kidney. They're not going to take anything else from him, not without a fight.

The first sign they're giving chase is the gunshot that slams into the trunk of a tree to his right. Jim throws up his arms and veers to the left as bark rains down upon him, cutting at his cheeks, almost taking out an eye. He hears them pursuing, and he curses himself for taking a seat on the bed earlier, for catching his breath, for allowing the pain in his back, his burning stitches, to cloud his mind. If he'd kept walking, if he'd kept checking, he would have seen them gather in the parking lot sooner. It would have galvanised him into action faster.

It's too late for regrets. Keeping moving is what matters now, and that's what he does. The pounding feet behind can't distract him. The gunfire that cuts through the trees, tearing up dirt and branches, cutting chunks out of the bark, he can't allow this to slow him.

But mental fortitude counts for nothing when a bullet finally finds its mark.

It hits him in the back of the right leg. In the hamstring. Jim goes down instantly, hot blood pouring out of him. He's dropped the Beretta. He can't worry about that. It's gone. He needs to keep moving, so he scrabbles and drags himself, his right leg useless behind him. He bites down on his lip to keep from crying out. It's to hide his position, but he's not sure how much that matters anymore. They can follow the blood. Can follow the marks in the dirt where he's dragged his leg along.

He reaches a fallen tree and throws himself over it. He knows he can't hide here. Needs to keep going, to keep pushing. He moves left and crawls along the length of the tree, but he doesn't get far before he hears footsteps all around him. Looking, he sees men from the parking lot in a circle around the fallen tree. They don't come any closer, but some of them have handguns, and they point them his way.

Another pair of steps comes toward him, crunching through fallen branches. Jim forces himself to roll onto his back. If this is it, if this is his death, he's going to face it head on, with a defiant sneer.

Two black men approach. One of them looks familiar. The taller of the two. Jim's mind races, and then he remembers – it wasn't long ago he saw him. After Tom and Hayley dropped him back at the motel. This man was at the vending machine. They passed each other as Jim made his way back to the room. Jim curses himself, but how was he to know?

It's the smaller of the two men who speaks. "Jim Belafonte," he says, and he's grinning, giddy, like meeting Jim is an enormous relief. "Usually, I never have to learn the names." He turns to the bigger man and nods. Jim notices the bigger man is carrying a gun. A Smith & Wesson M2.0.

Jim realises he's breathing hard. The pain from where he was shot in his leg radiates up to meet with the burning of his stitches. He stares into the barrel of the gun pointing his way, and he thinks of Rhonda, and suddenly all of the pain goes away. He sees her smile. She's holding her arms out to him. His breathing calms. He feels a warmth flood through him. Nothing hurts anymore. Nothing will hurt ever again.

The smaller man sees the change come over him. "What's he smiling at?" he says.

Jim looks at him. "You wouldn't understand," he says, and then he closes his eyes.

## 51

Hayley carries on with her job, but she's distracted. She thinks about Tom, and about Del. She thinks about Jim, and hopes that he's resting. She thinks about a lot of things – about Donny and his gang, and about the abandoned hospital in Santa Fe and the men who were harvesting organs there. She thinks about all of the people they must have killed. She wonders, too, how long it must have been going on for. How many people have suffered because of them. How many people have died.

She makes her way around the hospital, doing her rounds. Checking in on patients. It's a quiet day, and she's glad. She's had enough of emergencies for a while.

Moving between rooms, she comes across Jack Cooper, one of the janitors. He's moving his mop and bucket around, but he's not using it. It seems like he's looking for someone.

"Hey, Jack," Hayley says as she passes.

"Oh, Nurse Teller!" he says, seeing her properly. "There's something I think you should probably look at."

"What is it?" Hayley says, slowing to a stop, turning to face the janitor fully.

"There's a patient," he says, jerking his thumb over his shoulder down the corridor. "I was in the room emptying his trash, and he was complaining about a pain in his side. I said I'd see if I could find someone."

"Okay," Hayley says, "I'll go check in on him. Why didn't he ring for assistance?"

"He said he did," Jack says, keeping pace with her, dragging his mop and bucket along, its wheels squeaking on the buffed floor. "But no one came."

Hayley frowns. "I'll have to get someone to look into that," she says. "Which room is it?"

"This one here," Jack says, pointing. The room at the end, on the left.

Hayley wasn't aware of anyone being in there, but she can't know everything. She's not here at all hours. She goes to the room. Jack trails behind her. She motions to him, says, "It's all right, Jack. I've got it."

She steps into the room. There's no one in the bed, but there are two men present. She recognises both of them. Kyle Hobbs and Hal Redford. Kyle is pale. He looks like he's shaking and he might be sick.

As soon as she sees them, Hayley turns to flee. She's not supposed to have a phone on her when she's working, but lately she's broken that rule. It's tucked away in her back pocket. She reaches for it as she spins, to call Tom while she runs.

But she can't run. Her way is blocked. She looks up. Willie Shaw is standing before her. He grabs her before she can react, wraps his big arms around her and clamps a meaty hand over her mouth, silencing her. Eyes wide, Hayley looks beyond him, over his broad shoulders to Jack Cooper, silently screaming at him, pleading with him. Jack turns away like he hasn't seen anything. He pushes his mop along.

Willie bundles her toward the fire escape. He barks at Kyle and Hal. "Let's go!" he says. "Quickly!"

Hayley's mind races as they carry her toward the fire exit. When Tom rescued Jim, they escaped the same way. They set off the alarm. She's not sure if it's been reconnected since then. But, even if it has, Jack has led her to these men – he could know their escape plan in advance, and have disconnected it for them.

Hal gets the doors and checks the way is clear. Hayley attempts to bite down on Willie's hand, but she can't get loose enough. His grip is too tight. She can barely breathe.

Behind, keeping pace, she can see Kyle. He looks uncomfortable. She can see his hands trembling badly. He balls them into fists, but that doesn't help. Hayley stares at him, manages to catch his eye. Silently pleads with him, the way she did with Jack Cooper. It's not too late for him to change his mind about this – he can call for help, he can stop them from doing what they're doing.

Kyle looks like he's about to cry. He turns away, and then Hayley is taken out of the hospital. No alarm sounds. They go to a waiting car. Hal drives. Kyle sits up front with him. Willie is in the back with her. He pushes her low and crushes her with his weight. The car moves. None of them speak. Hayley doesn't know where they're taking her. They haven't given any indication of where they're going. She thinks of Tom. As if reading her mind, Willie becomes aware of the phone in her back pocket. He pulls it out and holds it in front of her face. "You ain't gonna be needing this," he says, and throws it from the window.

## 52

D el's Supplies is locked and in darkness. Tom hasn't been able to watch the building as long as he'd like. It's already been twenty minutes – five minutes over the deadline Donny gave him.

Tom peers in through the glass but the front of the store looks empty. He slips the key from his pocket and unlocks the door, taking care to be quiet. He steps inside. He moves silently, listening. There's nothing to hear. He's braced, ready for Donny's crew to launch themselves at him from one of the aisles of tools. No one does. He heads for the back. To the storeroom.

The lights are on back here, and it doesn't take Tom long to find Del. He's dead. Slumped in a corner next to a stack of boxes, a pool of blood beneath him. His sternum has been cut open with a chainsaw and his guts are hanging out. His head hangs to the side, almost severed, a bloodied hatchet lying nearby.

Tom's stomach tightens. It's hard to tell what has killed Del first – the gutting, or the decapitation. Whatever it was, they've gone overkill. They didn't need to do this.

Tom hears the click of a gun behind him. It's not close. It's not pressed up against him. This is their mistake. They should have gotten closer. They've left him too much space. He dives to his right, behind a shelving unit. The gun starts firing. Tom is out of view, and the bullets tear uselessly through the shelves behind him. Tom keeps running, to the end of the storeroom and the light switches next to the exit. He hits them, and casts the room into darkness.

The shooting stops. Donny's men can't see. Tom knows his way around. He heads to the right and creeps down through the next row of shelves, toward where the gunshots came from. He hasn't seen who is here, who has killed Del, but he can hear the shuffling of feet, and someone whispering, "*Find the lights!*"

Tom grabs a hammer from a shelf as he passes. He thinks of Del's dead, mutilated body. He sees a dark shape up ahead. It's holding a gun out in front of it. When Tom gets closer, he sees that it's Shawn Stark. When he's nearly on top of him, he sees who the other men present are – the Simmons brothers, and Donny himself. The Simmons brothers are both armed, but Donny is not.

Tom is holding his breath. His steps are light and silent. Shawn doesn't hear his approach. Tom swings the hammer into the side of his right knee, and knocks his patella out of place. Shawn's leg bends the wrong way, and he screams hard and loud.

Tom moves away as the other three men turn toward the sound. He throws himself into the nearest shelf and forces it to fall, crashing into the next shelf and toppling that, too. They fall toward Donny and the Simmons brothers. They have to scatter.

"Into the store – get into the store!" Donny says.

They flee into the store and leave Shawn behind. He's still screaming, and clutching at his leg. His fallen gun is gone.

One of the others must have grabbed it as they fled. Shawn cowers from Tom as he passes, raising his arms, but Tom leaves him for now. He moves on, slipping into the store, ducking low as he does so.

As soon as the door begins to open, it is fired upon. Tom expected this. He stays low and dives for the till area. He doesn't take cover behind it. Can't allow himself to get pinned down by their gunfire. Instead, he goes to the front of it and keeps moving, crawling to the nearest aisle.

Behind him, the Simmons brothers advance on the till, expecting that this is where he's taken cover. Tom leaves them to it, moving on while they're cautiously advancing, distracted. Tom goes to the end of the aisle. He puts down the hammer he used to break Shawn's knee, and instead picks up an axe from where it hangs. He keeps going. Finds a nail-gun. He tears it from its plastic, then loads it. It needs to be plugged in.

"He's not here," he hears one of the Simmons brothers say.

"He can't have gone far," Donny says, panicked. He's on the opposite side of the store to Tom. Tom heads straight for him, axe in one hand and nail-gun in the other. It's not as dark in the front of the store as it was in the storeroom. Tom has to be more careful here. To duck lower, and move softer. He sees Donny cowering ahead, breathing hard. Tom reaches a socket in the wall. He's close enough for the nail-gun to be in range. He plugs it in, and fires at Donny's leg.

Three nails bury themselves into the meat of Donny's left leg. He screams but doesn't go down. He's smart enough to move away from Tom's fire. He jumps forward. At his screams, the Simmons brothers come running. Max arrives first, rounding the corner. Tom is ready. He fires the nail-gun. A nail embeds itself into Max's right eye. His screams are worse than both Donny and Shawn's. Max goes down. Micky is right behind him. Tom drops the nail-gun and moves up fast, swinging the axe. He buries it deep in Micky's chest and, after a grunt, Micky goes down in silence.

The front door opens, and Tom looks to see Donny escaping, moving as fast as he's able, favouring his injured leg as he limps away, the nails still embedded there.

On the ground, Max writhes, clutching at his face, too scared to touch the nail. Tom stomps down on the nail with the heel of his boot, driving it in deeper. Max goes rigid. He begins to shake. Tom picks up his dropped gun, a Sig Sauer P220. He shoots Max through the face. The shaking stops. He goes still.

Tom returns to the storeroom, where Shawn remains on the ground. He's attempted to crawl away, but he hasn't gotten very far. He looks up as Tom approaches, terrified. He whimpers as Tom points the gun at his head.

"You killed Del," he says.

"Please," Shawn says, "*please–*"

"That's not going to bring him back."

"It was – Donny did it," Shawn says. "He – he made us kill him. We can't – none of us can stand up to him. I knew Del, I knew him, I used to work here when I was a kid, but Donny, he–"

"I don't want to hear it," Tom says. "Who are you working with? From Santa Fe, who is he – tell me!" Tom's nerves are fraught. He doesn't have the patience for Shawn's babbling.

"He – he's called Kendis! Hal used to work for him!"

"Kendis who?"

"Kendis, uh – Kendis *Dukes!*"

"He harvests organs," Tom says.

"Yeah, yeah he does, and I'm sorry, I'm sorry, man, but Hayley's blood is rare–"

Tom's own blood runs cold. His stomach tightens again, the same way it did earlier, but now he fells it in his chest, too, like a vice around his heart. He kneels down closer to Shawn, presses the barrel of the Sig Sauer into his forehead. "Hayley?" he says. "What about Hayley?"

The back of Shawn's head is pressed down into the ground by the gun. "She – her blood's AB-negative, and Kendis needs that! He needs her liver – hell, he's probably gonna take all her organs! But, but he's already got a buyer for the liver. He's really desperate for that liver, man."

Tom grabs him by the throat and raises him off the ground. "Why did you kill Del?" he says, but he thinks he already knows. His mind is racing.

"It was to get you here," Shawn says, swallowing. "But – but Donny didn't need to do that to get you here. He got him to call you. We could've just held him prisoner until you came. Donny wanted – he wanted to pay you back, for what you did, what he thinks you did – to the flakka, and to his house."

Tom hasn't seen Willie, or Kyle, or Hal. They could be at the hospital, now that he's gone.

"Tom, I'm sorry–" Shawn says.

Tom shoots him through the forehead.

## 53

K endis and Big Ron are leaving the motel when Kendis gets a call. He's expecting it to be Donny, but instead it's Alec. He slips back into the room to answer.

"Where the hell are you?" Kendis says. "Everyone else got here hours ago, and they say they don't have a fucking clue where you've gone. I've tried calling you about a dozen times, motherfucker. What the hell is your phone doing off? Now of all fucking times."

"We need to talk," Alec says.

"You're damn right we do," Kendis says, pacing the floor.

"I mean now."

Kendis stops short. "Are you kidding me?" he says, struggling to maintain his composure. The room's door opens and he looks up to see Big Ron. Big Ron raises an inquisitive eyebrow. Kendis waves him in and motions for him to close the door. "Now is not the time for you to be pulling your shit, Alec. You need to get here *now*. We have the fucking liver."

"Which makes me think that now is *exactly* the time we need to do this," Alec says. "Do you understand how good I am at my job, Kendis? Do you understand that if I were to put the word around, just how in demand I would be? I think it's high time we discuss my pay."

"You're unbelievable."

"Oh, you had best believe it, Kendis. I'm not stepping foot in Hopper Creek until we've talked money."

Kendis looks to Big Ron. He can't hear the discussion. He stands by the door, waiting and looking concerned.

Kendis takes a deep breath. Alec has him cornered. He needs him for the surgery. They *need* the liver. They need it more than they've needed any other organ.

But it's fine, he tells himself. It's fine. Once they have the liver, once it's sold, he'll never have to see, or deal with, Alec ever again. He can agree to anything Alec demands right now, because he's never going to see a penny more than he's already earned.

"All right," Kendis says. "Fine. Whatever you say. Just come to Hopper Creek and–"

"I'm not coming to Hopper Creek," Alec says, "and I'm not negotiating over the phone. You will come to me. Right now."

Kendis bites his lip. "Where are you?"

"I'm not far. When we get off this call, I'll message you the directions. And bring Big Ron with you. I know how you don't like to go anywhere yourself, Kendis, and I don't mind his being present. Something tells me he already knows more about the financial structuring of your organisation than a bodyguard would be expected to."

Kendis doesn't have any choice. "Fine. But right *now*. We need to get this over with."

"I agree," Alec says, and hangs up.

"What was that all about?" Big Ron says, stepping forward.

"It's Alec," he says. "Being an asshole, as per usual. We need to go see him, me and you."

Big Ron frowns.

"I know, I don't like it either," Kendis says. "But we *need* him, unfortunately." He shakes his head. In his hand, his phone buzzes. He glances at it. The message is from Alec, directing him where to meet. He looks back at Big Ron. "Let's get this over with."

## 54

Tom has raced back to the hospital, very aware that not all of Donny's men were present back at the store. He can't find Hayley. No one knows where she is. They try paging her. They put out a call. She doesn't answer. All the way here, Tom tried calling her. She never answered. He feels sick.

He can't keep still. Staying at the hospital is no good. He heads to the motel. He'll pick up Jim, and then they'll go and find Donny and his unaccounted men. They'll find Hayley. He calls him on the way. Again, no answer. Tom fears the worst. He doesn't go straight to the room. He watches the scene first, though he's antsy doing so. He thinks of Hayley. Of where she could be and what could be happening to her.

The motel looks clear. Tom goes to the room. The door is locked. He lets himself in. The room is empty, but he can feel a breeze blowing from the back. He goes to the bathroom. The window is open. Tom grits his teeth and climbs down. He's careful. Keeps his head on a swivel, looking around, prepared for an ambush. He's kept hold of the Sig Sauer he took from Donny's guys at the store. It's in his hand as he inspects the ground, picking up on a trail. He finds many pairs of feet. Deeper into the woodland, he sees bullet holes in the trees. He finds spent casings. He follows the route. Once the shooting has started, it's easy enough to keep on top of.

Then, he finds blood. His heart pounds. Up ahead, the dirt is scuffed as if something has been dragged through it. Off to the left, Tom spots something familiar. His Beretta. He retrieves it and checks it. It's short four bullets. Tom tucks it into the back of his jeans. If Jim does not have the weapon, it doesn't look good for him. Tom presses on, his sense of dread growing as he reaches a fallen tree. He doesn't have to go any further. He looks to the left, and he can see Jim's body.

They've barely attempted to conceal him. Just laid a few branches over him, mostly obscuring his face. Tom moves them aside. There are two bullet holes in the middle of his forehead. Jim looks like he's smiling, but Tom doesn't think too much of this. He's seen men's faces do a lot of strange things in death. He places a hand upon Jim's chest and closes his eyes.

## 55

Tom can't stay in the woods with Jim's body. He needs to be proactive. Needs to do something. The longer they have Hayley, the worse it is. The less chance she has of surviving. He starts moving, heading back through the woods, leaving Jim's body where he found it. He marks the location in his mind. He won't forget.

His mind is racing. He doesn't know what to do. Enough time has passed since they'd drawn him away they'll have gone to ground with Hayley, no doubt. Into hiding while they perform the operation. Although Shawn said they'd probably take all of her organs, on account of her rare blood giving them extra value. For that, they'd need to take her somewhere secure. Somewhere safe.

Tom can't afford to waste time running around, hoping they'll turn up somewhere he's familiar with. They could be somewhere he's never known about. Then he thinks of something. He thinks of some*one*. Someone who might be able to help him.

He calls the only friend he can turn to. Someone who has a history of finding seemingly untraceable people. Someone who can manipulate computers and security systems in a way he can't, and especially not with such limited time.

He calls Cindy.

It rings three times. Four. Tom isn't a praying man, but he closes his eyes and he starts.

On the seventh ring, she answers, sounding breathless. "Tom, hey!" she says. "Fuck, I've just moved into my new place and I've got things *everywhere* and I could hear the phone ringing but I couldn't find it, and anyway, I'm sorry it took me a while to answer–"

"Cindy," Tom says. "I need your help."

She picks up on his tone. From light and airy, pleased to hear from him and laughing at her own mess, she turns serious. "What's happened?"

Tom tells her the abridged version. Gives her everything relevant. If she needs further details, she just has to ask.

"All right," Cindy says, talking fast. "I'm grabbing a pen and paper – give me the details of the cars you know about. Start with Donny, his crew. Tell me their vehicles."

Tom reels them off from memory.

"Okay," Cindy says. "I'll track them down. I'll go through security footage, find out who they've been meeting with and get their vehicle details. You said they took Hayley from the hospital?"

"Yes, I think so. I don't see where else they could have got her from."

"Okay, that's good. I can work with that – there's gonna be security footage all over the hospital. Listen, it's gonna be faster for me to get off the line and work through this. I'm gonna have a lot of cameras to check, and I wanna do it as quick as I can. The thing is, a small town doesn't usually have as many security cameras as a city, but if they've started at the hospital that's good. I'll do the best I can, Tom."

"I know you will," Tom says, balling his fists, squeezing the phone tight.

"I'll call you as soon as I have anything." Cindy hangs up.

Tom stands in the woods and stares down at the blank phone. He looks around. Staying here won't help anything. He needs to be prepared for when Cindy calls back. He hurries back to the motel and returns to the car – Hayley's car. He keeps the phone in his hand all the way. He doesn't want to miss a call.

## 56

Alec recognises Kendis's Lexus as it approaches, and he steps back down the hill out of view. This area is off-road, and concealed. The Lexus will no doubt struggle across the terrain. Alec leans against the car he drove here, and he waits. He feels cold steel pressing against the inside of his right wrist.

Eventually, the Lexus comes into view, bumping around the corner of the hill. Big Ron is driving. He doesn't look happy. Alec can see why, as the car rocks on its suspension, and the top of his head hits the roof of the car. Alec raises his left hand and wiggles his fingers in a little wave.

The Lexus comes to a stop and Kendis and Big Ron are quick to get out. Kendis strides over. He stops a couple of paces away. Close enough. Not within arm's length, but Alec would just need to take a step forward to reach him.

"All right," Kendis says, waving a hand in a circling motion. "Let's get this over with. What do you *want*?"

Alec wonders if, on their way across the uneven terrain, they questioned why Alec would want to meet them here, in a spot so secluded.

Alec gets straight to the point. "I've spoken to Palmer Elliot," he says. "I know how much he's offering for the liver."

He sees Kendis stiffen, and he grins.

"And I know that I won't see so much as a *fraction* of that amount," Alec continues. "Which gets me to thinking, how much *else* have you shafted me out of over the years?"

Kendis has to clear his throat before he can speak. "You were a junkie when I found you," he said. "I've kept you clean. I've given you purpose. *This* is how you want to thank me?"

"I would always land on my feet, Kendis," Alec says. "A man like me? Of course I would. They can strip away my medical license and send me to prison, but so what? None of that can dull my skills. All I've allowed you to do over these years is put a roof over my head. I stayed in that hospital and performed those operations because *I* wanted to. Do you understand that? And now I want something more."

"Money."

"Of course!" Alec laughs. "We *all* want more of that, don't we?"

"I'll be honest, Alec, I've never been sure if you did," Kendis says. "Truth be told, I always thought you just liked cutting people open and sewing them shut again. I thought playing God was what got you off."

"True, but money's the second best thing."

Kendis glances back at Big Ron. Big Ron stands in front of the Lexus. He's a few paces behind Kendis. It wouldn't take him long to close that distance.

"Give me what I want, and then we can go and get this precious liver," Alec says. He smiles as Kendis turns back around. There's only one way Kendis can give him what he wants, truly, and it isn't with hollow promises of a pay rise. For now, Alec is enjoying toying with him. He's lulling him, making him believe he wants one thing when, really, he's here for something much different.

Kendis lets out a begrudging sigh. "*Fine*," he says. "Name your price."

"Half."

Kendis's eyes bulge. "*Half?* You know I've gotta run the fucking place, right? I've gotta pay the men, I've gotta pay the licenses and the–" He stops and holds up his hands. He grits his teeth. "Half," he says, conceding.

Alec understands the sudden compliance, why Kendis stopped himself mid-rant. They're all playing each other here. Neither of them intends to fulfil their promise to the other. When Palmer Elliott makes the payment, Kendis is gone. Never to be seen again. Alec wonders if Big Ron is in on this. No doubt he is. No doubt he knows all about it.

Alec holds out his hand. "Shall we shake on our new arrangement?"

Kendis stares at the hand like it's a snake rearing back to strike. He isn't wrong. He reaches for it. Alec slips the scalpel into his hand, careful not to catch it by the blade, then raises his arm out of Kendis's reaches and steps forward. He slashes at Kendis's throat. Blood sprays. Kendis's eyes are wide. He doesn't understand what has just happened. He falls to his knees, clutching at his neck, his blood spilling through his fingers.

Big Ron steps forward. He's reaching for Kendis. Alec moves on Big Ron. He slashes through the air again and drags the scalpel across his throat. Big Ron falls back, his right hand going to his neck. He clasps it tight, but he doesn't go down. His eyes blaze, and he lurches forward, left arm outstretched, grabbing for Alec. Alec keeps his cool, though this is unexpected. He backs up and slices at Big Ron's grasping fingers, severing them at the tips, splitting the skin between his index and middle fingers.

Big Ron falls to a knee. The blood loss is getting to him. Alec presses his foot to his chest and kicks him over. Big Ron tries to move, but he can't. He's covered in his own blood. His hand slips from his neck. His eyes flicker closed.

Alec steps over him and crouches down beside Kendis. Kendis is already still. He's dead. Alec reaches into his pocket and takes out his cell phone. He uses Kendis's thumb to unlock it, and then searches through his recent messages. For the first time, Alec wishes he'd paid more attention to the names of Kendis's men. He reads through the messages for context. One of the latest sounds promising. A man called Len telling Kendis the hospital is cleared and he's on his way to Hopper Creek. Alec transfers the number to his own phone and then messages Len.

> This is Alec. I'm going to call you. Make sure you answer it.

He waits a moment, and then dials Len's number. "Alec?"

"That's right," Alec says. He pokes Kendis's dead body with his foot. "Now listen up. Kendis and Big Ron have had to go out of town to deal with an emergency. They've left me in charge."

He can hear Len's hesitation. His doubt. "Uh..."

"Uh *what*?" Alec says.

"Why – why isn't Mr Dukes calling me himself?"

"Did you hear me say it was an emergency? Of course you heard me say that. Work it out for yourself."

"Okay..." Len still sounds doubtful.

Alec presses on. He expected this. "Kendis gave me your number. That should tell you enough. Do you think *I* had your number before today?"

"Mm," Len says, and it sounds like this makes sense to him.

"Do you have the girl?"

"Donny's men have her, yes. We're on our way to meet them now."

"Good. Gather everyone up, and bring her back to the hospital."

"The hospital?"

"In Santa Fe."

"Yeah, I figured. But is that such a good idea?"

"It's one operation," Alec says. "It's our best option. Get her there, get it done, and then we find somewhere else to set up. We leave that to Kendis." He grins to himself.

"Okay..."

"Don't keep me waiting." Alec hangs up. In his other hand, he still holds Kendis's phone. He waits. Sure enough, Kendis's phone starts to ring. It's Len. Alec is not surprised. He leans against his car and waits for it to ring out. Len starts calling again almost instantly. He calls three times altogether, and Alec ignores the call each time. Len sends a message.

> I need you to call me back.

Alec needs to use Kendis's thumb to unlock the phone again. He responds to the text.

> What's up?

> I need you to call me.

> Busy. What do you want?

> Alec says you've put him in charge. Says you've had to leave town for some kind of emergency.

Alec smiles to himself as he types.

> That's what's happening. I'll explain when I get back. Less said the better. But yes, Alec is in charge. Do as he says. Don't have time to discuss further.

Alec waits, wondering if Len will respond. He does.

> Got it.

Alec drops Kendis's phone onto his dead body. He doesn't need it anymore. He gets back into his car and leaves the Lexus and the two dead bodies behind, out of view of the road. Alec wonders how long it will take before they're found out here. By then, he should be long gone. He crosses the rugged terrain and gets back onto the road, and then points the car back toward Santa Fe, whistling to himself as he goes.

## 57

Donny drives, his left leg bloody and aching. He keeps it to one side and tries not to move it. The nails are still inside. He touched one tentatively but it was too painful to attempt removal. He tucks his phone between his ear and his shoulder and calls ahead to Willie.

"Did you get her?" he spits, gritting his teeth in pain.

"Yeah, we've got her," Willie says.

"Where is she?"

"She's right here beside me. I've got my arm around her as we speak."

"She putting up a fight?"

"She *did*, but we've sedated her. Forced some pills down her throat, and that's knocked her woozy. She's been all right since then. How'd it go for you? You deal with him?"

Donny looks down at his left leg, and then quickly looks away. The three nails are poking out and it feels like they're mocking him. He's going to need help to get them all the way out. His jean leg is soaking through with blood. "Ah, fuck – he was a damn wild man, Willie. He's killed everyone else."

"*What*?"

"The Simmons brothers, and probably Shawn, he's killed them. He went fucking nuts. Jesus Christ, there was no stopping him."

"What the hell? What set him off?"

"You know exactly what set him off."

"He found Del?"

"Yeah, and I assume the fucking red mist descended. Listen, if we've got his girl, he's gonna be on the fucking warpath. We're gonna have to tell Kendis about this. He needs to shore up his men. We've gotta be prepared for him." He knocks his leg, the nails hitting against the door. "Ah, *shit*."

"What's wrong? What's happened?"

"I've got nails in my fucking leg, Willie, that's what's happened! That motherfucking psycho shot me with a nail gun!"

"Holy shit, are you okay? Do you need me to come get you?"

"I can drive – just tell me where I'm going."

"We're going to Santa Fe. Kendis has had to split, apparently. He's put some guy in charge – the surgeon or something, I don't really know. But we're taking Hayley there to meet up with him, and he's probably gonna get straight down to it."

"Send me the location."

"Will do."

Donny hangs up and heads out of Hopper Creek. His left leg throbs. Bracing himself, he prods at one of the nails. Pain shoots up into his hip. He spits in pain, not caring where it lands.

"Son of a bitch," he mutters to himself, thinking of Rollins. "You goddamn son of a *bitch*."

## 58

Cindy calls back and Tom answers instantly. It's been a half-hour. Every minute of waiting has been agony.

"What you got?"

Cindy sounds exhausted. "Okay, so I've managed to follow the car that Hayley was bundled into and they've gone to Santa Fe. Thing is, in Santa Fe they've disappeared – but don't be alarmed. They've hit a stretch of road where it seems like all the cameras have been turned off. Also, I've followed some of the other vehicles they've been meeting up with, and they've gone to the exact same black spot."

"Where is it?" Tom says, but he thinks he might know.

She gives him the street name. "I've taken a look on Google Maps, and Tom, there's a lot of buildings there – it's next to a bus station, and there's an old hospital, and–"

Tom is already starting the engine. "They're at the hospital." He turns the car around.

"You're sure?"

"That's where they were running their operation out of.

They'd cleared out when we went to take a look, but it's probably the most convenient place for them to take her."

"Listen, Tom, if you need anything else–"

"I know, Cindy, and I appreciate it. One way or another, I'll be back in touch soon."

"Tom, there were a lot of men in those cars I saw. I counted about a dozen."

"That's good to know."

"Listen, I know you don't always have the odds in your favour, but I get the feeling you're a little more emotional than usual. Just – just be careful, okay?"

"I always am."

Cindy hesitates. Tom is ready to hang up. Before he can, she asks, "What are you going to do?"

"They killed Del," he says. "And they killed Jim. They've killed who knows how many other people, just to gut them of their organs and throw away the parts they don't need. And now they've taken Hayley, and they're going to do the same to her." He grits his teeth, putting his foot down and racing out of Hopper Creek, calculating how long it will take him to get to Santa Fe, and to the hospital. He has his KA-BAR, his Beretta, and the Sig Sauer he took from Shawn. There's no time to get anything else. No time to be careful, not the way Cindy means. He knows he shouldn't rush into a situation like this, and especially not in such an emotional state, but he has no choice. Hayley's life depends on him. He can't think – he needs to *do*. Needs to rely on his instincts and his abilities, and hope that they'll be enough.

"Tom?" Cindy says. "Are you still there?"

Tom squeezes the steering wheel. "I'm going to kill them all."

## 59

Hayley is sedated and being prepped for surgery. Alec tends to Donny's leg first, at Donny's insistence. "It's hurting like a motherfucker," he says. "Get these goddamn nails out of me."

Alec rolls his eyes, but he laughs and plucks out the nails with his gloved fingers.

"Jesus Christ, I could've gotten Willie to do *that!*"

"Yes, well, you asked *me*," Alec says.

Donny's crew are in the room with them. What's left of them. Willie, Kyle, and Hal. Willie and Hal are close, watching Alec as he works. Kyle is apart from them, in the corner, his arms folded. He bites on a thumb.

Kendis's men are scattered throughout the hospital, guarding it. Men equally spread across every level, and all of them armed.

"All right," Alec says, the nails out and dropped to the side. They lie on the ground, blood pooling beneath them. "Take off your jeans so I can clean and dress the wounds."

"Shouldn't we clean that up?" Donny says, pointing to the

blood that has dripped from the nails and is now pooling under them.

"I'm sure one of your men can deal with that while I'm getting ready for surgery," Alec says.

Donny slides his jeans down to his ankles. He sees how blood pulses out of the wounds. "Are they gonna need stitches?"

"No," Alec says. He wipes the leg down, and cleans it with stinging disinfectant. He puts a dressing over each hole, and then wraps bandages around them. "Try to keep your weight off it," he says, finished, removing his blood-smeared gloves. He stands. "Now, I have somewhere important I need to be."

"Wait a minute, wait a minute," Donny says, reaching for his bloody jeans. "Where's Kendis gone? He's so desperate for this liver, and then he just ups and disappears when we get it for him. What's that all about?"

"Family emergency," Alec says, his face impassive. "He's left me in charge."

"Yeah, I get that, I get it, but when are we gonna get *paid*?"

"Don't worry about that," Alec says, with a wry smile that Donny doesn't like. "Once this is all over with, if Kendis still isn't back, I'll be sure to see that you're handsomely rewarded for your efforts."

"I've lost three of my crew," Donny says. "You gonna take that into account?"

Alec flashes him that same wry smile again. "Of course," he says.

Alec leaves them. Donny turns to his boys, pulling his jeans back up. "Jesus Christ, he's a creepy guy," he says, shaking his head. He points to the blood on the floor. "Someone clean that up. I don't want my blood lying around this place."

Willie and Hal go in search of something to tidy up with. Kyle remains behind. He watches until they're gone, and then steps closer to Donny. He's still chewing his thumbnail. Donny looks up at him. His leg is aching. "Kyle," he says, "if you wanna make yourself useful, you could go and find me some painkillers."

"Donny," Kyle says. He doesn't continue. He bites his lip.

"What?" Donny says. "Spit it out."

"I, uh, I'm having some real doubts about what we're doing here, man."

"What kind of doubts?"

"Well, I mean, we *know* Hayley – we've known her for, like, forever – and we've served her up for this surgeon guy to just butcher her like a piece of meat. And did I hear you killed *Del*?"

Donny stares at him. "What do you expect me to do, Kyle? We need to do this. We're getting paid. We don't have money coming in from anywhere else. If *this*," he circles a finger in the air, "is what we need to do, then we're going to do it. And Rollins has pushed us to his – keep *that* in mind, too. This is on *him*."

Kyle doesn't respond. He starts chewing on his thumb again.

"Kyle," Donny says, "trust me, now ain't the time to start doubting what we're doing here. We're already in too deep. What's got you all inside your head? Del? Fuck that old dude. He was an asshole. *Hayley*? You think she gives a shit about *you*? Hell, man, we're gonna get rich off this bitch. She's worth more to us dead and in pieces than she ever was alive. And, what, you think I've never had to get blood on my hands before? Shit, Kyle, we've kept you too sheltered."

Kyle winces at this talk. Donny rolls his eyes, seeing that he's not getting through. He gets to his feet, favouring his left leg.

"When the others get back, tell them I went looking for some painkillers."

Kyle nods and steps back. As he passes him on his way out of the room, Donny notices that he's chewed the skin around his thumbnail bloody.

He stops close to Kyle, their shoulders touching. "You're gonna have to swallow this down, Kyle," he says. "I've let you leech off my crew all these years because we go way back, and because I'm loyal like that. Because the other boys like you. But these guys here, they don't know who you are, and they don't give a shit. They look at you, they just see some junkie hanger-on. You let them hear any of this soft shit you're saying now, they're gonna eat you alive. Man up, you hear me?"

Kyle closes his eyes. He manages to nod. Donny slaps him on the shoulder, and then goes in search of painkillers, leaving Kyle alone with what he's told him.

## 60

Tom makes his way straight into the hospital, going around the back to the window he broke the last time he was here. Inside, he moves fast, but he remains quiet, and careful. His KA-BAR is drawn. If he comes across anyone, he wants to keep it quiet.

He peers out from the room he's in and looks down the corridor. Off to his left, he sees two men standing guard by the main entrance. They're close to each other, and talking. Tom notices they're both armed. Handguns. They're not carrying their weapons. They're holstered. From the right, he hears footsteps approaching. One set. They're casual. There's nothing hurried about them. Tom opens the door a little wider, but keeps himself hidden from view, pressed up against the frame. He watches the two men by the exit at the end as the footsteps get closer. Neither of them notices. They don't turn around.

The footsteps are nearly parallel to Tom now, and his open door. He braces. The man comes into view. He's armed too, but again he's not carrying his weapon. Tom grabs him and drags him into the room, hand clamped around his mouth to keep him silenced. As he does so, he glances left and right. There's no one off to the right, and the two men down to the left don't hear.

Tom deals with the man quickly. There's no point questioning him – the other two men are too near. He can't risk uncovering this man's mouth, giving him a chance to cry for help. Tom slides the KA-BAR under his ribs, into his heart, and keeps his mouth covered until he's still. Tom dumps his body in a corner of the room and then slips out, closing the door behind him. The two men at the entrance are still talking. They haven't noticed anything. Casually, Tom walks to the right and gets to the corner, out of view. There's an elevator nearby. If it's in operation, it would make too much noise. Nearby, there are stairs that head up, but they're too exposed. Opposite him, there's a door that leads to the fire stairs. Tom has no doubts they'll be guarded, but it's his best option. His only option.

Silently, he steps inside the stairwell, carefully closing the door after him. He listens. There is movement one level above. The shuffling of feet. Tom peers out, looks further. The stairs are steel grating, and easier to see through than if they were solid. He spots another guard, two levels above the other. They're not close enough to be in easy communication.

Tom could pick off the man directly above with his Beretta or the Sig Sauer, but it's too early for guns. He doesn't know what he's up against, other than the dozen men Cindy mentioned, the remnants of Donny's crew among them. That's still too many for him to get caught up in a gunfight with, and that's not to mention that there could be men who didn't come to Hopper Creek, who Cindy never saw on any of the footage she combed. Tom needs to keep things quiet for as long as he can, until he has no other choice.

He goes to the stairs and starts making his way up, but he doesn't walk. He gets down and he crawls on all-fours, staying low to the steps. He's silent. His breathing is shallow. The KA-BAR is in his right hand. He keeps his eyes on the man directly ahead at all times. The guard shifts his weight from foot to foot. He's wearing a cap. His back is turned. He's looking out a window. His weapon looks more promising than the abundance of handguns Tom has seen so far. He has a Remington R4. It's not strapped to his back or slung over his shoulder – it's in his hands, ready for action.

The guard, however, is not as otherwise prepared as he should be. Tom gets up behind him and covers his mouth, sliding the knife into his back. The guard's spine arches. His grip on the rifle tightens, but his fingers are nowhere near the trigger. Tom lowers him to the ground, watching the guard two levels up as he does. He's leaning against the wall, on his phone. Not paying attention to his surroundings, or what's happening just below him.

*Amateurs*, Tom thinks.

The man in his arms dead, Tom takes his Remington R4 and his baseball cap. He checks the magazine. It's fully loaded – thirty-five rounds, but no extra magazines. He pulls the cap on, and lowers it over his face. He straps the Remington to his back. He starts making his way up the stairs to the next guard. His footfalls are quiet at first, but even if the other guard sees him, all he's going to notice is the cap obscuring his face. He'll think it's his buddy from lower down the stairwell. He won't know otherwise until it's too late.

The guard sees Tom when he's only paces away. He doesn't move from the wall. Barely lowers his phone. He can't see Tom's face. "Hey, where you going?" he says.

Tom doesn't respond until he's on top of him. This guard doesn't have a rifle. Just another handgun. Tom pins him against the wall, left arm across his chest, and presses the KA-BAR to his throat. He lets the guard see his face. "Where is Hayley?" he says. He presses hard on his chest, to keep the air in the guard's lungs at a minimum, choking off any screams before they can happen.

The guard's eyes are wide. "Who – who's Hayley?" His voice is hoarse, choked.

"The woman with the liver you want," Tom says.

"They're – they're prepping her for surgery. They might already be doing it now, I don't know–"

Tom presses on him harder. "*Where*?"

"Another floor up," the guard manages to gasp out. "In the operating theatre."

Tom cuts his throat and lets him fall to the ground, then runs up to the next level, not needing to worry about making noise in the stairwell anymore. There's no one left to hear.

He stops at the door. Cracks it open a little and peers out. He sees a familiar sight. Donny. He's limping, favouring his left leg, and using the wall for support. He disappears into a room. The rest of the immediate corridor is clear. Tom pulls the Sig Sauer and follows.

The remnants of Donny's crew are all present. Donny himself, Willie Shaw, Hal Redford, and Kyle Hobbs. Tom enters with the gun raised in his right hand, his left still holding the KA-BAR and held steady against the Sig Sauer's handle. Tom scans the room. Hal is closest, leaning against the wall to his left. Willie is kneeling down, leant over something on the ground. It looks like he's cleaning. Donny is making his way to a seat in the corner. Kyle is opposite Tom, standing rigid, a bloody thumb in his mouth, smearing red across his bottom lip. He sees Tom first, his eyes going wide. He doesn't make a sound.

Tom strikes at Hal first, burying the knife in his throat all the way to the hilt. Donny and Willie hear his choked cry turn to gurgling. They turn. Without hesitation, Willie launches himself at Tom. Tom is able to side-step him and brings the knife down into his back. Willie grunts and hits the wall. Tom takes aim at Donny.

He's tackled from behind, Willie throwing his bulk into him and driving him up to the other wall. Out the corner of his eye, Tom sees Donny flee from the room, as fast as his injured leg allows him. Kyle, however, doesn't move. He watches Willie and Tom with wide eyes and a slack mouth.

Willie gets his hands to Tom's neck. Before he can squeeze, Tom brings down both of his fists into the inside of Willie's arms, at his elbows, bending them and breaking his grip. He kicks at Willie's ribs closest to the stab wound. Willie cries out, but he's undeterred. He launches himself back at Tom, keeps him pinned against the wall. Tom feels the Remington digging into his back.

"Kyle!" Willie says, snarling. "Help me!"

Even wounded, bleeding, Willie is strong. Tom lowers the gun toward his face, but Willie manages to grab his arm and push it back, up against the wall.

While struggling, Tom sees Kyle make a move. But he's slow, hesitant. Thinking about what he's doing. He goes to the chair where Donny was going to sit and picks it up. It's a stool. Its top looks hefty, like it could do some damage. Kyle is moving slow, still, as he comes toward them, and Tom thinks he'll be able to avoid it as it's inevitably swung at his head. When that happens, it should catch Willie off guard. His grip will loosen. When it does, Tom will shoot them both. The time for silence is through – no doubt Donny is already raising the alarm. With the Remington, Tom is ready for noise. He's ready for them to come charging. He's ready to cut a line through them all to get to Hayley.

Kyle gets close. He raises the stool. He bites his bottom lip. With all his might, he slams the edge of it into the back of Willie's head.

Willie's grip slips away. He stumbles back. Tom cracks

him across the face with the Sig Sauer. Willie goes down. Tom turns to Kyle, confused.

"I didn't – I didn't know they were going to do that to Del," Kyle says, and his eyes are glassy, wet. "I didn't know–" He sounds like he's about to cry. "I didn't know what they were going to do to Hayley–"

Tom drives the KA-BAR through Willie's temple. Kyle flinches. Tom grabs him by the front of the shirt and pulls him close. "Is she still alive?"

"I think so," Kyle says, defeated. Out the corner of his eye he looks to Willie's corpse. "I don't think Alec has started the operation yet."

"Where are they? The operating theatre?" Tom knows where that is. Hard to believe it was only this morning when they were last here. The smell of bleach is still strong in the place, but it's being overwhelmed by blood.

"I don't know if they're in the theatre," Kyle says. "They're along the corridor, on the right, third door from the end."

Tom looks into Kyle's eyes. Sees the sorrow and the remorse there. He pulls him closer. "Leave this hospital," he says, "leave Hopper Creek, and never look back. *Run.*"

Tom lets go, and Kyle doesn't need to be told twice. He bolts for the door and Tom can hear him racing toward the stairs. With the door open, Tom can also hear calls, shouting. Rushing feet. Donny has raised the alarm. They're coming for him. He tucks the Sig Sauer back down his jeans, and slips the KA-BAR into its sheath. He takes the Remington from his back and heads for the door.

## 61

Alec is watching as Hayley's eyes begin to flutter open. "It looks like you're going to need another sedative," he says.

She looks up at him, frowning, blinking against the bright lights in the room. Her clothes have been cut from her and she's in a gown. She's bound to the table by her wrists and ankles, padded straps that have held dozens, if not hundreds, of patients in place before her. Her hair has been tied back and covered with a net. She struggles to focus on his face. She's confused. She doesn't know where she is, and she likely doesn't remember how she came to be here. The sedative has affected her short-term memory.

Alec is in his surgical scrubs. A mask covers his mouth and nose. Seeing that she's awake, he pulls it down. "I can only apologise," he says. "You should still be asleep right now. I gave you quite a strong sedative, but then I was dragged away to deal with someone's minor injuries." He sighs. "You know how it is – someone finds out you have medical experience, and even though they have a wound they're more than capable of dealing with themselves, they just *insist* that you do it for them. You're a nurse, isn't that right?"

Hayley blinks hard. She's struggling to focus.

Alec continues as if she's answered. "Then I'm sure you know exactly what I'm talking about. Anyway, I'm a little behind schedule. We'll get some more sedative in you and it'll be as if this conversation never even happened."

He moves away from her, but Hayley starts to make choking sounds. His head snaps back to her. She's not choking – she's trying to speak.

Alec waves at her dismissively. "I'm sure whatever you're trying to say is very important," he says, "but it doesn't matter."

"He'll find you," she finally manages. Her voice is a rasping croak. She swallows.

Alec looks at her. "Who?"

"Tom," she says. "He'll find you. I know he will. Just let me go. You don't want him to come after you."

Alec leans closer, resting his arms on the operating table near to her head. His face is close to hers. "He'll never find me," he says. "After today, I'm in the wind. No one will ever find me again." He straightens, smiling down at her. He strokes her brown hair through the net. "I can see why he'll be upset. You're a very beautiful woman. It almost seems a waste to empty you out like this. But there's no woman on this planet who is more beautiful than millions and millions of dollars, and I'm afraid your blood and your organs are far more valuable to me than your face."

Hayley takes a deep breath. He knows what she's going to do. She's about to scream.

"Feel free," he says, cutting her off. "Do you think you'd be the first? No one will hear you." Alec turns his back on her to show how little he cares. He prepares the sedative. Hayley does not scream. When he turns back to her, needle in hand, he sees how fully awake she is now. She's alert, and she's scared.

Alec strokes her hair again. She strains against her restraints. Alec hushes her. "You're not going to feel a thing," he says. "Just relax." He lowers the needle to her exposed arm.

From outside, he hears frantic shouting. He pauses, the needle an inch away from her flesh. Hayley raises her head. They both look toward the door. The voice is calling Alec's name.

The voice stops outside and pounds on the door. It isn't locked. Alec has never had to lock it before. The men out there – the men who used to work for Kendis, but who now belong to him – know better than to ever consider disturbing him while he's in surgery. He recognises this voice, though. Donny. Sure enough, the door flies open.

"What do you think you're doing?" Alec practically screams, struggling to restrain himself as he straightens.

Donny looks terrified. Alec can see that the bandaging on his leg has soaked through, his jeans darkening with a fresh torrent of blood. He's been putting weight on the leg, no doubt. Donny gasps, catching his breath. He jabs a hand back down the corridor. "It's Rollins!" he says.

Without a moment's hesitation, Hayley screams. "*Tom!*"

Alec strikes her across the face with the back of his hand to silence her. He's losing control of the situation and he doesn't like it.

Donny leans into the doorframe, chest heaving. "I've told everyone," he says, sucking down air. "They know he's coming."

Alec hesitates. He doesn't know what to do. This wasn't in his plans. He wasn't expecting this. He looks down at Hayley. She's smiling back at him, grimly defiant.

"I told you he'd come," she says.

Alec sets his jaw. He leans close to her. "*Let* him come," he says. "Do you know how many men I have out there? They'll gun him down like a feral dog."

Then Hayley does something he isn't expecting. She throws her head to the side, into his face, and bloodies his nose. Alec stumbles back, dropping the sedative and holding at his face. He sees the blood, his blood, on his gloved hands. He can feel it soaking into his mask where it hangs down by his chin. He tears it off. Enraged, he grabs at his table. Picks up a scalpel.

"What're you doing?" Donny says, watching.

Alec steps closer to Hayley. She struggles beneath him, still trying futilely to break free.

From the corridor comes the sound of gunfire. Alec's attention snaps toward it. He hears return fire. Donny dives further into the room. Automatic gunfire fills the air at the end of the corridor. Alec hears men crying out, but the shooting doesn't stop. Donny cowers in the corner.

Alec turns his attention back to Hayley. He takes deep breaths, calming himself. Things aren't going how he'd like, but it's fine. He has *her*. So long as he keeps hold of her, the mess occurring out in that corridor doesn't matter. He touches her arm, runs the bloodied fingertips of his gloved hand up it. He holds the scalpel up near his face in his other hand. "It looks like your operation is going to have to wait," he says. "But don't worry – we'll get to it soon enough."

# 62

Over the gunshots, Tom hears Hayley scream his name.

He knows the room she's in. The one Kyle told him. It's not the operating theatre – it's next to it. The prep room, he's guessing. From the corner where he takes cover, he can see it. Four men guard it, firing back at him, tearing chunks out of the walls around him. Three of them are armed with handguns, but one of them has an M4. It's doing the most damage.

The door into the stairwell opens and a man comes running out, Glock raised. Tom guns him down easily. He should have been more careful. Should have checked the situation. There's another man still in the stairwell. He *does* take his time. He attempts pot shots at Tom from the cover of the doorframe. Tom hooks the Remington over his shoulder and grabs the Sig Sauer, dropping down to one knee and holding it outstretched in both hands. He takes careful aim and waits for the man to peer out again. When he does, Tom shoots him through the eye. Blood sprays out the back of his head, painting the wall, the door, and its frame.

All the while, the men guarding the room Hayley is in have continued to fire. They're pinning him down. They just need to keep him busy, unable to pass, while they cut out her liver.

Tom puts the Sig Sauer away and braces with the Remington again. He checks the magazine. Twelve rounds left. He listens to the M4, waits for a lull. It comes. He hears the man changing the magazine. Tom ducks low and swings out with the Remington, eyes darting fast as he squeezes the trigger, picking out the man with the M4. He drops two of the men. One of them had the rifle. Tom's bullets also take out the legs of a third, and he goes down screaming.

Tom ducks back behind cover. The man remaining shoots one more time, and then Tom hears him curse. Tom peers out to find him frantically reloading. Tom strafes the area, and takes out both him and the man screaming on the ground.

He steps out into the corridor, keeping the rifle raised. Despite the ringing in his ears, he hears footsteps further away, but they're not coming this way. They're fleeing. Before long, he can't hear them at all.

He moves down, faster than he'd like but making sure to sweep the area. He watches the door to the room where Hayley is. The door is closed. When he reaches it, he presses himself to the wall beside it. "The men out here are either dead or they've ran," Tom says, calling through. "Come on out here, and you better fucking pray you haven't hurt a hair on her head!"

A voice calls back. Tom doesn't recognise it. "I'm afraid you're going to have to come in here," it says.

Tom grits his teeth. He doesn't have much choice. When he opens the door, they could gun him down – *if* they have weapons in there. They haven't shot through the door as he spoke, hoping to catch him through it. That doesn't mean anything. They could be careful. Trying to catch him unaware.

Staying at the wall, behind cover, Tom kicks the door open. Gunfire doesn't immediately erupt. He steps into view, Remington raised, and then he sees why no shots have come from this room – they don't have any guns.

What they *do* have, are scalpels. And Donny is pressing one of them to Hayley's throat.

There's an operating table between them, and Tom can see unstrapped wrist and ankle braces. On the other side of the table, Donny is pressed up against the wall with Hayley in front of him, almost like a human shield. He holds a scalpel to her neck, grasping it in a shaking hand. To their right stands a white-haired man in surgeon gloves. His nose is bloody. Tom hasn't seen him before, but he assumes this is Alec. He's holding a scalpel too.

"You must be Rollins," Alec says.

"That's him all right," Donny says.

Alec ignores him.

Tom moves the Remington between them. There's only a few rounds left in the magazine. He doesn't want to use them. The room is too enclosed with Hayley in it. He can't run the risk of hitting her, especially when Donny is using her as a shield.

"Come on now, Rollins," Alec says. "We all know you're not going to use that gun. Not when your lady love is right here."

Tom doesn't falter. He doesn't lower the rifle.

Alec holds out his hands. "It appears we're at a stalemate."

"Let her go," Tom says.

"You're not in any position to be making demands," Alec says.

"And yet here I am," Tom says, "demanding."

Alec smirks. "Let's be honest, Rollins. Even if we were to let your lady love go, what are you going to offer us in return?" He holds up a hand to show he doesn't expect an answer. "Nothing. Isn't that right? You're still planning on killing us. And, as it is, we have no intention of letting Hayley go. She's far too valuable to us. So, the way I see it, either you die, or we do. How does that sound to you?"

"It sounds about right," Tom says.

"I thought it would. But you know as well as we do that you can't fire that thing in here. Not when *she's* so close." He points at Hayley with his scalpel. "And we don't have any guns on us. So put yours *down*, Rollins, and we'll handle this some other way." He waves the scalpel.

Tom holds the Remington steady. Alec raises his eyebrows.

"All of them," Alec says. "I see the two handguns, too. You put them down, or I start cutting her right here in front of you."

Tom lowers the Remington. He looks straight at Donny. "You watch those shaking hands," he says. "Because once I'm done with this asshole, I'm coming for you, and if there's one scratch on her – well, that decides whether I make it fast or slow."

Donny sweats. Tom can see the beads that run down the side of his face.

Tom throws the Remington to one side. Alec motions to the Beretta and Sig Sauer. Tom takes them out and throws them to the Remington. He pulls out the KA-BAR, and this he keeps hold of.

"Fair enough," Alec says, and then he charges.

---

## 63

Hayley watches as Alec races at Tom, slashing through the air with his scalpel, backing him up out of the room. They disappear around the doorframe, down the corridor and out of view.

She feels Donny move her forward. He wants to get to the door, to watch them, to see what happens. He needs to be sure that Alec wins. He's too terrified of what will happen if Tom does.

"You should start running now," Hayley says. "You heard what Tom said."

"Shut up," Donny says, pushing her. "If he gets through Alec, *I'll* fucking kill him, just you watch."

The ground is cold beneath Hayley's bare feet as Donny shuffles her forward. Her toes nudge something. She looks down and sees that it's the needle. The sedative that Alec was going to pump into her before Tom arrived. Hayley hesitates, but she knows she can't. She has to act. Her life depends on it. She pretends her knees buckle, still weak from the sedatives she's already been given.

"My legs," she says.

"Get up," Donny says, and he has to move the scalpel away from her neck to keep her steady.

With the blade moved, Hayley seizes the opportunity. She makes like her legs give out again and she goes down. She lands on top of the needle, concealing it between her thighs. She reaches for it. As Donny drags her up, she grips it tight. She looks up, and sees his straining face. Again, she can't think. She must act. She jabs the needle up, and plants its tip into his right eye.

Donny lets go of her, screaming, rearing back. Hayley sees the stains on his left leg and slams down her elbow where the blood looks thickest. Donny's leg buckles, but his focus is on the needle in his eye.

Hayley scurries away across the ground, toward the door. Donny launches himself at her and pins her down. She lands on her stomach, the wind driven out of her as she's crushed between Donny and the ground.

"You bitch!" he screams, right into her ear. "You fucking bitch, I'll fucking kill you!"

Hayley throws her head back. She's not sure what part of his face she connects with, but it drives him off her enough that she's able to spin around under him. She gets her feet up and kicks him off.

She notices his hands are empty. Donny has dropped the scalpel. Hayley scans the floor. She spots it and dives for it. Donny, one-eyed, sees what she's doing. He dives at her again. Hayley grabs the scalpel and rolls out of the way. She comes up clasping it, pointing it at him.

He looks at her one-eyed, his right closed around the needle.

"Just give up, Donny," she says. "Just – just turn around and run. Look at you – look at how much you've already lost. Just go."

Donny snarls, showing his teeth. "I lost it because of *him*," he says, and he reaches up and pulls the needle from his eye. He throws it to one side and then charges at Hayley.

She keeps the scalpel up. Donny lands on it. She hears a gasp escape him, and then blood runs down her hands and arms. Donny pulls away, and the scalpel slips out of Hayley's grip. It's still inside him, in his chest. Donny looks down at it, and the spreading blood blossoming on his shirt. He collapses back, coughing. Blood sprays from his lips, and runs down the corner of his mouth. He presses his back against the wall. His breath is ragged, and fading.

"Donny?" Hayley says.

He doesn't respond. He doesn't look up. He just keeps staring down, his shoulders hunched and heaving. And then, slowly, his inhales become shallow, and his exhales become longer, and longer, until his head slumps down to his chest, his shoulders fall, and his breathing stops.

## 64

Tom backs up as Alec slices at him, keeping out of his reach. Alec is untrained, but he's wild, coming at Tom like a whirling dervish. Tom can't get close enough to him, and he thinks this is Alec's strategy. They move further and further down the corridor.

Tom ducks in, and slashes at Alec's midsection. Alec manages to avoid it, and cuts at Tom, catching him on the left cheek. Tom backs off, feeling blood pour from there.

"Another scar for your collection," Alec says, grinning. "You look like you have more than a few already, and those are only the ones I can see."

"They come with the territory," Tom says, tasting blood at the corner of his mouth.

"I'd ask what territory that is," Alec says, "but frankly, I don't care. Truth be told, you won't live long enough for that cut to heal. We can always imagine how it would look on you."

"You talk too much," Tom says, and jabs at him.

Alec manages to avoid the thrust, and slashes the scalpel

at Tom's face again. Tom anticipated this. His jab was purposefully sloppy. He was luring Alec in. He catches Alec's arm under his left, and wrenches up. Alec cries out, but has the sense to use his other hand to pin Tom's arm, to keep the knife away from himself. He headbutts Tom, right on the bridge of his nose, and splits the skin there. Tom feels blood run from his nostrils, covering his lips.

The blow dazes Tom, but he doesn't allow his grips to loosen. He can't. Alec attempts to headbutt him again, but Tom sees it coming this time. He lowers his head and they bang crowns ineffectively. Alec laughs, and then he lunges for Tom's neck with his mouth wide, intending to bite him, to take a chunk out of his throat. Tom snaps his head back out of his range, but the bite was a feign. Alec raises a leg and kicks Tom in the gut. As Tom bends over with the impact, Alec slashes at him again, aiming for his carotid. Tom ducks his head and barely avoids it. He raises the KA-BAR, but Alec strikes with the scalpel again on the backswing, and it slashes along Tom's right forearm. Blood splashes onto the wall, and across Tom and Alec's faces.

Tom drops the KA-BAR.

He backs up, clutching at his bloodied and burning forearm. He opens and closes his fist, making sure he can still use it, that no important nerves have been severed. It's hard to tell how deep the cut went. The hand still works, however.

Tom looks at Alec. Alec is very pleased with himself. "I thought you were supposed to be something special," Alec says. "Donny seemed so scared of you. He made you sound dangerous."

Tom has to admit to himself, he underestimated Alec. He hadn't heard of him before he reached the hospital. He wasn't expecting a surgeon to be so vicious. Alec advances on him, slashing left and then right. Tom has no choice but to back up. He watches Alec's movements. He shakes his right hand, keeping the feeling in it. Blood flies off his arm and spatters the wall and ground. Alec has a gleeful, sadistic look on his face. His tongue flickers out over his lips. He tastes Tom's blood there. He's fast. Tom needs to be faster, mentally as well as physically.

Tom feints left, and Alec strikes at him. Tom brings up his forearm and blocks the swipe. He hooks Alec's arm again. Alec goes for the bite again, or the headbutt – it's not clear but it doesn't matter – and Tom catches him by the neck. He wrenches up on Alec's arm again, and spins with him, holding him tight by the throat and slamming him up against the corridor wall. He slams him into the wall again, banging the back of his head against it. He sees Alec's eyes roll after the impact. They go glassy, struggling to focus. Tom locks his fingers and wrenches up hard until he hears a crack in Alec's arm. Alec cries out. Tom hears the scalpel hit the ground.

He lets go of the arm and, with both hands, grabs Alec by the face. He drives his skull back into the wall. There's a dull, sickening thud. He does it again, and again, and soon there is a bloody smear on the wall. Tom slams Alec's head into it over and over. Alec's body is already limp. Tom doesn't stop. They slide down the wall together. Alec is seated now, and Tom is on his knees. He slams Alec's head again, with the last of his strength. The back of Alec's skull is shattered and soft. Tom lets go of him and Alec slumps to the side, smearing blood and brain matter down the wall as he goes.

Tom forces himself to his feet. He leans on the wall as he goes, his arm dripping blood. He needs to get back to Hayley. He needs to deal with Donny. He's going to have to be smart about it. With Alec dead, there's no real reason for Donny to keep Hayley alive.

He grits his teeth, reaching for his Beretta. It's not there. Of course not. It's back where he dropped it with the others.

There's movement at the doorway ahead. Tom looks up.

It's Hayley. There's blood on her, but she doesn't look wounded. She rushes to Tom and drops to her knees, cupping his cheek while she looks him over. She looks past him, to Alec's dead body. She turns back to Tom, and she throws her arms around him.

# EPILOGUE

Tom has stitches in his right arm and his cheek. His right arm is in a sling. Every so often he wriggles his fingers, just to make sure he still can.

Two weeks have passed. It's been a busy fortnight.

Tom had lost a lot of blood from the fight with Alec. He and Hayley got out and she patched him up. They caught the news that night, and saw the report of what had happened at the hospital. The police were drawn after all the gunfire, no doubt. The cops were putting it down to a gang war, judging by the number of spent bullets and bodies they found.

The news also gave Alec's backstory – a brilliant surgeon brought low by drug dependency. He'd gone missing after his release from prison, and now he'd turned up dead at the scene of this battle. The theory they were going off was that he'd turned to crime, joining a gang and using his medical background to serve them in a medical capacity. The report didn't mention how he'd died, that his skull had been caved in against a wall.

With Cindy's help, Tom found out who owned the

hospital in Santa Fe. Kendis Dukes. They were able to track his Lexus driving out of Santa Fe, and Tom found his corpse off-road, along with another man's. Their throats had been cut. Upon closer inspection, Tom found they had been caused by a scalpel. He put it down to Alec. Clearly, something had occurred between the three men. Some kind of disagreement. Tom would never know and he didn't really care. He stuffed both bodies into the Lexus and then set it on fire.

Tom spoke with Duncan Mather. He was sitting in his cruiser at the side of the road when Tom slid into the passenger seat beside him. Before Duncan could say anything, Tom stared him into silence. "You know who I am," Tom said.

Duncan nodded, eyes wide. "I remember you from school," he said.

"Uh-huh. What did Donny tell you about me?"

"He, uh, he didn't tell me anything about you."

"What'd he tell you he burnt my house down for?"

Duncan didn't answer this.

"You've been turning a blind eye to things wrong in this town for too long," Tom told him. "That's over now. It's time for you to do your job. If you don't, you'll be seeing me again."

"I'm a cop," Duncan said. "You can't talk to me like this–"

"It's time for you to act like one," Tom said, cutting him off. "I know who you are and what you've been doing. If I have to come see you again, it won't be so friendly."

Duncan opened his mouth, but he saw the look in Tom's eye and promptly clamped up.

Duncan wasn't the only person Tom needed to go and see. Hayley told him about Jack Cooper, the hospital janitor who gave her up to Donny's men. She begged Tom not to hurt him. Tom promised, though it was difficult to restrain himself. He found Jack at home. He lived alone. He was in the living room, watching the television, and didn't look surprised when Tom let himself in.

"I know who you are," Jack said. "I know who you are to Hayley, and I reckon by you being here that you know what I did. So just hurry up and do what you're gonna do and get it over with."

Tom looked down on him from the doorway. "There's nothing I'd like more," he said. "But Hayley made me promise not to. She has a soft spot for sad cases."

Jack bristled at this, but he didn't say anything.

"Get out of town," Tom said. "Don't come back. You've got twenty-four hours. When I come back this time tomorrow, I might not be in the mood to keep any promises."

When Tom returned the next night, Jack was gone.

Jim was cremated. Tom and Hayley were the only people present. They took his ashes away with them. They took them to Santa Fe and scattered them in the park. Tom wasn't sure what else to do with them. He thought of what Jim had told him, about Rhonda and her death. About the essence of her being in Santa Fe still. Tom hoped that was true. That somehow, someway, they were able to find each other again.

The Hopper Creek Medical Centre, under the recommendation and guidance of Hayley, has requested funding to offer treatment and therapy for the town's growing number of suffering drug addicts. Hayley has told Tom that Dr Oswald thinks it might take a few more weeks for the funding to come though, but he thinks they have a good chance of getting it.

Today is the day of Del's funeral. Tom and Hayley go together. A lot of the town turns out. Del was an institution. For most people, he and his store had been a staple of the town as long as any of them could remember. His family were there too. They shook Tom's hand after the service. Everyone knew Del had been murdered. Word spread fast. They all knew who did it, too. Tom doesn't know how, but they seem to know he avenged him.

He and Hayley hang around the graveside after, foregoing the wake. Hayley holds onto Tom's arm and rests her head against his shoulder. "How are you doing?" she says.

"I've been better," Tom says, staring at the fresh earth on Del's coffin.

Hayley sighs. She strokes his arm. "This isn't your fault."

Tom doesn't respond to this. It feels like it is. He went after the flakka. He was trying to clean up the town. Now, Del is dead, Jim is dead, and Hayley was almost killed.

His right arm tingles where the cut is healing. His cheek feels tight. Hayley squeezes his arm. "Should we go home?" she says.

Tom takes a deep breath. "You go on," he says. "I'm not ready to leave yet."

"You want me to wait with the car?"

"No. I think I want to walk."

Hayley kisses him on the cheek. "Take as long as you need," she says. "You know where to find me."

She walks away and leaves him alone at the graveside. Tom breathes deep, staring down into it, at the coffin. At the dirt. He thinks of Del. Of his store. He thinks of Jim, and of Rhonda, whom he never met. He thinks of how close he came to losing Hayley. He closes his eyes and he breathes deep, and feels a light breeze run its fingers over his skin, and he thinks about what Jim said to him, about essence, and atoms, and dust. About finding the one you've lost. And he starts to think about Alejandra, and when he went down to Mexico to spread her ashes, to return her to her home. He wonders if her essence, her atoms, her dust, if they're too far away for him. If he'll ever be near them again.

When he opens his eyes, he's not sure how much time has passed. The breeze continues to run over him, to cool him. He says a silent goodbye to Del, and then he turns and walks away.

# ABOUT THE AUTHOR

Did you enjoy *Last Stand*? Please consider leaving a review on Amazon to help other readers discover the book.

Paul Heatley left school at sixteen, and since then has held a variety of jobs including mechanic, carpet fitter, and book-shop assistant, but his passion has always been for writing. He writes mostly in the genres of crime fiction and thriller, and links to his other titles can be found on his website. He lives in the north east of England.

Want to connect with Paul? Visit him at his website.

www.PaulHeatley.com

# ALSO BY PAUL HEATLEY

**Blood Line**

(A Tom Rollins Thriller Book 1)

**Wrong Turn**

(A Tom Rollins Thriller Book 2)

**Hard to Kill**

(A Tom Rollins Thriller Book 3)

**Snow Burn**

(A Tom Rollins Thriller Book 4)

**Road Kill**

(A Tom Rollins Thriller Book 5)

**No Quarter**

(A Tom Rollins Thriller Book 6)

**Hard Target**

(A Tom Rollins Thriller Book 7)

**Last Stand**

(A Tom Rollins Thriller Book 8)

Made in the USA
Middletown, DE
24 May 2023

31300219R00196